PRAISE FOR MORGAN CRY

'Sweaty, seedy, fun'   Ian Rankin

'An immersive thrill-ride through a wild expat Costa del Crime community'   Denise Mina

'Fast, furious and infinitely entertaining'   Lin Anderson

'Unputdownable'   Denzil Meyrick

'Morgan Cry has created the ultimate literary cocktail: perfect measures of thrills, tension, suspense, served on the rocks with a liberal dash of humour'   Sharon Bairden

'Pure escapism – pick of the month'   *LoveReading*

'A hugely entertaining, deftly told crime caper' *Irish Independent*

'Riveting'   *Sunday Post*

'Brown may have left behind the dark alleyways of tartan noir for the hot streets of Spain, but he proves that it can be just as dangerous out in the sun, and that he can still make his readers sweat'
Scotland on Sunday

'A character-driven crime caper that steers clear of grit and sadism without ever feeling too lightweight'   *The Herald*

'A fantastic mystery, compelling storyline, tense and gritty . . . Highly recommended!'

ABOUT THE AUTHOR

Gordon Brown was born in Glasgow, and lived in London, Toronto and a small village called Tutbury before returning home. His day job, for many years, was as a marketing strategy specialist, and he helped found Scotland's international crime writing festival, Bloody Scotland.

He has also written several short stories including one in the Anthony Award-winning *Blood on the Bayou*. *Six Wounds* is his ninth novel (his second writing under the name of Morgan Cry). He's a DJ on local radio, has delivered pizzas in Toronto, sold non-alcoholic beer in the Middle East, floated a high-tech company on the London Stock Exchange, compèred the main stage at a two-day music festival, and was once booed by 49,000 people while on the pitch at a major football cup final.

Six Wounds

Morgan Cry

First published in Great Britain in 2022 by
Polygon, an imprint of Birlinn Ltd.

West Newington House
10 Newington Road
Edinburgh
EH9 1QS

www.polygonbooks.co.uk

1

ISBN 978 1 84697 570 7
eBook ISBN 978 1 78885 489 4

British Library Cataloguing in Publication Data
A catalogue record for this book is available
on request from the British Library.

Typeset by Biblichor Ltd, Edinburgh

To all the artists who provided the soundtrack to my writing
(with a special mention to Orchestral Manoeuvres in the
Dark, Juho Paalosmaa and the world of trance dance).

PROLOGUE

The Raid

The door explodes inwards, ancient wood splintering, sending a hail of lethal flying daggers, some a foot long, into the pub. Everyone inside, hidden behind upturned tables, cowers as the staccato rattle of the wooden bullets crashes around the bar. The door handle, an ancient lump of brass, is a warhead, taking out the top gantry of spirits, vaporising bottles – some that have lain there, untouched, for two decades. The door's hinges, set free from their frame, embed themselves in the roof and reduce the banknotes, stuck to the ceiling by generations of drawing pins, currency from around the world, to confetti, spraying the room like the wedding from hell. A slice of oak the size of a boxer's glove rips the lager font from its mountings and the pressurised CO_2 forces a fountain of beer into the air. The eight-ball from the pool table is clipped by shrapnel and rises, ricocheting off the baulk cushion before bulls-eying the giant LED TV, which detonates, ejecting a wave of shattered screen. The room is now a murderous cocktail cloud of glass, wood, metal, paper and lager, forcing the already huddled patrons to hunker down further – to whimper, to cry, to moan, to pray.

Through the gap where the door stood, bodies begin to flow in, heads bent down against the settling debris. Figures rolling across the pub with a single objective. Thundering towards the bar: screaming, shouting, leaping. Kicking tables. Flinging chairs to one side. The patrons lying on the floor little more than living hurdles to be negotiated. Crash helmets crown many of the invaders' heads. They all wear leather jackets or heavy woollen coats and most are sporting steel toecap boots. Some are wearing dark sunglasses. One sports a welder's mask and, in his world of near perfect dark, he head-plants the pool table, potting two balls and cracking a cue into four pieces.

A light bulb is struck and pops. The circuit breaker kicks in and the pub is thrown into darkness.

But on they come.

The bodies.

The pub's patrons have no time to respond. No time to repel. No time to act. They only have survival on their minds – that and a ringing in their ears and flashes of light speckling their sight from the explosion. They are befuddled and scared, lying beneath the wave of invaders – their arms wrapped tight, legs curled up – trying to anticipate blows, avoid pain, cringing under the on-slaught.

A cry goes up as the bar top is breached, the office beyond invaded, and the fire door, blocked with filing cabinets, is wrenched open. The cabinets are thrown to the floor as the invaders, mere seconds inside the building, flow out of the rear. When they have left, a hush settles upon the scene, like the cowl on the dead. Remnants of plaster and currency float down as a lone pool ball rolls to a halt under a table, and a surviving pint glass falls to the ground, smashing. Beyond the ruined entrance there's the sound of cheering, engines firing up, spinning wheels and heavy metal music. That noise too fades.

Then there is nothing. And, for the briefest of moments a void exists where the universe once was: a momentary black hole, its event horizon a perfect sphere to the breeze-block building where the raid took place.

Then someone moves.

A patron of the pub.

Towards the office.

They enter and, a heartbeat later, there is a sigh from within.

Then a sentence from without.

'Did they get it?'

A pause from within.

For a moment there is hope from without.

Then a single word from within. 'Yes.'

'Well, team,' says the voice from without, 'that's us fucked.'

'Christ,' says the voice from the office. 'I think there's a dead body in here.'

'A dead body?' says another voice.

'Yes.'

'Dead?'

'I think so.'

'Who is it?'

'It looks like Pat Ratte.'

I

Carl Stoker

A Week Earlier

They say the sun shines on the righteous. At least my mum used to say that when I was wee. And it's true, but it shines just as hard on the less virtuous. It's just not as palatable to the masses that those with a more selfish agenda should benefit from others, with no comeback for their actions. It hurts more when the morally upright see the morally bankrupt showcasing their new super yachts, treading the glitterati's red carpets or ordering a bottle of the most expensive champagne the local pub has to offer, just because they can.

I don't count myself amongst those insolvent of generosity but I can see where they come from. I understand their contempt for those who they see as weak. I don't approve, but I'm not as sinless as I'd like to think, when it comes down to the brass tacks. That my existence was one of servitude and mindless drudgery in a call centre not long ago has imbued me with a sense of entitlement for the better life I now enjoy. That I am no longer a minion, bowing to some truly horrible people, augurs well for my future. I'm brighter, happier and richer. The source of this new existence is a little more ethically challenging to me than my conscience would like. I have more than my small toe dipped in the world of criminality to pay for my new life. But I've convinced myself, on a superficial level at least, that there is justification for all my actions. That somehow I am a worthy recipient of the spoils. That doesn't sit well with me. I'm of the mindset that if you haven't earned it you don't deserve it. And I sure as hell didn't earn the building I'm sitting in or most of the money in my bank account.

My name is Daniella Coulstoun and I'm the majority shareholder in one of the seediest bars on the Costa Blanca. Buried in the coastal town of El Descaro, Se Busca is a windowless breeze-block cell that serves as a drinking hole for, in the main, British expats. My mother, a stranger to me for most of my adult life, ran this place as her own personal fiefdom for over two decades. Everything in here, from the ceiling papered in cheap foreign currency to the gaudy pink furniture, is a shrine to her poor taste. My mother believed, during the final few years of her life, in the principle that the less cash invested in the pub, the more cash in her pocket.

I'm perched at the bar, *café con leche* in front of me, looking at three badly typed quotes. Each has a substantially higher monetary total than I feel is warranted. All three relate to my desire to lightly, on a budget, revamp the pub. I'm thinking that all three mistakenly believe I want to rebuild the place as some sort of five-star retreat. I'd envisaged a lick of paint and a few new chairs. The quotes are, in my mind, suggesting gold leaf trim and marble thrones.

When my mother died and I'd inherited the pub I was appalled by its lack of aesthetic appeal. But it has grown on me the longer I've been here, my mother's frugal nature surfacing in me. My journey from disgust to tolerance to tacit acceptance of the pub's decor has been a slow but sure one. The quotes in front of me are simply reinforcing my arrival at the end of the journey. I push all three pieces of paper to the side and sip at the coffee.

Clyde, a student who is also one of the minority shareholders in Se Busca, is on point at the bar. He's a nice lad, helpful, hardworking and a hit with the punters. He studies at university in Valencia when not working here – ploughing through a degree in art that he hates but is enduring to please his father's failed artistic ambitions. Clyde had planned to travel once he'd graduated but since I gifted him a small share in the bar he's been full of ideas on how we can expand and make more money – and has stopped talking about roving. Mum left me her flat as well as the bar. A two-bedroom apartment up in El Descaro's old town. She also happened to own a piece of land that a Russian bought from me to turn into upscale homes and that put enough money in my bank to take it easy for a while. And, as a sideline, has allowed me to leave the UK and take up residence in Spain.

I live in the attic above my head. It's a place that I recently had converted from a bare shell, installing an industrial quantity of sound insulation to keep the pub noise out, and splashing out for serious air conditioning to dampen the heat from the bar beneath and the Spanish sun above.

Tonight, in Se Busca, is darts league night. We're up against The Fabled Corner, a pub that nestles in the small village of Cuando, which lies about five miles from where I sit. The darts guys from all the participating pubs take the league seriously. Se Busca are the current champions, having beaten DB's last year by a single point – DB's being another, less successful, expat bar near the beach area of El Descaro. Sandwiches are already lined up on the pool table for the expected hordes and I've ordered in extra lager. The Fabled Corner usually bring a fifty-seater coach full of support with them and all of them drink like booze is about to be banned from the planet. Last time The Fabled Corner played us there was a bar brawl that would have graced John Ford's best scenes so I've hired in a man mountain called Jeep as extra muscle in case things get rowdy. Jeep is old school. Nothing fancy. Blunt force trauma his weapon of choice. He was a super heavyweight fighter back in his day, is twice the mass he was then and steroids have since tripled his muscles. They've also addled what brain cells he had. Words with more than one syllable challenge his intellect but he's effective and, importantly, cheap.

I'm not planning to stay for the darts game. Zia MacFarlane, my partner, has volunteered to help Clyde out at the bar. Zia is singing down at the seafront tonight so in return for pardoning me bar work, I'm the designated taxi driver to ship him to his gig later. As a one-hit-wonder pop singer from the eighties, Zia still harbours hopes of a return to stardom. A dream he has been carrying for forty years.

I decide I fancy a walk to clear my head. The thought of a night in a pub full of punters screaming for a double top isn't appealing to me right now.

'Clyde?' I say.

Clyde is serving Saucy a large vodka and a small tonic. Saucy's real name is Arthur Heinz and he was once a high-powered accountant who, when sober, still knows more about Spanish tax law than anyone I've ever met. He'd be a great man to trust your finances with, if he didn't prefer the lure of the distilled potato peel to that of the balance sheet.

'One minute, Daniella,' says Clyde.

Saucy smiles at me and raises his glass.

'Can you *please* make sure he pays,' I say to Clyde with a sigh.

Saucy is also a minority shareholder in the pub but before I made him such he had a bad habit of drinking for free. One of the conditions of becoming a shareholder was that everyone, except me, pays for booze.

'Already done,' says Clyde, holding up some euros.

Saucy staggers to his favourite table and the vodka is gone before he sits down. Clyde takes him another and returns to the bar.

'What is it?' he asks me.

'Do you mind if I go for a walk? Zia can help out with the darts game.'

'I'd *love* for you to go for a walk, Daniella' he says.

'Love? Clyde, why would you *love* for me to go?'

'Daniella, you might be the boss but you're rubbish behind the bar on nights like tonight.'

'I'm learning.'

'My great-gran is a quicker learner of nuclear physics and she's been dead thirty years.'

I smile and he does likewise. As I said, nice lad.

I drop from the bar stool and acknowledge a few customers as I weave my way to the main door. Clyde grabs the builders' quotes and stuffs them under the till. He's with me on the refurb – a quick visit to *la ferreteria,* a dozen pots of *pintura*, call in some brush holders and pay them in drink is his call. I agree.

As I leave the pub and push into the late afternoon heat, I breathe in the freshness and let the sunlight bathe my face. My pallor doesn't suggest that I'm a resident of a sunny corner of Spain. Since I moved here I've been more of an indoors girl than the outdoors type. Se Busca has a way of eating your life. Of keeping you prisoner. A time machine where the hours fly. There are supposed to be three shifts in the pub. Eleven in the morning to five. Five to midnight and then there is the late haul. The reality is less clear-cut. The bar staff consists of my partner Zia, Clyde the student and myself. There are a couple of others who help out now and again. Zia is a reluctant member of this chain gang and doesn't like working solo, a bit of a must to keep costs down. And since I'm not the best at pouring pints we are tight on good staff. But I pay better than other bars and job security is a given because we have the most loyal punters in the town.

'Daniella Coulstoun?'

The stranger shouting my name is standing in the pub's dirt-covered car park, leaning on a fresh-out-of-the-wrapper deep black BMW 7 Series. Dust covers every car in this town. His is sparkling, as if he's just rolled it away from the valet's white-gloved mitts. He has black, centre-parted hair that rolls onto his shoulders and is wearing a black shirt, loose at the collar, black jeans and black Vans. A silver chain hangs around his neck and, despite the temperature hovering in the late twenties, his armpits are as dry as the Sahara, his forehead clear of sweat. He looks trim and his arms bulge above and below his elbows. Popeye comes to mind.

I say nothing. I've learned that strangers come with a health warning in the world of Se Busca.

'My name is Carl Stoker,' he offers up.

The name means nothing.

'I'd like a quiet word with you, Daniella. If you have a minute.'

I can't place the accent. Not a Brit. Maybe a Scandi. I keep up the silent routine.

'I knew your mother, Effie,' he says. 'We had a small business arrangement. I'm sorry for her passing but, as a courtesy, I would like to talk to you about a mutually beneficial matter.'

'Arrangement?' I decide that silence isn't going to drive this guy off.

'Your mother and I were business acquaintances,' he says.

I'm still on an upward learning curve with my mother. We were all but estranged from each other for twenty years. When she moved to Spain I was sixteen. She left me with my aunt, no explanation, and, on a daily basis, I'm discovering Mum was something of a local legend – and not one with a clean record.

'What type of business acquaintances?' I ask.

'Could we conduct this conversation somewhere less inclement?'

He nods at Se Busca but I'm not for talking to anyone connected with my mother in there. My customers have noses that root out crap and I don't need them anywhere near family business until I know what is going down.

'There's a nice café on the front,' I say. 'Plenty of parking nearby at this time of day.' I nod at his car.

'As you wish,' he says and opens the passenger door.

Stepping into a stranger's car strikes me as not the smartest move this side of the Med but if there's one thing I've learned out here it's to keep all your playing cards, the packet they came in, the cellophane and the spare ace, superglued to your chest. And that means doing any talking away from here. Loose lips sink ships and all that.

The car is as crisp inside as it is out. It could have rolled off the production line yesterday. I point to the road that runs by the pub, and Carl spits some gravel as he exits the car park.

'Down there,' I say.

We slip into the port, buildings rising around us, entering a maze of apartments atop shops. Some of the roads are pedestrian only and I guide us to the main square. But I get the feeling he doesn't need directions.

With one end open to the sea, the square shines in the sun. A few yachts are in the bay playing tag with each other, and the main pier, protecting the marina, is dotted with walkers out for point-less strolls.

Once we are parked and out of the car, I deliberately steer us away from the seafront and into a back alley where a small café sits next to a dead end. It's a local's place. No pandering to tourists. A glass tapas bar with a single beer tap guards the open kitchen. The tables and chairs are traditional wood, the floor is tiled. The walls are all but bare, white and recently painted. A single fan beats above – air conditioning is something frowned upon. I pick a table out of sight of the large glass window that looks out onto the lane and order up a *café con leche*. The stranger asks for water. *Me das, un agua sin gas, por favor.* His Spanish sounds fluent, his accent good. My Spanish is two up from appalling.

'Okay,' I say, as the owner prepares our order. 'Who are you?'

'I told you, my name is Carl Stoker.'

I shake my head. 'That's not what I mean.'

He has a way of talking that reminds me of Capitán Lozano, a police officer I've had a run-in with. The sentences are well constructed, structured, almost as if he's reading a script.

'I know who you are,' he replies. 'You are Daniella Coulstoun. Your mother, Euphemia Coulstoun was the sole owner of Se Busca until her untimely demise. You now own the bar, or rather you are the majority shareholder. Your minority shareholders are the young student, Clyde, Zia MacFarlane, the ex-pop star, who is your partner, Arthur Heinz, accountant, who is known to all as Saucy, Peter Solo, a failed racing driver, who likes to be called Skid, Jordan Norman and his sister Sheryl, failed models, and George Laidlaw, a failed lawyer. Collectively Effie called them all the Ex-Patriots and, as far as I can ascertain, you have taken over the mantle of your mother as the de facto leader of this little gang. You also have a tie-up with Pat Ratte, pronounced rat, an ex-gangster who used to live up on the hill behind the town, in a large villa, but is now sweating it out in a hotel, waiting to see if he will be charged for killing your mother. Did I miss anything?'

The man has done his homework.

'My shoe size?'

'Probably a six.'

'Good guess. So what do you want, Mr Stoker?'

The water and coffee arrive and Carl drinks the liquid, taking his time.

'Your mother never mentioned me?' he questions – after the fourth sip.

'I hardly talked to my mother in twenty years. She was here. I was answering phones for an insurance company in the UK. But you probably know that as well. She died late last year and I never got to say goodbye. So the simple answer is no, she never mentioned you.'

'You came out for her funeral and never went home? So I believe.'

'Something like that.'

Carl's teeth have that whiter-than-white sheen that's bought with the sort of money that would pay for a half-decent home extension. They are picture-perfect straight and when he talks his gums show, singing healthy. I'm not close enough to smell his breath but I'm betting we are in minty-fresh-with-added-zest land.

'How did you know my mother?' I ask.

'As I said, we had a business arrangement.'

'What type of arrangement?'

For the first time, Carl looks around the café. We are the only customers and the owner is cleaning the kitchen range at the far side of the bar.

'An arrangement that benefited us both,' he says, as if that explains everything.

'And?'

'Do you bet, Daniella?'

'I've been known to put a quid each way on the Grand National, and I was a killer at pitch 'n' toss when I was at school. But other than that, I think it's a mug's game.'

'Many people enjoy it as a pastime.'

'I'm sure they do but I had a friend who gambled away his home, wife and eventually his life.'

'Unfortunate.' The word comes out with ice on it.

'Where is this going?' I ask.

'Daniella, your mother was a bit of a gambler.'

'Mum?'

Every day is a school day out here.

'Well, let me rephrase that,' he says. 'Your mum liked to be involved in gambling.'

I'm not surprised. When I'd arrived I'd discovered that my mother had been up front and centre on a million-euro-plus property scam that had gone south. The odd bet here and there seems a little underwhelming in the face of that.

'I never knew,' I say.

'Daniella, she was what could be called a middle man. Or rather a middle woman. Or should that be middle person? I'm never quite sure nowadays. A conduit between the individual who wishes to bet and people like myself.'

'You're a bookie?'

He laughs. A small unpleasant rasping sound.

'You could call me that. I prefer the term gaming consultant. I facilitate wagers.'

'I thought all that shit was done online nowadays.'

His face crinkles, just a touch, at my use of the word shit.

'For the more run-of-the-mill bets, that's true,' he says. 'But I am not interested in the run-of-the-mill. I am more a connoisseur of the exotic wager.'

'Which means?'

'Let me explain.'

He drains the water and signals for another.

'Daniella, have you heard of the *Puig Campana*?'

'The mountain near Benidorm?'

'That's the place. Well, it's a popular spot for a little hill walking. Unusually it has two peaks. Legend says a French hero, a commander of Charlemagne's army, cleaved a massive notch in the smaller peak with his sword while fighting a Moorish leader.'

'I must remember that one for the quiz night,' I say.

He doesn't smile.

'There is,' he continues, 'an annual foot race to the top. It's fiercely competitive and, as a result, generates a little side betting. A wide variety of side betting if truth be told. Money on the first runner to the top, first to both peaks, first man up and back, first woman up and back, first person with the name Jose to the top.'

'You made that last one up?'

'No I didn't and that's just the start. There are bets on last to the top, second last. You can bet on the forty-third up if you want. First person with a dog. First runner to be hospitalised. Heart attacks, broken legs, medical stitches, stretchered off. You get the gig. Some people will bet on anything. I satisfy that demand.'

'And that's a worthwhile commercial exercise?' I say, mimicking his clipped style.

'I'll let you in on a little secret.' He looks around the café again, ignoring my little jibe. 'The total sum waged on the *Cursa de Puig Campana* last year was just over one hundred thousand euros.'

Despite myself, I'm interested. 'In total?'

'No,' he says, laying a hand flat on the table. 'Just through my book.'

'And this sort of betting is prevalent elsewhere?'

'I cater for the bets that the big boys don't. Take La Vuelta last year. The cycle race. It came right through El Descaro. Knowing the route, I picked six points along the way. Call them imaginary finish lines. You'd be amazed how many people bet on who would cross those imaginary lines first.'

'But it could be anyone at that point in the race. The finish was fifty kilometres from here.'

'Exactly. And that allowed me to offer large odds and the punters flooded in. Same principle as your Grand National back in the UK. Most people bet on a name, not form. People like long odds.'

'And what has my mum to do with all of this?'

'She helped run my book. Se Busca is a police-free zone. Is it not?'

He leaves that hanging. I know it to be true. We have what can be best called an understanding with both the Guardia Civil and the Policía Local. They leave us alone and we ensure that the less savoury of our clientele don't crap on their own doorstep. And that would make us the perfect place to transact a bet offline.

'Effie,' he continues once his second water has been delivered, 'would set up a small table at the back of the pub for me at certain times. I'd then conduct my business and your mother would take a cut of the winnings. As the ad says, *Simples*.'

I have a feeling that nonsense like this coming out of the woodwork about Mum is going to be a less than favourite part of my life for a while yet. Her twenty years out here are a mystery novel to me that is being revealed, page by page, day by day, event by event. Effie, as everyone knew her, cut a huge figure in these parts. A figure that some think I need to replicate.

'And you want to set up shop in the pub for some event?' I ask. 'Is that it?'

'A big event.'

'How big?'

'Have you heard of the El Descaro Classic?'

14

I shake my head. 'Enlighten me.'

'A classic car rally. It's held every two years. Cars start from all over Europe and end up here. Your mum was involved in getting it up and running in the first place.'

'Bloody hell, what wasn't she involved in?'

'Not much, Daniella. Anyway, the finish point for the event is the Se Busca car park. Your mum would put up a marquee and lay on food and drink. It's a big deal. Once all the cars arrive there's a parade through the town and down to the seafront.'

Now I think about it I have heard of it. I'm not a car person but I seem to remember it being described as the London to Brighton Veteran Car Run on steroids. Instead of sixty miles we are talking thousands of miles covered in ancient cars.

'And this is a big betting thing?' I ask.

'Huge. There are eleven start points in nine countries and every one of those countries has expats out here living or holidaying. They'll bet on a range of outcomes for the race. It's one of my biggest pay days. But we are only seven months out from the start, and I went surfing on the Internet last night to discover that there's no update to the rally's website.'

'So?'

'Your mother ran the website. It is the hub for registration and info.'

'I know nothing about it.'

'That's why I'm here. Time to get it together, Daniella. Normally entries are taken from six months out. And you are *it* for getting the whole race up and running.'

I stare at the café window letting the coffee get to work. I've eased into a nice groove here in Spain over the last few months. Zia and I are rolling along just fine, even given our twenty-year age difference. The bar is ticking over and the days are melding into one. My ex-colleagues back in the UK are still sitting at their call-centre desks staring at a screen and wishing it was Friday, so pissed off at my Facebook posts that I've noticed I've been blocked or ghosted by most. There's only so many pictures of a cold glass of *vino blanco* with the Med in the background, sun above, that a wet UK resident can take. So the thought of organising some classic car rally really isn't on my agenda.

'I don't think that'll be happening this year,' I say.

Carl leans across the table, lifting his hands and placing them on mine. He presses down with the heels of his palms, crushing my knuckles. I yank my hands to try and free them, but he simply puts on more pressure. His face changes. The smile gone. Eyes solid. Nose flared.

My hands feels like they are about to explode.

As I struggle, he speaks in a whisper – almost inaudible. 'Yes,' he says to me. 'It.' Pause. 'Is.' Pause. 'Going To.' Pause. 'Fucking Happen.'

He leans back, freeing my hands, and the smile reappears. 'Do I make myself clear?'

I'm unsure what to say. That was down and dirty scary. A real *Sopranos* moment. Tony in full effect.

'Maybe a beer?' he says as if the incident had never happened. 'To celebrate our new partnership. The queen is dead. Long live the queen. Does that sound about right?'

Nothing about that sounds about right.

2

The Gen on Stoker

I skip on the beer offer, rise and leave without a word. My legs are shaking a little. Carl is a chameleon with a terror side. His welcoming demeanour, flash clothes and smooth talk hide an ability to scare the crap out of you. Seven words and I am reeling.

'*Yes. It. Is. Going To. Fucking Happen.*'

I exit the café and draw some fresh air into my lungs before heading for the sea, trying to calm my nerves. I drop onto the sea wall and boat-watch a clutch of small yachts dancing with each other. Beyond them, riding the horizon, is a container ship, ploughing its way south, probably aiming for Alicante or New York or somewhere else.

As I sit, I know I need some more info on Carl and the El Descaro Classic. I call Zia. He answers on the second ring.

'Hi, lover.'

That usually makes me grin. But not today.

'Hi, pop star,' I say with no heart.

That will still make him smile. Zia had one Top 40 hit back in the eighties and has been chasing that fame bubble ever since. He's currently working on an album although it seems to be taking an age to come together. When I ask about it, which I do a lot as I'm not allowed to go to the studio, he says good things take time. I point out how disappointing 'Chinese Democracy' was when Axl Rose eventually got around to releasing it after working on it for a decade – blowing some 13 million dollars in the process. Zia tells me it would be nice to have that much time and money.

'Where are you?' he asks.

'Down at the front. Zia, do you know a guy called Carl Stoker?'

'A bad bastard,' is his curt reply.

'Did Mum know him?'

'She did and as far as I know she was the only one that could handle him. He used to set up shop in the pub now and again. He's the go-to guy for under-the-counter betting around here. Why?'

'He doorstepped me outside the pub. I went for a coffee with him and he more or less told me that any deal he had with Mum, he now has with me. That and something to do with the El Descaro Classic.'

Zia sighs. 'A real pain. Your mum organised a lot of the rally. It's a ton of work and it's a big deal. The last one had close on three hundred cars enter. From all over Europe. As far afield as Russia.'

'That guy Stoker said they all finish at our car park.'

'They do.'

'You couldn't fit three hundred cars in our car park.'

'Your mum used the wasteland behind the pub. She paid a contractor to clear the scrub. The *ayuntamiento* help with some of the costs.'

Se Busca is located on a vacant plot midway between the port and the old town of El Descaro that sits up on a hill. The pub lives in a no-man's land surrounded by bush and trees. There's some sort of preservation order on the area and nothing else can be built near the pub. That suits everyone just fine.

'The rally sounds expensive to put on.' I say.

'It is, but your mum wasn't stupid. She made money on it all.'

'And what about this guy Carl Stoker? What's his background?'

'Not good. He isn't nearby, is he?'

I look around. 'No,' I say.

'Trust me, Daniella, you don't want to pry into his dealings. Even Pat Ratte is scared of this guy and Pat ran with the worst of them back in London.'

'And?'

'Rumour says Carl was some sort of gun-for-hire.'

'A hit man?'

'So they say. He hired himself out at big bucks if you believe the stories. Then, about a five years back, he rolled into El Descaro and next thing he's the new bookie of choice. He chased all the others out, and I use the word "chase" in its loosest sense. To this day a few of his competition have never been seen or heard from again.'

I swing my legs over the sea wall and bang my heels on the stonework. My heart is sinking faster than a shot-put being pushed off a cliff.

'So not someone to get involved with,' I say.

'You need to talk to George. He knows a bit more than me. He'd be in a better place to advise you on what to do.'

I'm wishing I'd been a bit slower to get into Carl's car. Thought it through a little.

'Is George in the pub?'

'I was downstairs five minutes ago and he wasn't to be seen. Why don't you WhatsApp him?'

'Love you, rock star.'

'Igualmente.'

I hang up and draw up the WhatsApp screen and type.

'George, can you talk?'

There's no instant response and I stand up, stretching out my nervousness. I console myself with the fact that Mum seemed to be able to deal with Stoker. And if she could, then maybe I can, although I'm not filled with joy at the thought. My mum was a very different beast to me. When she'd died of a heart attack on the pub floor, I'd been in the UK and the more I discover about her the less certain I am that I'm the chip off the old block that people seem to expect.

I cross to a café and buy an ice cream to try and calm myself a little. As I lick the cone the WhatsApp noise buzzes from my pocket.

'What is it?' It's from George.

I type back. 'Ever heard of a guy called Carl Stoker?'

A second later the audio on the WhatsApp bursts into life and I answer.

'Hi George,' I say.

George is a disbarred lawyer from the UK who came out with Mum two decades ago to set up a new life, only for Mum to dump him ten years in. Although he stuck by her to the end. He's also another of the minority shareholders in Se Busca.

'Why are you asking about Stoker?' he asks.

I give him the once-over on my meeting with Stoker.

'Scary bastard, isn't he?'

'He seemed so polite at first.'

'It's his way. He can be the nicest person on the planet and the devil's own pitchfork an instant later.'

'Did Mum know him well?'

'Your mother had the measure of him. Knew how to handle him. She was the only one who did. I was never sure how. I always thought she had something on him. It would be so like Effie to have gen.'

'How did you get on with him?'

'Okay. But I was always talking to him about stuff him and your mum were working on. As I said, when it came to your mum he was a different person.'

'Why did no one mention him before?'

'Daniella, no one has mentioned a lot of things to you before. Effie was twenty years out here. She built a business and a lot of relationships. Stoker is only one of many.'

'And this El Descaro Classic?'

'A lot of work but a nice earner. It's a bunch of car nuts getting to drive across Europe in their pride and joys.'

'And Stoker?'

'Makes the book on the side. Uses Se Busca as the bookies' shop for about a week leading up to the race and stays in place until the last car leaves. Then he goes.'

My ice cream is dripping. I flick some liquid to the ground and lick up the mess running down my hand.

'I take it Mum got a cut of the action?' I say.

'That's how it worked.'

'How much was the cut?'

'Twenty per cent of the net profit.'

'I'm thinking we don't need this.'

'I'd love to say it was your call but if Carl wants it to happen, I can't see any way to say no.'

'Can't we find someone else that would want to run it?'

'Not a chance. No one deals with Stoker unless they have to. And he doesn't like anyone sticking their nose in his business. He'll want it all arranged and a quiet corner set aside for him – with absolutely no questions.'

I listen, thinking. George knows a lot about how things work in Se Busca land. And there is nothing about that land that's normal. It's a hang-out for the disenfranchised. A place with its own rules and, if it had its way, its own passport – it's a state for the stateless.

'George, who would know how the bloody race is run?'

'You're in luck, Daniella. Skid is your man. He loves the bloody thing.'

'Brilliant.'

Peter, né Skid Solo, named after the Skid from the Tiger comic back in the day, is an Ex-Patriot racing nut who believes he still has what it takes to be a champion racing driver. He doesn't, but there's no convincing him. He is also, in non-PC parlance, a wheel short of full racing mode.

'Can he run such a thing?'

'Not well, he needs help, but your mum used him a lot to do all the crap work and heavy lifting. He knows the ins and outs better than anyone but he'll fall flat on his arse if you ask him to run it on his own.'

'Anyone else know much?'

'Zia, your partner, helped a little. To be fair we all did. Effie roped everyone in come the day.'

'And you think saying no to Stoker is a bad idea?'

'In the scheme of crap ideas then it's the crappiest of crappy ideas in a crappy field. My advice is to arrange the thing, give him a desk and just pray it all goes well.'

'Thanks, George.'

I kill the call and discard the half-eaten ice cream in the bin. I've lost my desire.

3

The Bubble

When I was ten years old I ended up in hospital. Three broken bones in my left leg, all as the result of crossing the wrong person at school. I'd been playing with a couple of tennis balls at break. Handballing the things off a wall. At my best, when I was about thirteen, I could work three balls at the same time but back then two balls was my limit. If I could get into a rhythm I could ride fifty or sixty smacks off the wall before I lost it. And it was the concentration required to hit those heights that had gotten me into trouble.

We had our share of the bad boys in my school class when I was wee. A small red-headed loon called Fraser Smart who thought it the queen's knickers to flick bogies into your hair. Or there was Neville Ralston. He considered peeing in his pants and then letting you sit in the chair he'd just soaked worth the hiding he got back home for pissing himself. There was even Robbie Dunn, a crabbit little shit who hid around corners and leaped out on you as you appeared. He'd do it all day long with a Tarzan-esque yell as he shoved you to one side. But the real bastard was Tommy Todd. An out-and-out mental case. He should never have been at our school. He needed round-the-clock attention, drugs and disciplining. He wasn't on the spectrum or classed as ADHD or diagnosed bipolar. He had no medical excuse for his behaviour – although heaven alone knows they looked for it. He was simply an evil, vindictive little prick who enjoyed other people's misery.

I always thought the source of his vile anger came from his height. He was by far the smallest person in our year and made Clive Jennings' life a living nightmare. Clive was three planets ahead of us all when it came to vertical inches and Tommy was relentless in his pursuit of Clive. That was until the day he pushed Clive over the edge when, literally, he shoved Clive from a twelve-foot wall onto the road below. Clive saw red. Tommy, for the first time in his life, came off second best when Clive picked up a slug of wood from the garden of Mrs Carmichael. He smashed Tommy's nose with one blow of the plank, earned a suspension for that and Tommy's reward was a trip to hospital.

The following day I was playing with the two tennis balls at the back of the school shelter, an ancient construction of stone and slate, designed to be a bolt-hole for the kids when it rained. I failed to see Tommy slip around the corner of the shed – which, given that he had a white bandage circling his face like some giant Polo mint, showed how engrossed in the game I was. Tommy nipped in between me and the wall and kicked one of the flying balls, sending it skiting away. Common sense should have told me to suck it up, pick up the other ball and leave. Common sense was having a day off and my anger bunny, with which I live to this day, popped out.

Instead of taking my medicine, I turned on him and launched the ball in my hand at his head. My aim was true and the ball smacked off his damaged beak. A blow that would normally have been little more than mild on the pain scale, registered with Tommy like an incoming cricket ball bowled by the Hulk. And, as the offending ball rolled up against the wall, I knew I was up the shittiest creek of my young life. As my old friend 'Trine said when telling the tale, 'Tommy went Radio Rental.'

I knew better than to stand and wait on the inevitable retribution, and hit the concrete with one destination in mind – the jannie's office. Our janitor was called Mr McLarey and he was a menacing son of a bitch. Tommy might have been mental but he would have had to be certifiably insane to square up to Scary McLarey. I'd have made it to safety had I not taken a swan dive over some P4 kids playing marbles. I slammed into a small brick wall, yards from Scary's door and Tommy was on me like an arrow from Robin Hood. I took half a dozen kicks to my legs before Scary saw what was going down and intervened. Hospital and a cast followed suit.

The lesson from that day stays with me. Don't cross scary bastards if you can avoid them and, if you do have to deal with them, do it on your own ground, on your own terms and when you are good and ready.

And Carl Stoker is a scary person who needs some quality thinking and planning time applied to him. Not so much a Plan A, B and C – more a bloody perfect Plan A with enough flexibility to allow for the mad nutter that he clearly was. And for that I will have to seek advice. Good solid advice. Advice from someone with the experience of a lifetime of dealing with nutters. I know two people I can approach on that front. And they couldn't be more different in their backgrounds.

In the red corner we have Capitán Lozano of the Guardia Civil. Lozano is still investigating the death of my mother. At the time, I, along with most other people, thought Mum had died of natural causes – a heart attack brought on by a love of junk food and booze – he had thought differently. He'd suspected someone else had been involved and that brings me to the man in the blue corner – Pat Ratte. Pat is the man who Lozano has down for my mum's death. Ratte is an ex-gangster from London, although the 'ex' is a matter of interpretation. Now in his late seventies, he's still a powerful man. Ratte is currently out on bail. Unusual for a murder suspect in this country but the evidence is circumstantial at best. He'd supplied Mum with some Ecstasy pills that she took and it's a matter of debate whether they triggered her heart attack or not. Before he was lifted by the police he had been renting my mum's flat up in the old town from me but I'd told him to forget that once he was connected to my mother's death. Pat has admitted to slipping her a half-dozen tablets of Ecstasy on the morning of her death. He says she'd asked for them as a pick-me-up. That she used them regularly. But Ratte is only *el investigado* at this stage and that's why he has been given bail. He had a quantity of drugs on him when he was arrested but that wasn't enough to keep him locked up. He is now in a hotel near the harbour awaiting a trial date.

Both Lozano and Ratte have a lifetime of experience under their belts with people like Stoker. Neither is an ideal choice as a shoulder to cry on. Lozano thinks me a crook and lucky to be walking the streets after my involvement in Mum's recent property scam. I'm also sure Stoker will be on his radar and I don't want word to leak back to Stoker that I'm talking to the Guardia Civil about him. That would be bad for my health.

My reasoning behind not wanting to talk to Pat is simpler. He killed my mother. I'd like to believe otherwise and that it was Mum's sedentary lifestyle that did for her. When we'd cleared her apartment, two freezers stuffed with microwave curries and six crates of rum had to be decanted. Her coffin had carried a triple XL badge on it. Regardless, I still have Pat down for her death. He gave her those pills. Full stop.

Ratte or Lozano. I know of no one else who can help me. As a time-served, call-centre grunt in the claims department of an insurance firm I've tackled my share of criminals, but, if I believe Zia and George, Stoker is shaping up to be an Olympic javelin thrower to my schoolkid shot-putting ability.

Ratte's hotel is two hundred yards, maybe less, from where I stand. Lozano is based about two hundred yards the other way. I've no doubt both know Stoker, but only Ratte knows him from the dark side. And I've a feeling that will matter.

Ratte has texted and called frequently since his arrest. I've blanked him. He's been told to stay away from Se Busca and, surprisingly, has done just that. I've seen him just twice since he was lifted. Once when he honked at me from his ageing Range Rover down by the harbour, and once when I'd seen him sitting in my favourite café in the main square of the old town. Both times I'd ignored him.

I think back on Tommy Todd and how much worse it could have been if I'd been further away from Scary McLarey's front door. And Ratte is Scary's front door, but how in the hell do you even begin to engage with a man who killed your mother? Forget the emotional jungle that surrounds such a chat, it could also be seen as a mitigating factor in his favour come court day. The daughter of the deceased happily in conversation with the suspected killer. That would be one for the defence counsel to use. Me talking to him would be a big lever for Ratte to reference as to his innocence.

What to do?

My go-to on these things is Zia. He's become my confidant in a way I thought no one would. His twenty years on me place a welcome sense of calm on my sometimes-racing thoughts. But I know his answer without calling. Neither Ratte or Lozano should be approached. He'll tell me that Pat Ratte isn't someone to trust, that he was involved in my mother's death and isn't above raising his hand to solve his problems – male or female. And he'll say that if I talk to Lozano it will get back to Stoker – and that is a bad, bad path. Zia would just tell me to wake up, smell a truckload of Nescafé and walk away from it all. Let things take their course. But if this guy Stoker needs a little taming then I need to learn a few things quickly.

'Ze bandit is ours, Señorita Coooolstone.'

The man shouting the words is a rotund, bald-headed figure wearing a pork-pie hat. His name is Davie Brost and he owns DB's, our less successful expat pub rival, better known to the customers as the Dog's Bollocks. George Laidlaw introduced me to Davie a month back and we exchanged a few words on the street. And that's been my total interaction with him since I arrived here. But he's a jealous son of a bitch. Se Busca does three times the business he does, and is the home of choice for many of the expats around here. Davie wants that mantle, especially now that Mum has gone. As to what he's shouting about, I'm clueless.

'We ees taking eet back to our casa, Señorita Coooolstone.'

The faux Mexican accent is obviously meant to add something to the message. He's grinning like a dung-chewing sloth and waving his hands in the air as he shouts. A few people around him are staring.

'One weeeek, Señorita Coooolstone, one weeeek.'

He turns up a lane and vanishes, laughing.

Another El Descaro mystery to solve. *Zee bandit is ours.* Hell knows what that means.

I look out at the water. Something I do a lot. It's postcard perfect. Two rising cliffs at either end of the bay curving towards the sea. A pebble beach breathing in and out in rattles as the waves come and go. The small harbour feeding and receiving a constant flow of boats. A few hardy, early season swimmers riding the small white horses. And, in the distance, a cargo ship is heading north, Barcelona bound probably. I stand in the shade of a palm tree, leaning on it, hand rubbing the wooden scales that make up its rough bark. A paddle boarder, a young woman in a cut-down wet suit, is making her way along the coast twenty yards from shore, long wavy strokes guiding the board along. She's gazing my way; she hypnotised by the shore, me by the sea. We lock eyes for a second then she wobbles, stops paddling, throws her attention to her feet, rebalances, dips the blade back in the water and takes up the stroke again. I don't recognise her but that's hardly a surprise. The beach draws from a world of locals and foreigners. Tens of thousands of people use this place. In the summer if you open your ears you can hear twenty languages in twenty minutes. Spanish wins out, but only just. In sheer numbers the place is as close as makes no difference to fifty per cent local and fifty per cent outsiders. Enclaves have sprung up over the years, the Brits hugging one of the hills, the Swiss nestling under the mountain, the Germans deep in the valley, the French down by the beach, the Dutch in the port. The bars and restaurants reflect this. You can eat your way around most of Europe if you take a fancy. Tapas rules, but from Sunday roast to Abendbrot and Mellanmål to Borreltijd: seek and ye shall find.

The thought of food stirs up my stomach but I'm trying to keep an eye on my weight. When I landed here I was proud of my figure. Six days a week I'd put myself through the purgatory of the spin class in the UK, following it up with fifty lengths of the local swimming pool. Out here my exercise regime is seven nights a week in a bar, and too often on the wrong side of it. My shorts fit, because I bought them two weeks ago; my jeans don't, because they arrived with me. There's a slimming club in the old town that's starting to look appealing. And that's not something I thought I'd ever find myself thinking.

I stroll out onto the harbour wall, aiming for the small lighthouse that squats at the end. A row of sailboats lines the harbour side of the wall, shrouds and forestays ringing off their masts in a chaotic chorus as the vessels bob. A few other souls are out for a walk. Come summer the place will be wall to wall with humanity. I stop short of the lighthouse and stare back at the town, running my eye up one of the roads until I spot the black tar roof of Se Busca framed by the old town above it. I let the thoughts around Stoker and Brost melt a little in the sun. A *bocadillo* would be good just about now, suggests the naughty part of my brain. *Jamon y queso* with all the trimmings, a small plate of *patatas bravas*, a cold Coke and some olives. Ladies and gentlemen, I thank you for your calories, my hips and tum are grateful for your contribution.

I sigh, the noise surprising a passing man out with his dog. Skipping food would be a far better, if less appealing, idea.

'We ees taking eet back to our casa.'

Davie Brost's words float out over the water and I wonder what he is talking about. Take what back to their house? *The bandit?*

Who or what in the hell is the bandit? If he means a person, it could describe almost anyone who frequents my pub. We're not short on the legally dodgy in Se Busca.

I walk back to the port, chewing over Brost and Stoker.

'Hi, Daniella.'

George Laidlaw is sitting sipping a glass of whisky at one of the harbour-front cafés.

'Hi, George. Did you come looking for me?'

'Given our call I thought you might need a little face-to-face time about your new problem.'

'Stoker?'

He puts his finger to his lips. 'Shh.'

George had taken an almost instant dislike to me when I arrived on the scene. That was until I cut him in on a share of the pub and fed fifty k in euros into his bank. Now we do what I would class as 'strained civility'. His patented chino, white shirt, neat trimmed beard and swept-back-hair look, coupled with an overly firm handshake, are his way of marking out his legal credentials – even if he has no Spanish qualifications to practise. That hasn't stopped him amassing a client base that trusts his advice. I wouldn't trust him if he presented me with a certificate of authenticity from John Grisham.

'Can we park Stoker for a moment,' I say. 'It's about Davie Brost.'

'Take a seat.'

I pull out a chair and the waitress approaches.

'*Me das una copa de vino blanco?*'

She nods and vanishes inside. I'll limit myself to one if I need to drive Zia tonight. Just one.

George watches the waitress's backside as she leaves.

'She could be your granddaughter,' I say.

'No, she couldn't. Not unless I've got kids I don't know about. So what is it about Davie Brost?'

'Not long after our WhatsApp call he appeared on the other side of the road. Starts shouting at me. Bloody weird and all.'

'Shouting what?'

'Something about coming to get the bandit.'

George laughs. 'Christ, is it that time of year already?'

'So you know what he's talking about?'

'Yip. The Steal.'

'The Steal? What's that? An annual conference for thieves?'

He laughs again as the waitress drops my wine on the table.

'Gracias,' I say.

'De nada,' she replies and George's eyes wander to her jeans again.

'You do know that people can see you doing that?' I say.

'I can look.'

'Sure, but a bit of subtlety would look less pervy.'

'Maybe I like pervy?'

'The Steal, George,' I say with a grump in my voice. 'What's the Steal?'

'An annual competition between DB's and Se Busca.'

'What type of competition?'

'A stealing competition.'

'Stealing what?'

The waitress reappears and I flick George on the nose as he turns to look at her.

'Stealing what?' I repeat.

He rubs his nose but still watches the waitress.

'Saucy started it,' he says.

'Saucy started what?' I ask.

'He stole Bernie about ten years back.'

I lean back in the chair. George can be like this. Instead of just telling you the story straight out, he strings it along. A hangover from his legal days when he charged by the hour. He can take a ten-minute pub chat and stretch it to last most of the night.

'George, just give me the non-chargeable version of the story.'

He gazes around looking for the waitress but she's inside. Once he's satisfied she's not nearby he continues. 'About ten years back Saucy was down on the front, pub-crawling. Effie had slung him

31

out as he was shit-faced and noising up the other customers. You know what he's like now and again.'

I do. Most times he's a harmless drunk but every so often he goes on the attack, offending at will.

'Anyway,' George says, 'Saucy reaches DB's. By that time probably the only place that would serve him. They are none too fussy about your state of inebriation. Not if you still have cash to spend. Daniella, have you ever been in DB's?'

I shake my head.

'A bit basic. If sawdust were still in fashion the floor would be an inch thick in the stuff. Anyway, the pub has a mascot sitting behind the bar. A large stuffed bulldog called Bertie. A monster of a thing that Brost brought from the UK. It wears a Union Jack waistcoat. Brost keeps his pork-pie hat on it when he's in the pub. Well, Saucy managed to steal it.'

'What? The hat?'

'No. Bertie. Heaven knows how. It's almost as big as him. Not only that but he managed to drag it the mile and a half back to Se Busca. Brost went ape but we refused to return it and he was forced to come and pick the thing up.'

'Is that it?'

'A month later Brost sneaked into Se Busca one afternoon and stole Busca.'

'Busca?'

'Our bandit.'

'*Our* bandit.'

'We have a mascot as well. A wooden bandit called Busca.'

'At Se Busca?'

'You've not seen him?'

'Obviously not. Busca the Bandit?'

'That's him. He usually sits beneath the big telly.'

'I'm lost.'

'He's a large carved model of a Mexican bandit. Sombrero, bandolier's belt and all.'

My blank look encourages him to keep going.

'I thought he was here when you arrived. Maybe not. His arm got broken off sometime back, and Saucy arranged to get him fixed by the guy who carved him in the first place. When I think about it he was sent away a couple of weeks before Effie died. In fact, he should have been back before now. Especially as the Steal is next week.'

I sip my wine and feel better informed but less knowledgeable. I wait while George orders up another glass of whisky and ogles the waitress.

'And how does this Steal work?' I ask when I get George's attention back.

'The Steal,' he eventually says, 'is an annual piece of nonsense that takes place every year. Each pub has to try and steal the other's mascot. Whoever has both mascots in their pub at midnight is the winner.'

I empty my lungs in one long blow.

'George?' I say.

'What?'

'When does this stop?'

'When does what stop?'

'All this drivel that comes with Se Busca.'

'Drivel?'

'Stoker, the Steal, El Descaro Classic and the mountain of other crap I've encountered in the last few months.'

'It's hardly drivel. It's what goes on here. What did you expect when you came over? A weekly game of bridge and the omnibus edition of *EastEnders* on Sundays? You're running a pub not a tea room. If you think that what you've seen so far is not to your taste then just wait. You're hardly out of the starting blocks. There's a lot more down the track.'

'This is so dumb.'

'You can always sell up.'

When I'd inherited the pub that had been my intention, but this place has a way of getting under your skin. The sun and sea are

33

only part of the attraction. There's also the fact that it's not my old life. And my old life is a great reason not to return to Blighty.

'Well, I could do with some warning on stuff,' I point out. 'You know, like a calendar of events – who is who? What to do? What not to do?'

'You're a slow learner aren't you, Daniella?'

That stops my train of thought. 'Pardon?'

'You're not the brightest. Effie had you beat hands down on that front.'

'Are you trying to insult me or just doing it by accident?'

He slugs his whisky back, emptying the glass. 'I'm just telling you the way I see it. You've been here what? Five, six months? And in that time what have you actually done?'

'I've been trying to run a business.'

'Sure, pulling pints, ordering stock, getting food in for the odd event.'

'And the rest.'

'I don't see much *rest* from where I sit. What about learning the ins and outs of this town? What about getting to *know* the lie of the land? The competition? What about meeting with the local officials at the *ayuntamiento*? Or the police or the Guardia Civil? What about setting out a plan to build the business? What about asking your fellow shareholders what they think of things? What about getting to know your other shareholders?'

I don't reply.

'Daniella, all I see is someone who has landed lucky. Someone that was gifted a pub, an apartment and a wedge of cash. Mummy came good and dropped it all in your lap.'

'My mother didn't gift me it. She died. Remember. She didn't bloody give me anything when she was alive.'

'Poor girl. Doesn't see much of Mummy for twenty years and feels hard done by. Is that it?'

'Why are you being like this? Is it because Mum dumped you?'

'No. That's ancient history and these things happen. Effie moved on from me a decade back.'

'But you never moved on from her?'

George had been, unknown to me, Mum's lover back in the UK for a few years even before she moved to Spain.

'I did move on.'

'You'd hardly notice.'

'Daniella, do you really want to know why I'm down here chewing shit with you?'

'I do.'

'Okay, open your ears and listen. It's time you saw what is what around here. You might have fobbed off the Ex-Patriots with a share in Se Busca and a little cash—'

'And keeping you all out of jail,' I interrupt.

'So you say.'

'I bloody did. That stupid property scam Mum set up would have sunk you all without me. And, I repeat, *I* stopped you going to jail.'

'No,' he says, 'you stopped us all getting the hell out of this place. In fact you've now tied us to it.'

'You ungrateful sod,' I shout and the other customer's eyes focus on us.

'You should've handed the money over to us.'

'And what? You would've run into the night and left me as the patsy.'

'You could've run as well.'

'I didn't have to. I wasn't the one who was involved in the scam.'

'So what?''Oh, wake up, Daniella. Do you think any of us want to be here? We were all but out of here in our heads and you changed that. Now there's no chance of leaving. And you just happily ignore that.'

I'm taken aback. I had dug them out of a 1.3 million-euro hole and now I'm being told I was the bad person in all this.

'Get to the point, George.'

'Daniella,' he continues, 'if you want this life to work out for you, you'll need to do a damn site more than open the doors of Se Busca and drink wine.'

I look at the glass in front of me as he says that.

'Daniella, you're in a bubble, and every time something comes along that could prick that bubble you act as if you've been done an injustice.'

'And what should I do?'

'For a start, you could take the whole thing a damn sight more seriously and get ahead of the wave. And while you're at it, plan an exit.'

'An exit? I'm only just here.'

'Not just an exit for you but for all of us.'

'You want out?'

'Se Busca is losing value as we sit, Daniella.'

'I built the new beer garden. Put in the flat above.'

'A beer garden that few use and a flat that adds bugger all to the business – but makes you and Zia very comfy. And inside the pub is still a shithole. Admittedly a profitable one but a shithole all the same.'

'What would you have me do?'

'You have money. Invest in the business and then sell it. Give us all some hope that our shares will be worth something more in the future – and not less. You might be young but a few of the Ex-Patriots are closer to the end of a gravedigger's spade than they like. So get your head out of your arse and run the place like you mean it.'

'Or what, George? Or what?'

'Or move on.'

'What? Just leave? And do what with the pub?'

'Sell it to us. One euro would be a fair price.'

I choke on my wine. 'You want me to sell the pub for a *euro*.'

'Unless you up your game, yes.'

'You've drunk too much whisky.'

'Not yet I haven't. Daniella, sometimes you can't see what's right in front of your face.'

'What does that mean?'

'Daniella, how much of this conversation do you think is spontaneous?'

'Bloody none.'

'Spot on. This isn't a stream of consciousness on my part. This is an official warning.'

'What kind of warning?'

'Step up to the plate or we'll take the pub from you. And not even give you a euro.'

'We?'

'Daniella, the Ex-Patriots could make the business walk away tomorrow. So get your arse in gear.'

He stands up. 'Thanks for the drinks.'

With this he walks away, leaving me staring at the empty whisky glass.

4

Reassurance

My walk back to Se Busca is a slow one. It's clear that George and the other Ex-Patriots have been talking behind my back and, given Zia is one of them, I'm wondering if he knew what was about to go down today. I cross to the shaded side of the road thinking that's not something I ever did back home. Sun is hard won in Scotland. A small one-man cleaning vehicle is scraping the gutter clean of debris. It slides past me in a cloud of dust, the driver hard-wired into a set of headphones. I slump onto the wall that fronts a charity shop and watch the truck scrub its way out of sight. A couple of elderly joggers are half running, half walking up the hill towards me. I recognise one as a semi-regular from Se Busca. He lifts a weary hand to me as he passes and mutters the word *torture*. I unconsciously rub at my stomach. My lack of exercise is obvious to me in the softness of my paunch.

If George is serious, and I've no reason to think he isn't, it would be easy for the Ex-Patriots to ruin the trade. Call in a favour from their friends and acquaintances. Boycott the place and starve me out. Shut it down and pick over the bones after. Except I have deep pockets at the moment. Easily enough cash to see me through a boycott. Maybe enough to try and re-invent the pub. And how effective would a boycott be anyway? Would everyone stand by them? Where would they go instead? DB's? For they sure as hell need somewhere to be. Mum had created Se Busca as the home for the unwashed of this town. A place with its own set of rules. *What goes on in Se Busca, stays in Se Busca.* The authorities tolerate us because we keep our clientele out of their hair. Add to that the fact that the Ex-Patriots, and Clyde, own 2.5 per cent of the place each and they would also be cutting their own throats by closing it down. None of them are exactly flush with cash. Se Busca is the bread that keeps them from keeling over from hunger.

'*We could make the business walk away tomorrow.*'

They could but I don't buy it. On the flip side, George isn't one to make empty threats. He's not above a bit of violence by proxy either. A few broken fingers and I'd probably sign over the clothes off my back. And I can see George happily watching me scream. His threat needs to be taken seriously.

I look at my phone. Three thirty-five p.m. Less than two hours ago there was no Carl Stoker, no El Descaro Classic, no Steal, no threat from George. Less than two hours ago I was living the very existence that I thought I never would. A life in the sun with money in my pocket and a clear horizon. A horizon that is now murky and uninviting.

I stand up and trudge up the hill to the pub. As it comes into view it reflects my feelings. Dirty, bleak, dark-souled. I see a flicker of movement from the newly installed first-floor windows. Zia. Is he in on this? He's known George the best part of two decades. I've known him less than six months. And when he got wrapped up in the property scam a few months back he didn't step in when George hired some muscle to damage me if I didn't help out.

One of them?

I cross the gravel car park, dodging the few cars that are baking in the spring solar rays. Most of the customers leave their vehicles at home. Few come to Se Busca for the tea and coffee or soft drinks, and the Guardia Civil frequently set up shop in the nearby petrol station to breath-test.

I stop at the front door. It could do with a coat of varnish. I rest my hand on the door handle, let it go, spin on my heel and walk around the building. I climb the stairs at the rear and push into the flat above. The cool of the air conditioning wraps itself around me.

Once the attic for Se Busca, a single bare room the size of the pub, it now has two bedrooms, one with an en-suite, a bathroom and a single open-plan kitchen/living area. I can hear the sound of the kettle hitting the top of its boil as I push into the living room. Zia is sitting on one of the sofas, staring out of the window that looks down on the port where, above the apartment blocks in the distance, a sliver of the Med shines.

'Hi, pop star,' I say.

'Look at me,' he replies.

'Look At Me' was his lone Top 40 hit back in the day.

'I saw you walk up,' he says. 'You looked like you were carrying the weight of the world on your shoulders.'

Zia is Glasgow-born but his parents are from south India. He could pass for ten years younger than he is and dresses another decade down on that. His hair has a sheen to it that is now bottle bought and a small bald patch at the crown is the bane of his life. I've tried to tell him to shave down to a number one but he is now in that place that demands he grows his fringe and uses it to hide the protruding scalp.

'Are you making a cup of tea?' I ask.

'Sure.'

He rises, an athletic grace to his movement, and gets down and busy with tea bags, milk and cups.

'Zia,' I say as I sit.

'Yes.'

'I met George down at the front.'

'Good for you.' He grins.

'Not really,' I reply.

'Why?'

'How do you think I'm doing?'

'In what way?'

'Well, I'm not long here. I've taken on the pub. Something I've no experience in. I've taken up with you, left the UK and—'

'—and entered the dark and dangerous locale of Se Busca. A den thick with thieves and outlaws.' Again, he grins.

'Kind of. But how am I doing?'

He plonks a mug of tea on the coffee table and sits next to me.

'What's brought this on? What did George say to you?' he asks.

'Just tell me how I'm doing?'

'In what way?'

'In all ways. Running the pub. Living with you. Life.'

'A bit deep for a Thursday afternoon.'

I pick up a tea mug and roll the liquid around a little. 'Just tell me.'

'Okay. I like the *you and me* thing and I think you like the *you and me* thing. It was a little stiff at first, still is at times. We were kind of flung together in adverse circumstances and that doesn't always bode well for the future. But I think we're making it work. Or at least *I* think it's working. I have a little question over the future – in that twenty years between us might work now, but later? Not sure on that one. And I'm also no longer a party animal and I think you still have some dance shoes you need to wear out. But on a scale of one to ten I'd say we're a good eight and heading for a nine.'

He stops to drink.

'Is that what you wanted to hear, Daniella?'

'What about the non-me-and-you stuff?'

'Do you mean the pub?'

'Yes.'

'The pub is doing fine.'

'Fine? My friend, 'Trine, tells me that fine stands for Freaked-out, Insecure, Neurotic and Emotional.'

Zia smiles. 'Ah, *The Italian Job*. The newer one.'

'Sorry?'

'It's where your friend got the acronym from. Donald Sutherland and Mark Wahlberg chatting. Donald asks Mark how he's feeling

41

and Mark says *fine*. And Donald and Mark play out a double act of saying that fine stands for Freaked-out, Insecure, Neurotic and Emotional.'

'I'm going to cancel the Amazon Prime subscription, Zia. You watch way too many movies. So what do you mean by fine?'

'Are we on the honest island here?'

'Surrounded by the ocean of sincerity.'

Zia puts his mug down. 'The pub is losing its zing.'

'Go on.'

'It's not your fault, well, not entirely. In the last few years your mum decided she'd had enough and let things drift. She used to roll out new shit all the time around here. New events. New ideas. But that stopped a few years back and you haven't restarted it. Apart from installing that lurid set of used tables and chairs the place hasn't changed in an aeon. And with you in charge I can guarantee that our calendar of events for this year will be exactly the same as last year. Maybe less.'

'I thought that's what people liked about the place. The consistency. The surety. The comfort.'

'True, people don't like change until it happens, and then sometimes they surprise themselves and find they like change just fine.'

'And you're saying I'm slacking on the job.'

'I'm saying you asked me how the pub was doing and I'm telling you it's doing fine.'

'But not great.'

Zia's eyes wander to the window. 'What did George say to you?'

I use my tea as punctuation. Weighing up what to say.

'Have you been talking to George about the pub, Zia?'

'No more than usual.'

'No chat like the one we've just had. About how things could be better?'

He places the mug down and looks me in the eye. 'What has George been saying?'

'He says I'm not stepping up to the mark. And what you've said suggests he might be right. That I could be doing better. That I've been kicking back.'

'So what? It's your pub. You can do what you want with it.'

'It's not mine. It's *ours*. You, Saucy, the Twins, Skid, George, Clyde and me. I might hold the lion's share but we are all in on it. And now George is saying I'm not up to the job.'

'Did he?'

'More or less.'

Zia sighs. 'You're really pushing this to a bad place, Daniella. What do you want me to say? That you're lazy? Uncaring?'

'Am I?'

'No. None of those. You lost your mum. You shifted out from the UK. Left a crap job. You're entitled to take it a little easier. And, as I said, your mum had taken her foot off the gas long before you got here.'

'I'd just assumed that what was should be "what is and what will be."'

'Man, where did you get that from – an old fortune cookie?'

He gets a smile out of me.

'Zia, I need you to be straight with me.'

'Of course.'

'George Laidlaw has just told me that if I don't get my finger out of my arse and start making things happen around here, he is going to take the pub from me.'

Zia slides forward on the sofa, crossing his hands on his lap, a sign that I've grown to know indicates unease.

'Zia?'

'Tell me exactly what he said,' he says.

I play out the conversation and he listens. When I finish he interlaces his fingers, rubbing his wrists up and down his thighs. Increased unease.

'Zia, did you know about this?'

'Not directly,' he says.

'But you knew something?'

'I know that Saucy, the Twins, George and Skid have been avoiding me. The *you and I* thing doesn't sit well with them.'

'Are you surprised?'

'No. I can see it from their end. You're the outsider. They're unsure about you and I'm in your camp now. But how could George take the pub away from you?'

'He says he'll make the business walk.'

'That would be dumb. He'd kill the golden goose.'

'That's what I think.'

I watch Zia closely, studying him for any signs he's being disingenuous. Trust is central in any relationship and I think I have that with Zia. The key word being *think*. That seed of doubt born of my nattering inner voice. *You're thirty-six, he's fifty-six. You're the newbie in town. He's got two decades here. You were a call-centre grunt. He was a pop star.* This is a well-worn path in my head. I say none of it to him, but he reassures me all the same, over and over. Says all the right things in all the right places. And I still have that buried doubt. That small niggle that things are not quite right. And it's moments like this that bring it to the fore. I look into his soft brown eyes and search for the lie behind his words, knowing that each time I do this I'm harming the very thing I want to thrive. But I can't help myself. I don't *want* to help myself. I need the constant reassurance that comes when you challenge people to reaffirm your place in life. It's a trait that some have commented on.

'And you really didn't know George was going to front me up on this, Zia?'

Zia's face crumples at the edges, highlighting the wrinkles that give away his age.

'I just said I didn't.'

Don't you trust me?

I can hear the words behind the words.

'But you do think I've been kicking my heels?' I ask.

'I think you've been dealing with your mother's death and moving to a new country. That's what I think.'

'And what should I do?'

Zia pushes up from the sofa and stretches out. His stomach is flat against his T-shirt. He's taken to the gym recently after I mentioned he was developing a paunch. And, as is his wont, he went from zero to hero with the local health club. Five nights a week, five different classes. I rub my stomach again and think about how often in the last few months he's asked me to join him.

'I'd do nothing, if I were you,' he replies.

'You think?'

'Daniella, what can George really do?'

'I'm not sure, but he was serious.'

'Let me have a word with him. I'll suss out what's going on. Does that work for you?'

I nod with a smile.

'Anything else you need my wisdom on?' he says.

'Stoker and something called the Steal?'

'Stoker wants you to get the Classic up and running. Is that what he said?'

'While being a frightening SOB, but yes.'

'The Classic is a lot of work but it makes the pub money. Even if you could dump Stoker, which I doubt you can, it would still make sense to run it.'

'And the Steal?'

'It's nonsense. Who cares? Let DB's have Busca if they want. He's up at the repair shop anyway. If it was me I'd give Davie Brost the address of the wood worker and let him do us a favour by picking it up.'

'Would our customers not be a bit pissed off?'

'Probably, but they'll get over it. It's such a stupid tradition anyway. And last year two people ended up in hospital because of it. Geoff Stirling and his son tried to get into DB's through the roof and both fell off the bloody thing. Halfwits.'

And that's what I love about the man. In half a dozen sentences he's parked my mind in a quieter place. He'll talk to George, I should run the Classic and ignore the Steal. Of course, that presupposes that George hasn't got a non-Zia orientated, Machiavellian plan to remove me, that the Classic will be easy to run, that Stoker might back off, and that the Se Busca punters don't mind losing the Steal. All of that sounds like a little longer odds than I'm totally happy with. On the upside my head feels a little clearer. On the downside George's stab at my perceived laziness is not unjustified. Deep down I know it to be true.

5

The Note

'Pat Ratte's here to see you.'

Clyde is standing at the door to the office that hides behind Se Busca's cellar – a small box of a place that could barely hold a three-Chihuahua convention. I have left Zia to his tea, feeling an urgent need to study the finance books for the pub. I'm not really sure what I'm looking at or looking for, but something in George's warning has sparked a heightened interest in paying attention to where the business is and where it's going. So far I've gleaned that turnover has slipped about five per cent a year for the last four years, although profit has held up better due to Mum's increasingly frugal approach to the variable over-heads. It's making me realise that George might have just given me the kick up the backside at the right time. This can't go on.

'Ratte?' I say, looking up at Clyde.

'Says he has an appointment with you?'

Clyde sees the confusion on my face.

'It's what he says,' he replies.

'Tell him I'm busy and don't want to see him.'

'Too busy to listen to my side of the story.'

The voice comes from behind Clyde. Pat enters and pushes Clyde to one side. A monster of a man, dressed in a suit and tie with his coat slung over his shoulder, Pat cuts an imposing figure.

A lion's mane of swept-back grey hair above dark-grey eyes gives him a presence that has served him well as a gangster.

'Pat, I've no desire to talk to you,' I say.

'So why ask me to come here?'

Clyde vanishes and Pat steps into the tiny space.

'I never asked to see you,' I say. 'In fact, as far as I'm concerned, you can turn right around and leave.'

Pat leans on the wall, resting an elbow on the filing cabinet that's squeezed into the corner. 'I got your message at the hotel reception.'

He reaches into his pocket, extracts a piece of paper and drops it on the table. I read it.

Come up and see me. It's urgent. Daniella.

'Is that not your handwriting?' he asks.

I pick up the message. It's scribbled on lined, cream-coloured paper. Much like the paper in the pad that's lying next to the phone on the desk. I study the writing, trying to keep the surprise out of my eyes and probably failing. The handwriting looks a hell of a lot like mine. A hell of a lot.

'Not mine,' I say, throwing it down.

He reaches over and grabs the cream-coloured pad of paper before I can react. It's full of my scribbles.

'Looks like the same writing to me,' he says, examining the pad.

'Okay, it looks like my writing,' I agree. 'But, trust me, it isn't. I don't want to see you.'

'The receptionist at the hotel reception said a young lad wearing a baseball cap dropped it off. Said it was a note from you.'

'What lad?'

'No idea. But if it wasn't from you, who would go to the trouble?'

Who indeed?

'I've no idea,' I say, yanking the pad from his hand and placing it back next to the phone. 'But I don't want to see you.'

'Well, now I'm here do you not want to hear my side of the story about your mum?'

I slide back in my chair. I'm not sure who is playing what game here. I do want to hear his side. But only so I can debunk it and scream at the bastard.

'I don't want to know,' I lie.

'She asked for those pills,' he says.

'I said I don't want to know.'

'Had been using them for about a year,' he continues. 'Liked what they did. Effie's Es she called them.'

The police report said that my mum had ingested a significant quantity of Ecstasy just before she died of a heart attack.

With his back resting on the wall, Pat is cool and relaxed, his hand fingering the lock on the filing cabinet.

'I don't want to know,' I repeat.

'That morning she died here,' he continues, ignoring my words, 'she phoned early and asked me to drop some more pills off. A bit early for me but she asked me to deliver them here, not to her apartment. So I did what she asked. She usually took delivery of half a dozen at a time, said she didn't trust herself with any more.'

'What part of—'

'Told me that they helped her a lot. Took the edge off ageing were her words.'

'Are you deaf?'

'If I'd known she was going to neck them all I'd never have given her them. I knew she had heart problems.' He pauses and then says, 'I loved your mum. You know that.'

I slump. Pat told me a while back that he'd asked Mum to marry him and she'd said no. I'd wondered if the pills were his way of saying *If I can't have you, no one can* – except that didn't make much sense when you think about it. And I think about it a lot.

'Pat—'

'I'd do anything to take those pills back, Daniella. Not to have come down that morning. But I did and she's dead.'

He stops and stares at the ceiling, his eyes wandering across the grotty tiles. Neither of us speaks for a minute.

I break the silence. 'Is that it?'

He lets his eyes drop and shrugs. 'More or less.'

'What are you looking for here? Forgiveness? Absolution?'

'No. Just understanding.'

'Sorry? *Understanding?* Are you for real. *Under – fucking – standing?*'

Another shrug, as if this is a lightweight pre-cocktail discussion on the merits of dress etiquette for the gentrified.

I stand up, throwing the chair back against the wall. A cork in my mental bottle flies out. 'Understanding. I'll tell you what I understand. I understand that you have a history of violence. I understand that you are a vicious bastard when you want to be. I understand that you handed my mum a pile of pills that killed her. I understand that you knew she had a heart problem. I understand that my mum would probably be sitting in this bloody office today if you hadn't played the junkie dealer. I understand that you are in the shite for this and with luck will go down for a long, long time. I understand that at your age, you'll probably never get out of prison, other than in a coffin. I understand a lot, but what I'll never understand is why you killed her.'

He stands up, straightening his back. He's not a man to provoke. Even in his seventies he could probably rip my arms from their sockets, and my being female won't faze him in the slightest. His London gangster roots run deep and he comes from a world where face is everything, and I've just rubbed his in a pile of manure.

But he surprises me by flicking at his hair, nonchalant.

'Finished?' he asks.

'Just leave,' I spit.

He doesn't move.

'I hear that Carl Stoker has been in touch,' he says.

His words whip the wind from my lungs, and I try to get a handle on what this is really about.

'Just leave,' I repeat. It's the best I can come up with.

'He's a mad bastard,' Pat says. 'A real mad bastard. Scares me and, trust me, I take a lot of scaring.'

'Look who gives a—'

'Psychotic is the word. Not an empathetic gene in his body. That's Carl. Nice as ninepence one minute, complete nutter the next.'

'Just like you,' I utter.

Again, he doesn't rise to the bait.

'No,' he says. 'Not like me. Carl doesn't give a monkeys about anyone else. Carl comes first, second and last. And then some. What Carl wants, Carl usually gets, and he doesn't care who he hurts in the process. I'm a sane pussycat on Valium compared to him.'

I drop back to the chair. I've no control here. Not in this moment. Pat's used to commanding the room and he's in his stride. And, to boot, part of me actually wants to hear this.

'He'll want to set up in the pub for the Classic,' Pat continues. 'And he will also be taking a book on the Steal – but he'll do that face to face, not here. He'll not show favour to us or DB's by setting up shop in either for the Steal.'

'He'll take bets on a stupid pub game?' I can't help but ask.

'Carl will take bets on how long it takes for two rats to mate. The Steal's an annual wager. Some people take it seriously. A few grand will change hands on it.'

When I first landed here I thought the pub and its clientele a bit off the wall. A sort of home for the bewildered and rootless. But the reality is far darker. Se Busca lies in murky waters within a dark swamp occupied by a pond that doesn't like the light. The longer I stay here the less I seem to know.

'He told me to set up this Classic thing,' I say, despite my desire to say nothing.

'I bet he did. That's a real big deal in his diary. But the good news is that I can handle Carl for you,' he offers.

'Pat, I think I've had about enough of this.'

'You don't get it, Daniella. I'm trying to help. I'm on your side. I can't bring your mum back but I can be useful around here. And Carl isn't the only one that you need to watch out for. I'd keep an eye closer to home if I were you.'

'What in the hell does that mean?'

'Come on, don't play the dumb lassie. The Ex-Patriots were Effie's crew, not yours. I wouldn't trust any of them an inch. And I mean *any* of them, including your boyfriend.'

With this he slaps the top of the filing cabinet and whirls away, his coat arcing out around him. Enter with style, leave with style.

I sit for a few minutes working the conversation back through my head before shouting, 'Clyde.'

He appears.

'The shopkeeper,' I say to him, a little calmer now Pat is gone.

He looks at me as if I've just spoken Swahili. 'Who?'

'You appeared from nowhere. Just like the shopkeeper in *Mr Benn*. Look up kids' programmes in the UK from the seventies. You'll see what I mean.'

He still looks confused.

'Sit down, Clyde.'

He drops into the seat in front of me. He must have heard the entire conversation between Pat and I; he was too quick through the door when I shouted to have been much further away than the cellar.

'Clyde, what do you know about this Steal thing?'

'It's next Saturday and we don't have Busca.'

'Zia says it doesn't matter. If this Busca thing isn't here then there is no Steal.'

'Whoa, not cool,' Clyde says. 'Zia's off the mark there. The guys in the bar will be very unhappy if we forfeit. That hands the win to DB's. It's a matter of pride.'

52

'Pat says they bet on it.'

'Sure, and then some. Side bets are the norm. If we forfeit, a lot of guys in here lose cash.'

'Who won last year?'

'It was a scratch. They didn't get Busca and we didn't get Bertie. Year before was a draw.'

'A draw.'

'We got Bertie, they got Busca. The year before we won. That means we still hold the bragging rights. If we forfeit, then they'll crow about it all year.'

'And that matters?'

'It does to the guys out there.' He throws a hand towards the bar. 'They look at the Steal in the same way that someone would look at their football team losing the cup final to their biggest rival.'

'I don't like football.'

'What do you like?'

'What, sport-wise?'

'Yes.'

'I enjoy tennis.'

'Who's your favourite?'

'Andy Murray.'

'And you'd be happy if, come Wimbledon, Andy makes the final and then says screw it I can't be bothered.'

'I'd not be happy. But I'd get over it.'

'That lot out there won't.'

'What are you saying?'

Clyde steps a little closer. 'Given the talk in here, I'd say you should think about trying to win it.'

'Talk?'

He tilts his head. 'Talk, look, I need to get back to the bar.'

'Okay.'

Talk.

I wonder if it's too early for more wine.

6

Six Wounds

The Morning After The Raid

'Okay, Señorita Coulstoun, let us start at the beginning and take it slowly. My English is not the best.'

'Let's start,' I say, 'with the fact that a bunch of hooligans broke into my pub last night, wrecked the place, stole my property and a dead body appeared in my cellar. Let's start with you finding them. Let's start with why I'm sitting here with you. Let's start with anything other than inaction.'

The tiny office behind the bar feels smaller than ever with me facing a police officer. Capitán Lozano of the Guardia Civil turns every so often to look out on the cellar where an officer is standing, talking on his mobile. The fire door to the car park that surrounds the front of the pub is ajar, the hordes from last night having broken the lock getting out. Back in the pub the damage is extensive. Zia has been onto the insurance company already but they are taking a back seat until the police give the all-clear.

'Please, Señorita Coulstoun. What happened?'

'I wasn't here last night, Capitán,' I say. 'You need to be talking to Davie Brost. It was his lot that did this.'

The Capitán, a small man with close-cropped hair, is holding an old-school notepad in one hand and a pencil in the other.

'We will talk to everyone, Señorita Coulstoun. Where were you last night?'

'I was up at Mejor Comida in the old town.'

'For food?'

'No, for line dancing.'

'Is that a joke?'

'Look, I wasn't here and a bunch of morons from DB's broke into my bar, wrecked it and killed a man. I was up at the restaurant from seven through to, well, after this shit went down.'

'Can someone verify this?'

'Apart from the owner, three waiters, my boyfriend and half the clientele at the place? No.'

The Capitán rises. 'Do you think this attitude is helping, Señorita Coulstoun? As you said, a man is dead. A man who knew your mother well. A man who was under suspicion for being involved in your mother's death. Your *mother's death*. And now he is dead and was lying in what is now *your* pub. If you were me, Señorita Coulstoun, who would you be talking to about it? The owner of the premises? Someone who knows the deceased? The daughter who thinks the deceased killed her mother? – or all three? Because that's where you fit in, Señorita Coulstoun. An angry pub-owning daughter who knew the deceased and thought he killed her mother.'

I say nothing.

'When did you last see Señor Ratte?

'He came to see me nearly a week ago,' I reply.

'Did you invite him to see you?'

'Invite him? No.'

'Are you sure?'

'Yes, I'm sure,' I add.

'And that is all you have to say about it?'

'I'm not going to say I'm sad he's gone, so don't look to me for it. But while we're at it, he should never have been on the street in the first place. Why wasn't he locked up?'

'Señorita Coulstoun, Señor Ratte was not in our custody because the most we have on him is possession of MDMA. And not in enough quantity to hold him.'

'So you let him go? Even though he gave my mum the pills that killed her.'

He leans forward. 'Let me make a few things clear, Señorita Coulstoun. This is not the UK. We are more tolerant of the consumption of drugs, up to a point, because we believe that punishing the end user is counterproductive. We try to *cure* the users and punish the traffickers. We have been doing so since the 'eighties. In due course we *would* have punished Señor Ratte for his drug dealing. But it is all but impossible to prove that the MDMA killed your mother.'

'She had a bad heart and took a pile of tablets.'

He nods. 'And she had been taking the same drug for over a year. So how can we say that taking those pills that morning was the dagger to her heart?'

'That's bollocks. And you know it.'

'Why? Do you have evidence that Señor Ratte gave her the pills knowing she would take them all and knowing it would be fatal?'

'He could have forced them down her throat.'

'Again, where is your evidence? There were no marks on your mother's body. The person in the pub who saw her die that day said that she was acting normal until she had a heart attack.' He continues. 'So, do you know something we do not?'

'Oh, come on. For fuck's sake. She had a bad heart. That bastard gave her high-strength drugs. She ate them and died. Case closed.'

'Is that what you believe?'

'Yes.'

'Enough to want revenge, Señorita Coulstoun? Enough to say to yourself *the police are doing nothing about Señor Ratte so maybe I will*. Is that what you are saying?'

I clamp my mouth shut. Clever bastard. I shake my head at how easily he has pushed my buttons. Less than a year ago I was sitting at a desk, head-mike on, screen flickering, handling insurance claims back in the UK. I was good at controlling my emotions in the face of some wild customers. You have no idea how angry people can get if you decline their claims. And the Capitán has, with surgical precision, bypassed my cool button.

'No, that's not what I'm saying,' I reply.

'It sounds very much like it to me,' he says, scribbling some more.

'Don't put words in my mouth,' I say. 'I had nothing to do with Ratte's death. Nothing.'

A police officer knocks on the door.

'*Dime*,' says the Capitán.

'*Necesito hablar contigo un momento*,' the officer says.

'Excuse me, Señorita Coulstoun. My presence is required next door.'

He leaves, closing the door behind him, and I hear the faint sounds of Spanish being spoken. I'm feeling a little hemmed in here and not fully up to speed with the events of last night. I had got a call at just after midnight telling me that Pat Ratte had been found dead in the cellar. I'd asked the restaurant to call me a taxi, but by the time Zia and I arrived at Se Busca the police had sealed the pub tight. I'd been interviewed by a local officer and was told that someone would be in touch. Between then and now I'd had a series of phone calls with George and talked most of the night away with Zia in our apartment above the pub, listening to the sounds of the police processing the place.

The Capitán returns. 'Señorita Coulstoun, tell me about this Steal?'

'It's a daft game that DB's and Se Busca play out each year. Each tries to steal the other's mascot. It's what was behind last night's crap.'

'And this involves breaking down doors and wrecking furniture.'

'It all got out of hand yesterday.'

'Why? Has it descended into violence before?'

'Not that I know of.'

'And you approve of this Steal?'

'No. And yesterday I'd decided that we weren't going to be part of it. All week the damn thing had been building up. It was getting nasty.'

'Nasty? In what way?'

'DB's were making noises about an all-out invasion of the pub.'

'Who in DB's?'

'It was all online. Check out the eldescarorocks.com website. No, strike that, you won't be able to – I asked for the thread to be taken down by the administrator. You'd need to ask them if they can recover it.'

'What was on this thread?'

'Empty but angry threats. Like kids going at it. Only with more swear words. We're going to do this and we're going to do that shit. From both sides, but mostly from DB's punters.'

'And do you know who was involved in this thread?'

'All the names are there.'

'And you tried to cancel the Steal?'

'Yesterday morning. I was supposed to be on a day off but made the mistake of checking my phone. Someone had posted that they were going to ram a car through my pub's door to get the mascot. It had all gone mental. I contacted the site and put out a message that we were not playing this year.'

'Yet they still came.'

'The bloody website went into meltdown when I said we were quitting.'

'And did you not think of calling us?'

I laugh and Lozano's face hardens. 'Sorry,' I say. 'But at least three of the buggers on the site are Policía Local.'

'There are Spanish police officers using this website?'

'There always are. They monitor it. It's well known. You'd be amazed what they find out because of indiscreet posts. They sometimes post themselves. Usually to try and calm things down. But it didn't work yesterday.'

He writes a few more lines in his notebook.

'And then what happened?'

'All went quiet on the Western Front,' I say, struggling not to just get up and walk. 'The administrator pulled the plug on the thread and I thought it was over. And I was wrong. It must have all gone underground. Arrangements made. Probably by Whats-App. Then last night a gang turned up and raided the place, taking the mascot. But you know all this. And what you need to do is catch them all and make them pay for the bloody damage.'

The Capitán rolls his pencil around his thumb with his fore-finger. He is looking past me at a spot on the wall, thinking.

'My first priority, Señorita Coulstoun, is to apprehend the murderer of Señor Ratte.'

'Ask the mob from DB's. As far as I know, Pat wasn't here last night.'

'Yet his body ends up here.'

'He must have come with the crew from DB's.'

'I understand Señor Ratte was a loyal patron of Se Busca.'

'He was.'

'So why would he be with the people from DB's?'

'Ask them.'

I'm not sure where that will go. Pat hated Davie Brost. There were stories about a fight over a woman. But around here there are stories about everything. Even so, Pat wouldn't be seen dead in DB's. So what he was doing with the crew that broke in here last night is a mystery.

'I will ask them, Señorita Coulstoun. But why do you think he was with them?'

'I've no idea and, as I was at the restaurant last night, I'm not sure I can add anything else to this conversation.'

'Señor Ratte might not have been killed here.'

That stops me in my tracks.

'Are you saying,' I half whisper, 'that Pat was already dead and that bunch of idiots brought him here?'

'Maybe.'

He studies me as he makes the revelation. I have no idea what it means.

'If not here, where was he killed?' I ask.

'I do not know.'

'So,' I say, 'someone at DB's killed him and dumped him in the cellar when they raided the place?'

'Again, I will say maybe.'

'So how was he killed?'

'That is a good question and I am glad you asked it.'

'Glad?'

'The guilty don't often ask that question, Señorita Coulstoun. Human nature, you understand. The guilty want to avoid talking about what they have done. Although the really clever ones know this and they make a point of asking.'

'Are you saying I'm clever?'

'You are certainly not stupid, Señorita Coulstoun. But whether you are *that* clever is something that I haven't decided yet.'

'So you don't think DB's was involved, and I'm a suspect?'

'Señorita Coulstoun, everyone is a suspect. From what I understand there were maybe twenty or so people who blew out your front door and entered to steal the wooden figure. And do I know who they all are? In this town, of course not. You say the ones that raided here were from DB's. If I'm to believe the people that I have talked to so far, everyone from DB's was tucked up in their beds last night, drinking cocoa. But someone stole the mascot, someone killed Señor Ratte, and someone may have dumped his body in your cellar. And the one thing I know for certain is that Señor Ratte did not die of old age.'

'So how was he killed?' I repeat.

'He was stabbed.'

'Stabbed?'

'Six times.'

'Six?'

'Six wounds, Señorita Coulstoun. Six clear wounds.'

'Six wounds? That's not an accident,' I say. 'Not with six wounds.'

'As you say, no accident. Murder.'

'And he wasn't killed in my cellar?'

'That I do not know. The scene is confusing. He may have been killed elsewhere. Or he could have been killed here.'

'Why don't you know?'

'The lack of blood – but there is something also wrong about that. At this stage I do not know. Which is why I'm interviewing you.'

'When was he killed?'

'When?' He looks at me as if I'm playing him. 'That was the coroner on the phone to my officer outlining the initial cause of death. Time of death is estimated as sometime yesterday, no earlier than yesterday morning. But we will need a full post-mortem before we can be conclusive.'

He leans forward, placing his hand on his chin. 'So, Señorita Coulstoun, where were you all day yesterday?'

I let the question hang, not because I have anything to hide but because I have the distinct feeling that I'm being reeled in. Hook in mouth, a gentle tug pulling me to a bad place.

'Do I need a lawyer?' I ask.

'That is up to you. I am only ascertaining the facts. You are not under arrest. Are you willing to say where you were?'

'I took a rare day off. I went up the hairdressers in the *pueblo* for an appointment at eleven thirty. Then I drove up the coast and I came back in time to change and meet Zia for dinner that evening.'

'Can anyone confirm that?'

'I had lunch at a beach-front bar. They'll probably remember.'

'And the rest of the afternoon?'

'I just wandered. Am I under suspicion?'

'As I said, I have many potential suspects. Were you in the pub at any time?'

'Unusually, no. When I got back I was running really late for dinner. Zia called to say he was already at the restaurant, so I didn't have time to check in at the pub. I just changed and headed straight for the restaurant. Look, have you been to DB's this morning?'

'Why do you ask?'

'Because that's where I'd have gone. You said twenty people burst in here last night, and after they left, Pat was found. And that he may have been killed earlier in the day. I'm not a police officer but my first thought would have been that they brought the body with them. So why are you sitting here, talking to me?'

He reaches into his pocket and takes out a small plastic bag. Inside is a slip of very familiar paper.

Reeled in.

It's the note that Pat claimed he got from me.

'We found this on Señor Ratte.'

I shake my head. 'I told Pat I never wrote that.'

'You also told me that you never invited him to see you.'

'I didn't. That's not my note.'

'Is this your handwriting?'

'It looks like it but I never wrote that.'

'What about this?'

He reaches into his pocket and extracts another plastic bag. In it is a key.

'Do you recognise this key?'

I study it. 'Could be the front door key for the pub. Where did you get it?'

'Señor Ratte had it on him. Why would he have a key to the premises?'

'I've not a clue. Are you sure it is for here . . . ?' I pause and shake my head again. 'Of course you are, you've already tried it.'

'I have. It took a while to find the lock amongst the debris of the door, but it fits. We also found this.' He lifts out a third bag from his pocket. I recognise the gold key fob immediately. It looks exactly like the fob that hangs from the spare pub key I keep in the flat above.

'Is this yours?' he asks.

'I have a similar one back in the flat.'

He spins the bag round and I sigh. My initials are plain to see. Who in the hell gave Pat my key?

7

A Person of Interest

The rest of the interview rides over the same ground. Pinning down my movements, my connection to Pat and what I knew of the Steal. I'm at a loss as to how or why Pat had my key. At one point, more out of desperation than any real hope, I ask if I can go upstairs and check if my key really is missing. The answer from the Capitán floors me.

'We have some officers coming over to look at your flat. I would rather you did not go up there until they are finished.'

'Officers?'

'*Forensic* officers,' he says. 'My colleague told me the necessary paperwork has come through. I will give you a copy when it arrives.'

'You think Pat was killed in my flat?'

'I think that Señor Ratte may not have been killed in the cellar. And I think you have good reason to hate Señor Ratte. And by your own admission you were in your flat alone yesterday. And beyond that I think I'll wait and see what we find upstairs, if anything.'

'What are you saying? I killed Pat and dragged his body down here. Why the hell would I do that?'

'I do not know.'

'And what am I supposed to do in the meantime? I need into my home.'

'We will be finished as quickly as we can and then, if all is well, you can go up to your apartment.'

'And what about the damage out there?' I say with a wave of my hand.

'I have a lot of legwork ahead of me, Señorita Coulstoun. When I know more I will let you know what we intend to do about that.'

'My insurance company will not act until you are finished.'

'I cannot help that.'

He stands up and shouts to the officer in the cellar, who appears.

'I will be in touch,' the Capitán says to me as he leaves. 'Please give my officers any help they need when they arrive to look over your apartment. Jorge here will wait for them to arrive.'

And Jorge will undoubtedly ensure I don't sneak into my home and remove anything, not that there's anything to remove. *Or is there?* A cold shiver ripples down my spine. I follow the Capitán out through a cellar that is now coated in black fingerprint powder.

'And who cleans this lot up?' I say to the Capitán's back.

'We are finished here,' is his reply. He doesn't look around as he speaks.

I watch as he skirts the wreckage of the pub and leaves through the gaping hole where the front door once hung. I take in the scene of devastation. My head is a mess. The whole maelstrom around Pat's death seems to be suddenly centring on me. I pull one of the surviving bar stools away from the bar, pour myself a glass of Coke and slump onto the seat. After twenty minutes of fruitless looping, conflicting thoughts, I try and detach myself from the emotional waves rocking me by putting on my old insurer's claim hat. I pull out my phone and start photographing every inch of the bar. Every smashed chair, every broken glass and every trashed fixture. I miss nothing, working methodically from one corner to the next. Circling into the middle of the bar, I then head for the cellar, clicking away, avoiding the police tape that surrounds the dark stain on the floor that may or may not be Pat's blood. I finish up in the office and then exit through the busted fire door. Once outside I keep photographing, ensuring I get as many angles of the fire door and the main door as I can. Satisfied I have everything on the phone, I call Zia.

'Hey, pop star,' I say.

'Hi, lover,' he replies. 'Are the police still there?'

I tell him about the interview.

'They think you killed Pat?' His tone is incredulous.

'If they thought that, I wouldn't be talking to you. I'd be sitting down in the police station and calling my lawyer. Where are you?'

'Up at Skid's place.'

Before the Capitán had appeared for my interview Zia had left early, telling me he needed to pick something up at Skid's.

'Did you get what you wanted at Skid's?'

'Sorry?'

'You said you were picking something up.'

'Oh, yes. I got it.'

'What was it?'

'Eh, just a CD I lent him.'

'A CD. Was it that urgent?'

He avoids that question. 'Do you want me to come down?'

'Not yet. I need to talk to the insurers myself and try and move them on a bit first.'

'Well, you'd be the one to know how to do that.'

'Then we need to clean this place up. And for that I need all hands on deck. I want to reopen as soon as possible.'

Zia doesn't reply right away.

'Zia, are you still there?'

'You want to reopen?' he eventually says.

'Tonight, if we can.'

'But it's a crime scene.'

'Lozona said they were finished here. There's some police tape we can work around. If Lozano or the others want to stop me, fine. If not, I'm opening.'

'When?' 'Why so fast? No one will blame you if you close up for a few days.'

'And what will that achieve? George has me down as a lazy bastard. Here's a chance to prove him wrong.'

'But Pat was killed there.'

'According to the Capitán, Pat may not have been killed here.'

'Sorry?'

'He thinks Pat may have been killed elsewhere, that's why they are about to search our place.'

'They are going to do what?'

'They are sending officers up shortly and word will get around on that. We'll be the talk of the steamie on this one, so I want Se Busca back open and things as normal as they can be.'

'Normal isn't a death in a pub and police searching our home. And isn't the cellar off limits?'

'I told you, they've finished down here. And it all might help the takings. There's no such thing as bad PR, Zia.'

'You don't mean that. A man lost his life, Daniella. It's not a publicity stunt.'

'Sorry,' I say.

But I bet we do a hell of a trade tonight when the rubberneckers appear.

'Zia,' I say, 'tell the Ex-Patriots, those that can make it, that I want them all down here at three o'clock. Skid, Saucy, the Twins, George and you – even Clyde – all of them. You all have a share in this place so you all should share in the clean-up. I'm going to call the insurers now. See you at three.'

I kill the call before he can respond and I feel the anger in me beginning to boil again. I've had it on a peep and haven't realised. Anger at Pat for what he did to Mum, and anger at him for dying. Anger at the Capitán for his accusations. Anger at DB's and at Davie Brost for the raid but mostly anger at whoever is screwing with me with that note found on Pat, with my keys and my key ring. It all means someone is royally fucking around. I gave

Pat none of those things. Did Pat make the note up and steal the keys? If not – then who?

I try and put my professional head on, go back to the office and dig out the insurance documents. I know George has talked to the insurers but they are just about to get a lesson on what it's like when you talk to someone who knows exactly how your own game works.

The call takes ten minutes and I get the okay to start cleaning up. I've an email address to send the pictures to and an assessor will be coming up from Malaga in a few days. I'll stack all the broken stuff I can easily carry outside, behind the bins, for the assessor to look at if they want to. I grab another drink before digging out the old pair of work gloves we use to move the kegs around. I stare at the mess in the bar, sipping Coke. I decide that I'll start by piling all the unbroken furniture in one corner, although I should probably wait for the others to come to help with the heavy stuff – but I'm in need of something to do to take my head away from Pat's death.

Halfway through identifying the undamaged from the damaged, Jorge, the police officer who had been with the Capitán, comes in.

'*¿Me das las llaves de tu casa?*'

I know *llaves* means keys and *casa* is house and I fish the flat keys out. Behind him, in the car park, there are three men pulling on white Tyvek suits.

'Oh, for fuck's sake,' I say to Jorge. 'Could they not do that once they're in the flat? It's bad enough they've been here once for Pat but twice will make the front bloody page of the local rag.'

Jorge looks at me with a blank expression. I don't have the Spanish for what I've just said and in frustration chuck a leg of a chair at the wall. He visibly stiffens at my actions.

'*Lo siento,*' I say, apologising.

When he leaves I continue shifting furniture. One of the lurid pink tables that Mum bought on a bulk deal has been heavily wedged into the plasterboard next to the door. Surprisingly, it looks like it has survived the trauma intact and I eventually manage to yank it free. A slab of plaster falls away and I reach into my pocket to get my phone to take a picture of the new damage. Even with the front door wide open the wall is in shadow and my phone automatically uses its flash. The light catches an object. A glint of reflective plastic from something buried in the wall. I flick on the phone's torch and examine the hole. Wedged to a chunk of plaster-board is a photograph, the sheen from the surface-coating having caught the flashlight. I pull the photo free and hold it up to the light from the door. And my mouth drops open.

Taken from a high angle it's what looks like a grainy print from a CCTV feed. I recognise the setting. Pat Ratte's office. At least it used to be his office. A while back he had owned a stunning villa on the hill that rises behind El Descaro. Built on an old sixteenth-century castle, he had called it the Ratte's Nest. The picture is of me tumbling backwards with Pat, back to the camera, watching. It looks like he has just pushed me. I remember the moment well. A stupid dispute a while back and Pat making it clear who was in charge. But just how in the hell did the picture get into the wall of this pub? Who the hell put it there and, to add cream to an already too sweet cake, why?

It takes me a second to realise that someone is standing behind me.

'And what would that be, Señorita Coulstoun?'

I whirl around to find the Capitán standing in the doorway.

'I, eh . . .'

He steps forward and looks at the photo in my hand. 'May I see that?'

I find myself handing it over. He pulls a small latex glove from his pocket and, without putting it on, uses the palm section to grab the photo to keep his fingers off the surface. He looks at the picture.

'We searched this place this morning,' he says. 'I don't remember being told about a picture of you and the deceased.'

I'm at a loss.

'This doesn't look like a very friendly photo, Señorita Coulstoun. This looks like Señor Ratte is pushing you. Not very friendly at all. Where was this taken?'

The implication of the photo is as clear as the water in a south Pacific lagoon. Lozano is already looking at me for some involvement in Ratte's death and he's now holding another little gem to add to his growing bag of suspicion.

'It's not what it looks like,' I say, knowing it looks exactly like what it looks like.

'Then what is it?' he asks.

I can't get into the real reason I was at Ratte's house. We've all but buried the nonsense that my mum and the Ex-Patriots were involved in back then. Lozano was suspicious enough when it was all going down. He'll be like a scalded squirrel up a drain pipe if he gets a sniff that the photo is connected to the property scam Mum ran.

'It looks like it's a grab from Pat's CCTV up in his old house,' I say. 'God alone knows why it's here.'

'When was it taken?' he asks.

'Not long after Mum's funeral. I don't know how it got into the wall, and I've no idea why it even exists,' he says as he crosses the bar.

He pulls out a plastic bag from his inside pocket and slips the photo inside.

'That's not your property,' I say.

'It is evidence,' is the curt reply. 'I think maybe I will stay here while my colleagues are working upstairs.'

'Is that why you came back?'

'I came back because I left my pen on your desk. Do you mind if I get it?'

I look at the hole in the wall where the photo had been and Lozano follows my gaze.

How in the hell did that photo get in there?

'Maybe a little chat about this photograph is in order while we wait?' he says as he crosses to the bar. 'Please do not go anywhere, Señorita Coulstoun.'

He slips through the door that leads to the cellar, and a large slice of me wants to put the pedal to the metal and get the hell out of here. I'm now certain that someone is screwing with me. That photo couldn't have been behind the walls. Someone planted it. Maybe left it on the table in the stramash last night. Probably expecting the police to find it but, in the chaos of the invasion, the picture had been buried in the plasterboard with the table. If I add up the note, the key, the key fob and now the picture, I've no doubt that I'm being lined up to take the full heat on Pat's death. I hear scraping from above as the police officers begin to search my apartment and I'm wondering what they are going to find that wasn't there twenty-four hours ago.

The Capitán re-emerges.

'Look,' I say, 'you've got to know that someone is playing around here. That photo is just plain dumb.'

'It says to me that your history with Señor Ratte is not good.'

'It says nothing of the sort. It's out of context. A still taken from a video. Find the video and you'll see what I mean.'

'I intend to.'

'And if someone does think I was involved in Pat's death why not just come to you direct and say so. Why plant a photo or steal a key?'

'Maybe they are scared of you.'

It takes me a few seconds to understand the full implications of that statement. That the Capitán is putting me square into his gun sights. That he's thinking through a range of possibilities and likes the ones where I feature. I take a good grip of my mental handbrake and yank it hard.

The Capitán has a small tic in his left eye that I've never noticed before. Was it always there or is it a tell when he thinks he's onto something? A killer ready to be bagged?

'We will wait and see what transpires upstairs. I am a little confused over the photograph myself. '*Un poco conveniente.*'

'What does that mean?'

'A little too convenient.'

A small wave of relief passes through me.

'You've got that on the nail,' I say.

'While we wait, would a coffee be possible?'

I look over at the coffee machine. It has survived last night. I'm still a novice at the thing although it is a piece of piss to work. Grind the coffee, stick the powder into the portafilter, bang a button and jet wash the milk to hot. *Simples*, as Carl Stoker said. But I've got a small patch of red skin on the back of my left hand that's the result of a steam burn a month ago. It still bloody itches just to prove that the machine can get the better of me. Another scrape from my apartment above acts as a signal for me to get busy with the bubble and froth, while praying that someone hasn't undercoated my walls in Pat's blood or dipped my sheets in his semen.

Lozano pulls out a chair near the dartboard and drops into it. I fire up the coffee machine and think about who might want to put me up front and centre for Pat's death. Which, logically, must tie into why Pat was killed. Or does it? Maybe Pat's death was a random act of violence and I'm the most convenient patsy. Except I know that my key wasn't hanging on the usual hook when I left for the restaurant last night. I'd noticed its absence and I'd simply assumed that Zia had it. And the photo in the wall would need to have been extracted from the hard drive of Pat's system some time ago. He has been out of the villa for months. Then there's the note in my handwriting. It's at least a week old. If all three are connected to Pat's death then whoever is behind this planned it all well in advance. That would suggest that I'm not just some random fall guy. I've been chosen for a reason. Taking that thread, running it through the eye of the needle and sewing up the pieces means that Pat's death and someone framing me has to be connected. I consider telling the Capitán this but he's plenty smart enough to have it all thought out.

I suddenly laugh. An involuntary action as a sporadic thought runs through my head. The Capitán looks up. I focus on the coffee machine thinking that if I really had killed Pat then framing myself might be the best way to throw mud into the water. I know that I *really* don't want to air that one with the Capitán.

With the coffee starting to dribble into the cups I flick open my phone. If the Ex-Patriots have jumped to do my bidding they will be here in less than an hour.

I steam zap the milk and mix it with the coffee in two cups.

'Weren't you going to talk to the crew at DB's,' I say to the Capitán as I hand him a cup.

'I told you, I left my pen here.'

'And you only have one pen?'

'It is a good pen.' He sips at the liquid. '*Muy bien*. Not bad coffee.'

'We used to stock a real cheap bean but everyone moaned so I sprung for the good stuff,' I explain. 'However, they moaned when I upped the price. Man, you should have heard them bitch about that one.'

'How much is a coffee?'

'It used to be a whole euro.'

'And now?'

'A euro twenty, but you'd think I was robbing their kids' piggy banks in plain sight of their offspring when I told them the new price.' Then I get back to DB's. 'So when will you talk to those that wrecked my place?'

'I have two colleagues over there right now.'

He's going nowhere at the moment, and I don't think he ever intended to. I think he wanted to wait a little while and return to see if he could catch me in the act of something suspicious. Hiding the knife maybe?

8

Team Work

The Capitán puts down his cup and is about to speak when Jorge comes in. He whispers in the Capitán's ear – an act designed to imply something major has been discovered – and, with a *perdon*, the Capitán leaves me to my own devices again. As I sip at the coffee I move a few pieces of pub debris around. But when it becomes clear that the Capitán is not coming straight back, I return to serious sifting and shifting.

Forty minutes later, with the Capitán still not present, there's a noise from outside as an overpowered car screeches to a halt. I don't have to look out to know it's a bright red Ford Escort XR3i with an exhaust the size of the River Clyde tunnel. Skid Solo bounds through the door, replete in a yellow and white vertical striped shirt, over-tight jeans and a pair of loafers. Skid has a failing ability to age gracefully. He claims to be ten years younger than he is, dyes his hair and fills in every wrinkle on his face with make-up. He's also a man who gives the impression of firing on one cylinder less than ideal. I've not figured out if it's because he's got some genuine mental health issues simply can't pay attention for more than ten seconds, or was born without the common-sense gene. Zia trails in after him looking a little shell-shocked. Skid can do that to you with his driving. I refuse to get in his car with him. He scares me shitless.

'This place doesn't look any better in the daylight,' Skid says to me. 'You haven't done much since last night.'

Zia throws him a look but he ignores it.

'Being interviewed by the police,' I say, 'and then spending time contacting the insurance company would do that. Oh, and the fact that no one had the foresight to think that I might need a little help to clean up didn't help either – as if the magic *clean-up* fairy had been expected.'

Skid sits on a chair which promptly issues a fatal crack and he leaps up as it folds to the floor.

'Thanks, Skid,' I say. 'Just what I needed. Someone to make the damage worse.'

'That thing was dangerous. I could sue you for that.'

'Really, Skid, and given you own two and a half per cent of the pub, you'd be suing yourself.'

Zia steps in before I can say any more, 'Okay, Daniella, what do you want us to do?'

'I'm waiting on the Capitán to come back but, in the meantime, try separating the good stuff from the bad – good in that corner,' I say pointing, 'and bad over there. Then we'll put the bad out the back of the pub. And, Skid, if you're not sure what goes where, ask! Okay?'

He's already lifted a functioning chair, his head swivelling as he tries to remember which corner is which.

'Good stuff next to the pool table, bad stuff next to the toilet,' I say to him.

He walks the chair over to the good corner.

A few minutes later the crunch of heavy tyres on dirt signals that George Laidlaw's Jaguar has arrived. He's trailed into the pub by Saucy and Clyde. Saucy makes a beeline for the bar and I step in.

'Saucy, leave behind the bar to Clyde, you fix it.'

'I was only going to try and sort out the good stuff from the trashed,' Saucy moans.

'Sure, with some of the good stuff making its way down your throat. I don't think so, Saucy. Go help Skid and try and keep him right. I want two piles of stuff. Good there and bad there,' I say, pointing again.

Saucy is about five feet six inches tall and dressed in the worn green two-piece suit he seems to be welded into. His hair is of the vintage Bobby Charlton comb-over era. His head is visibly liver-spotted where the comb-over isn't working.

George walks up to me. His heavyset beard has had a bit of a trim since I last saw him. Neatly clipped.

'Daniella, I have an appointment in fifteen minutes down at the port,' he says. 'I'll be back to help after that.'

'Señor Laidlaw, Señor Solo, Señor Heinz and young Clyde. Now this is very convenient.'

The Capitán enters and crosses the floor.

'It is nice of you to all gather together. This will save me and my officers some time. We are having some problems getting to the bottom of the events that unfolded last night.'

George passes the Capitán heading for the door. 'Well, you'll have to hold that thought from my end. I have an appointment I need to keep.'

The Capitán touches George on the arm. Nothing more than a light brush but enough to stop him moving.

'I need to talk to you, Señor Laidlaw, and we can do it here or I can have you brought down to the police station later tonight. It is up to you.'

George stares back at the Capitán. 'We are not the guilty ones here. Go talk to the people that trashed this place.'

'People seem keen on telling me who to interview and I do not like that. As we speak I have interviews going on at DB's. All I need at the moment, from everyone here, is a list of names of who was in the pub last night and where everyone was all day yesterday.'

'Oh, naming those that were in the pub will be easy,' says Saucy, kicking some broken glass to one side. 'Let's see Capitán, I'll start when the doors open, will I? Then I'll just work my way through everyone that came and went. That'll only take a couple of hours.'

The Capitán moves towards Saucy. Firm, sure steps.

'Señor Heinz, let us remember that a man died here. Or would you rather join Señor Laidlaw at the station? What shall we say, midnight? Or maybe my diary might mean it needs to be a little later. And I'd prefer you sober. Does that sound like a plan?'

'I don't have to do anything you say,' Saucy says. 'I've done fuck all.'

'You were an accountant to the deceased, were you not?'

'I did a little work for him.'

'And all of this *work* concerned money obtained legally?'

Saucy, sensibly, says nothing.

'So let's start again,' says the Capitán. 'I do not need to know the names of everyone here yesterday. Only the ones that were still here when this so-called raid took place. I'll worry about the others later.'

George wanders back to the bar. Saucy sits down and Skid pulls up a chair next to Saucy; this time he checks it carefully before sitting on it. I perch on the edge of the pool table with Zia.

'Okay, who is going to tell me what went down last night?' the Capitán asks.

9

The Night Before –
As Told by George Laidlaw

'I'll tell you what happened,' says George, 'but, Clyde, do me a favour. Can you nip down to Raffy's place and tell Rab Fairbairn I'm running late. His mobile is on the fritz and he's too good a client to piss off.'

Clyde nods and exits.

'Okay, if you really want to know what went down,' says George, 'this is what happened, Capitán.'

'George?' Saucy said to me as he asked Clyde to double up on the vodka in his glass.

I was sitting across the table from Saucy trying to watch the latest UK news on the main TV. I blanked Saucy.

'George?' More insistent from Saucy.

I kept my eyes on the TV but muttered, 'What?'

'Do you think DB's will come for Busca?'

'Saucy, I don't care, I'm watching the news.'

'You heard that Daniella told everyone this morning that we aren't playing this year. She had all the comments pulled from eldescarorocks.com,' Saucy said. 'I talked to Milo Foreman and he says that DB's are calling us chicken.'

'So what?'

'Well, there's talk of us going over to try and snatch Bertie anyway.'

'Feel free, knock yourself out, why don't you?'

Saucy tipped the rest of the drink down his throat. 'George, the Steal means a lot to some people in here.'

I grunted and swung away from the telly.

'Saucy,' I said, 'it means a lot to the idiots who thinks it means a lot. Those that don't think it means a lot, don't give a shit. Those that do, do. It happens to be that those that do are louder in the mouth than those that don't. That doesn't mean that those that do are the guiding voice in here. If those that do want to go and do whatever it is they want to do, then good, let them do it. And if you want to do it as well, feel free. But for those that don't, of which I'm one, we want to do whatever it is we want to do and in my case I want to watch the bloody TV – does that clarify things?'

Saucy's face crinkled at the edges as he worked his way through what I had just said. He was still this side of the alcoholic oblivion he was heading for that day so I figured he might just be able to work it all out.

'So, you're with Daniella on this?' he finally asked.

'No. I'm not with that girl Coulstoun on anything. Ever. She can no more cancel the Steal than the bloody United Nations can. But let her think she has. For my tuppence worth I'd hand the damn wooden bandit to DB's if they appear here, just to get them to piss off.'

'Milo thinks they'll try an out-and-out, no-holds blitz.'

'Oh, for crying out loud. What is this? Assault on Precinct 13? DB's will try their usual inane stupid tricks, regardless of what Daniella has said about cancelling. But they won't be kicking the door in to do it. The police would be on that like a flash and who in here, or in DB's, wants the police involved in anything we do? Eh? So give it a rest.'

Saucy rose to head for the bar. 'I'm only telling you what Milo said. Out-and-out, no-holds blitz. Those were his words. And he's not one to bullshit.'

And, to be fair, Saucy was right on that.

'Clyde,' I shouted. 'Do me a favour and turn the TV up as loud as it can go. I'm getting tired of the chat in here. Let's see if Huw Edwards can drown it out.'

'Only saying,' said Saucy as he staggered to the bar. 'Only saying.'

'Did anyone from Se Busca try and steal DB's trophy?' interrupts the Capitán as he listens to George's version of events.

'No,' replies George. 'Saucy was talking out of his arse.'

'And who else was in the pub?'

'I'll get to that. Do you want to hear the rest of the story? I'm on the clock here. My appointment is a paying client and I'm already late.'

'Si.'

'George,' said Jordan Norman to me as he flew into the pub, trailing his twin sister behind him.

I sighed. 'What?'

'Have you heard the DB's are going to ram raid Se Busca?' said Sheryl.

'For heaven's sake,' I said. 'What in the hell has gotten into everyone today?'

'It was on the eldescarorocks website before it got pulled. Ramraid tonight. That's what it said,' squeaked Sheryl. She was almost birling with excitement.

'An army truck,' said Jordan.

'A what?' exclaimed Saucy, returning with his next drink. 'An army truck? I heard it was a car. At least that's what it said on the website. DB's are going to crash an army truck into the pub? Really?'

'An army truck? Really?' repeated Clyde, joining the conversation.

*

'An army truck,' says the Capitán.

'There was never an army truck in this,' says George.

'Who told you this?' I said, giving up on the news on the TV.

'The website,' replied Jordan.

'Then it ain't going to happen,' I pointed out. 'The police monitor that chat forum. You'd have to be clean off your head to announce something as dumb as that on that stupid forum. Now, has anyone else got any more half-wit news or can I get back to watching the real news?'

But it was too late. Huw had given way to the weather man who was telling me that the UK was going to be damp and experience tit-freezing temperatures interspersed with miserable patches of sleet.

I pulled out my novel and sat back to read.

The rest of the afternoon panned out as usual. Comings and goings. Saucy passed out at some point and slept it off under the dartboard. Sheryl and Jordan played gin and sipped at beer. I asked for the late afternoon movie to be put on the telly about four. Broken Arrow. *A Western – Jimmy Stewart trying to appease the locals. About seven o'clock Zia left to meet Daniella for dinner and a few people arrived to watch the FA cup game and that was that till gone ten.*

'Who was there at ten o'clock?' asks the Capitán.

'Saucy, the Twins, Skid, me, Clyde and the Charles brothers – although the brothers left about ten thirty. A quiet night because I think people had heard about DB's planned raid and avoided Se Busca that night. Can I continue?'

'*Si.*'

'Quiet, isn't it?' said Saucy, rousing from his stupor.

'That bloody website,' I said. 'It's got people scared. Clyde, is the back door locked?'

'I checked earlier,' he replied. 'It's solid.'

That's when the car arrived. Jordan was over by the main entrance and when he heard the engine he cracked the door to look out.

'George,' he shouted, 'that's Davie Brost's Porsche arriving.'

'Really? Anyone else?'

'No, just him.'

I got up and decided that if Brost wanted a chat it was better to do it outside. If there was some stupid plan going down it would do no harm for Brost to think the pub might be full of people.

'Jordan, I'm going to talk to Brost. Lock the door behind me and do it quickly.'

I exited, and caught Brost as he approached the pub. The lighting out there is poor at the best of times. There are a half a dozen bulbs out around our door, and the nearest street light went on the fritz a week ago. I met Brost halfway across the car park in almost complete darkness.

'Davie,' I said.

'George.'

'What brings you here?'

'You know why I'm here.'

He sounded nervous, scared almost.

'Out of lager?' I said.

'Funny man.'

'Okay, so you want to sell up and let us take over DB's?'

'I've got a spot on the comedy night this week that's still free, George. Are you auditioning?'

'Davie, from what I hear, a dead dog and a blind tortoise would be funnier than anyone you have on.'

He stopped talking for a second to look back. He wasn't looking at his car but over towards the entrance to our car park and out to where the side road cuts into the main avenue. There's a strip of nose-in car parking spaces on that road, usually empty at this time of year, but it looked fairly full to me. That set my alarm bells ringing. Chances were that Davie was the advance guard on this one. And what he said next confirmed it.

'Look, George,' he said, 'just give me that bloody wooden monstrosity of yours and this will all end here and now.'

'That easy, Davie. Just hand it over?'

'That easy, George. Your boss has already declared you are all out of it, so what's the beef?'

'Boss? You mean Daniella Coulstoun? Not my boss. She doesn't speak for me. Never will. But she owns the majority stake in the pub and she doesn't want any of the nonsense that comes with the Steal. That's why she canned it from this end.'

'And she was disrespectful with it,' said Davie. 'She had the eldescarorocks website pull down the chat and reported a few of the people.'

'People were saying some real nasty things.'

I didn't know that, but having been on the site when other shit was kicking off, I know what it can be like.

'Hot air, George. Nothing but hot air.'

'Sure, Davie. Just hot air. Hot air driven by a half bottle of vodka or a few joints, a darkened room and a pair of trousers round their ankles as they flick from their favourite porn site to eldescarorocks. All brave behind a screen. Mouthing off. Rank cowards most of them. Tell them to say some of that crap to people's faces in the street and they'd cack themselves for a month. You and I both know that.'

'She also said that the Steal was a dumb idea that attracted dumb people.'

'And she's bloody right. It's a kid's game being played out by adults. Okay, I'll give you that, in the beginning, it was a bit of fun, but when someone says they are going to ram an army truck into a building then you know we are in a whole new world of dumb-arsery.'

'I told Jimmy to delete that.'

83

'Only because the police would have had him in a cell if he hadn't. Who says something that bloody stupid?'

'Just hand over Busca,' he said.

'Or what, Davie? What will you do?'

His voice rose, quavering slightly as he spoke.

'I'm not in control of this, George,' he admitted. 'It was the devil's own bloody job to convince my lot that I should try and talk you into handing the thing over first. They were all ready to storm your place right now.'

'Your lot? Who is your lot, Davie?'

'Just hand it over.'

'All this over a bloody wooden statue?'

'Give it a rest, George,' he spat. 'You know it's more than that.'

'Davie, I can guarantee that the clientele of Se Busca don't give a toss about the Steal. Your lot, on the other hand, well, that's a different matter.'

'What does that mean?'

'You know.'

'I don't.'

'For fuck's sake, do you really want to do this here, right now?'

He looked at me, his expression hard to read in the dark. But I'd swear there was a wash of pleading across his face. As if somehow, I could be his saviour. As if he wanted this conversation. Maybe to delay things a bit. Maybe he knew what was coming and wanted to hear it from me. Or maybe he was just scared.

'They gave me ten minutes before I'm redundant,' he said. 'So if you're not going to do the sensible thing and hand over the statue then you have the floor. What is it I should know?'

What I said next wasn't breaking news but I don't think anyone outside of Davie's circle had said it to him directly.

'Davie, let's be honest here, everyone knows you are running a busted flush of a pub. You scrape by on a combination of a few semi-loyal expats and the odd lost tourist. DB's is off the beaten track of an unbeaten track. Your old man ran a great ship ten years ago. Rivalled us back then. Large expat custom base, thriving social scene. Old Effie, God rest her soul, took a few pointers from your dad on how to make a pub work around here. Your dad made being off tourist central avenue look like an advantage. But since he passed you've taken that legacy and fucked it up.'

'Have I hell,' he said.

'Oh, get off your oversensitive horse, Davie. I'm only telling you what every bugger in town knows. You're no pub man.'

'We are growing as a business this year.'

'Even if you are, you're still way down on where your dad was. Tell me this Davie, what do you charge for a beer?'

'What's that got to do with anything?'

'I'll tell you. You charge a whole euro less than us and you're never out of the local rag with some new drink deal or other. We haven't discounted booze in twenty years. Your dad never did either. A fair price, yes, but never short-term discounts. As to your business growing, I know you've picked up a few offcasts from here in the last twelve months. Malky Robertson and his crew in the main. And I'd bet you an even gold coin to a brass farthing that he's behind tonight's shite. But Malky is a wallet-sealed skinflint. What did he ask for when he came knocking at your door? Did you cut him a deal on booze prices to switch from us? I bet that'll work out well in the long run when word gets out to your other punters. I'll say it again, you're not a pub man. You don't even rule the roost in your own world. Otherwise, why are you here pleading with me? If Effie had told everyone in here to stop with the Steal, they would have listened. But you, in your pub, no bugger listens to you.'

'George—'

'Let me finish,' I said. 'I also hear that you've been looking for help from here to try and get DB's on an even keel.'

'Rubbish.'

'No, it's not. You tapped up our Saucy for the heads-up on Se Busca's accounts. Offered him free drink if he'd 'fess up to our wholesaler deal and other running costs. And don't say you didn't. I heard that he damn nearly took you up. Saucy can't keep his mouth shut when he's drunk and he's drunk a lot.'

'I never talked to him,' slurs Saucy.

'Yes, you did. You bloody told me so a month ago. We'll talk about it later,' George says, pausing the story. 'But let me finish this bloody thing.'

'All the wrong clientele at DB's and you know it,' I continued. 'You've a smattering of expats that are living on a shoestring and a few tourists that don't want to pay beachfront prices. And there's bugger all loyalty in either of those. But I'll let you into a little secret, just in case you think that Malky and his crew are the turning of the tide. You see, Malky Robertson and his dead-heads were kicked out by Effie. Malky was caught trying to dip the till a year ago. Tell me that wasn't exactly when he alighted on your doorstep.'

'I have Karen Dorset,' he said.

I sighed at that.

'Yes, you do. Karen Dorset and the knitting crew,' I said. 'I heard they were at yours. Big deal. Six women who drink a coffee each every couple of hours and take up two tables for days at a time, knitting.'

'And who have booked a twenty-first at mine,' he threw back.

'You do know that she's also booked her wedding reception for her daughter here? A hundred guests and a marquee outside. She's only at yours because she and Effie were close and she struggled to be in the pub after Effie died – but she's getting over it. She'll be back soon. Trust me, DB's has only one future – a long lingering death – unless you change shit. I've no idea why I'm telling you this. I should let you sink without trace but, trust me, Davie, I think Malky and some of the others are making a play for DB's. Taking it over through the back door. The plan is simple. Bleed you dry and pick up the pub for a song. This stupid Steal is just another step in their power play. They win this, they brag to the world, you look like a weak arsehole and they continue to wring you arid. Davie, you know the game out here. You just don't know how to play it well.'

'And you have the crème de la crème of customers in your place.'

'Oh, for fuck's sake, Davie. We have the arse end of customers in here. The fucked off and fucked up. The expats with nowhere else to go. But they put their hands in their pockets and appreciate the anonymity of Se Busca. What do you have? You have the guys you see propping up every cheap bar around here, blowing hard about what they could have done had they just had the breaks, and moaning about every fucking thing on the planet. That's who you have. Our lot might moan but they pay well and moan – and that we can live on and with. You've lost control of your own bar. Your dad would be flipping three-sixties in his grave if he knew you were here on bended knees. He would have told Malky to fuck himself in a public place with a tent pole and been done with it.'

Davie couldn't help but look at the street with the parked cars. 'That's all for shite, George,' he said, looking back at me.

'For crying out loud Davie, no it's not. I'm trying to give you some solid advice. You need to wake up and smell the fucking Nescafé or you'll be out on your ear. How will Rhona cope without her three shopping trips to Madrid a year? And who'll pay Derek's school fees? You need to look after your family, Davie. As I said, I should just let you sink, but I figure I'm not telling you anything you don't already know. If I was you I'd man up and tell that bunch of wankers back there that this game is off. Bar them all. Kick them out. That's if you still have the balls, or the ability, to do that.'

*

And what did he say to that?' asks the Capitán.

'Nothing,' replies George. 'He just walked away.'

'What time was this?'

'About eleven.'

'And the raid?'

'Thirty minutes later, give or take.'

'Why did they leave it so late in the day? Isn't the game to get the mascot to theirs before midnight?'

'That's exactly why it was so late. The closer to midnight they grab it, the better,' says George. 'That way there's less chance we can get Busca back off them before the deadline. Whoever has the other's mascot at midnight is all that counts.'

'Why did you not call the police?'

'And say what?'

'What you suspected.'

'Why? For all I know, my talk with Brost might have worked and he'd managed to get them to stand down.'

'But he didn't achieve that. Go on.'

'I need to leave for my meet.'

'Please finish.'

George looks at his watch. 'For f . . .' Then he finishes the story.

For the next half an hour nothing went down. I returned to the pub and told everyone what had been said between me and Brost. Jordan periodically checked the door, but nothing was stirring. I was conscious that they could easily come around the back, but Sheryl was listening at the back door and could hear zip. The closer we got to the witching hour the better as far as I was concerned. Too close and there wouldn't be enough time to lift Busca and get it back to DB's.

'Skid, Jordan,' I said, 'do me a favour. Pull a table and some chairs across the front door.'

'It's nearly eleven thirty,' said Saucy. 'I think they've called it quits. Anyway, that bloody door has got to be three inches thick. Why the table?'

'I'm just belt and bracing,' I said. 'If it was me in charge of the raid I'd be thinking of hitting in the next few minutes. And while we are at it we should move Busca into the back office and lock the door.'

'If they come in the fire door you are making it easy for them,' Saucy pointed out.

'The fire door is solid metal, Saucy. Overlapping joints. Easy to open from this side. Not from outside.'

'I thought you didn't care if they got Busca?' Saucy said.

'I can't see how they're going to get in here, but if they do there's no point in making it easy. Another ten minutes and they'll have no chance of getting Busca back to DB's. All I'm doing is making it as hard as possible – if they are coming.'

So, Jordan, Sheryl, Skid and I moved Busca to the back office.

And there was no sign of Señor Ratte in the cellar?' asks the Capitán.

'I think we might have noticed a dead body,' says George.

We had just come back from dumping Busca in the office when we heard the noise. A thump against the front door. Like someone had just slung a wet sandbag at it. We all turned and I shouted, 'Down, everyone down.'

I pulled a table over on its side and threw myself behind it. A split second later the others were all diving to the floor. Then the door exploded with one hell of a bang. The lights went out, and, next thing I knew, there were people swarming all over the pub, screaming and shouting. I buried my head behind a chair as the furniture was turned over all around me. Torchlight flashed and I caught a glimpse of the invaders, but but some had crash helmets on. I even saw one small man with a welder's helmet on.

Bloody weird. They made straight for the cellar, and then there was a cheer and I heard the fire door being battered open.

It took a few seconds to gather my thoughts before I moved towards the office and I heard Sheryl shout, 'Did they get it?'

I checked the office but Busca was gone and I shouted out, 'Yes.'

'Well, team,' said Sheryl, 'that's us fucked.'

That's when I saw Pat's foot, sticking out from behind the kegs. I checked and shouted, 'Christ, I think there's a dead body in here.'

A dead body?' said Saucy.

'Yes,' I replied.

'Dead?' said Saucy.

'I think so,' I replied.

'Who is it?' he asked.

And I said, 'It looks like Pat Ratte.'

'And does everyone agree with that story?' asks the Capitán as George moves towards the front door.

They all nod.

'Señorita Coulstoun?'

'You know fine well I wasn't here, Capitán.'

'Ah yes, you were in the pueblo, eating?'

I don't answer.

'Sénor MacFarlane?'

'I was with Daniella.'

'Ah, so you were.'

'Look, I'm going,' says George. 'You know where I am.'

'One last question, before you leave, Señor Laidlaw.'

'What?'

'You say Señor Ratte's body was not there minutes before the raid?'

'Correct. We placed Busca in the office and there was no body there.'

'So Señor Ratte was brought in by the people that raided the pub?' says the Capitán.

'How else?' replies George.

'But why, Señor Laidlaw? Why bring a dead man into this place and leave him to be found?'

'I've no idea.'

'And no one saw a dead body being dragged into the pub?'

'It was chaos. They had just blown off the door.'

'All a bit extreme, is it not?'

'Yeah, well, Malky Robertson's brother works in construction. He's currently overseeing the extension to a new road, and I know they're blasting. That's what made me tell everyone to get down. Go ask him if any explosives are missing.'

'I will.'

'And I'll tell you something else, Capitán. I know that Pat had been in DB's recently.'

'You do?'

'In fact I saw Pat down near DB's yesterday.'

'Near? What do you mean by near?'

'Actually, he was going into DB's.'

'What time was this?'

'Early, ten o'clock that morning.'

'You saw Señor Ratte alive at ten yesterday morning and he was entering DB's.'

'Yes.'

'And you think he was there for what reason?'

'I could guess.'

'Go on.'

'Remember I told you that Brost was looking for help to save the pub, that he had approached Saucy? Remember?'

'Yes.'

Everyone is looking at George now.

'Well, it's no secret that Pat wanted to take Se Busca over from Effie, but Daniella well and truly spiked that gun when she arrived.'

'And what has that to do with Señor Brost, Señor Laidlaw?' says the Capitán.

'Well, and I'm only spitting wind here, what if Pat was muscling in on Davie's place instead? Davie was looking for help. Saucy blanked him. He turns to Pat and maybe he asked the wrong guy. You do know that Pat had Malky Robertson under his thumb? Malky was shit-scared of Pat. Maybe Pat planned a little coup of his own with DB's. Maybe the whole Malky defection from Se Busca was a set-up. Malky told to dip the till here. Get in Effie's bad books. Then put himself and his team inside DB's, so to speak.'

'Señor Robertson was barred from here a year back,' says the Capitán. 'That would mean long-term planning.'

'Pat was bloody good at planning,' says George. 'Bloody good. What if he told Malky to destabilise DB's? If Pat thought he was onto a loser here in the short term but could control DB's, he could make a pretty penny – he'd simply force some of our customers to switch allegiance.'

'But Señor Ratte is dead.'

'He is that.'

'And you think that maybe in the chaos of last night his body was dropped here for what reason? To cover up his murder that happened at DB's earlier?'

'Davie Brost was as nervous as a priest in a strip club last night when we had our chat out in the car park.'

The Capitán scrubs at the small bald patch that's poking through the crown of his head. 'But, Señor Laidlaw, if you had acceded to Señor Brost's request to hand over the wooden statue then they would never have broken in. And in that case, they would not have been able to leave Señor Ratte here.'

'True, and then maybe Pat would have turned up elsewhere. Or maybe Davie Brost was setting up his alibi. To be able to claim exactly what you just said. All I know is I saw Pat Ratte at DB's yesterday morning. The rest is me taking a wander down speculation alley.'

'This is serious, Señor Laidlaw. Why did you not say this earlier?'

'Because no one asked. Now one way or the other I'm going to my meet.'

With this he leaves and the Capitán is out behind him like a shot, shouting at Jorge, '*Cuando el equipo termine en el piso de arriba, llévalo a DB's lo más rápido posible.*'

10

Cold Blood

I wander out into the car park and see the Capitán vanish around the back of the pub as George walks quickly towards his car. If George is right about Pat being at DB's yesterday morning then he's put Davie Brost right in the frame for Pat's death. Which is good news for me and also makes Davie a prime suspect for framing me. Him or this guy Malky Robertson. I've seen him around town a few times, and I'd heard that Mum kicked out a few leeches from the pub now and again. It was her way of controlling all the others. No one wants to be barred from Se Busca. So what better way of keeping everyone in their training reins than by barring a few every now and again? Nothing like exclusion to sharpen the sense of loss. I return to the pub and ask everyone else to get back to work.

The Capitán makes a brief appearance fifteen minutes later but, as I'm not arrested, I have to assume that my apartment has not yet given up anything suspicious. I ask when I can get back in to my home and he says he will phone and let me know.

Ten minutes later and the officers searching the apartment head off. Jorge is left at the bottom of the stairs to my apartment on his own to stop me getting into my place. He's at such a loose end that I manage to get him to help out with the clear-up in return for a coffee and time out of the sun.

By five we've cracked the back of the clear-up. With one last Herculean effort we transfer all the busted stuff outside and I distribute a mop, a Hoover, a few brushes, a clutch of cloths, some polish, bottles of window cleaner and toilet gel, telling everyone to get scrubbing. While the place is given a buff, Jorge, Zia and I nail a dust cover over the gap where the door stood, to keep the weather out. It's hardly secure but I'd forgotten to phone the joiners earlier and it will need to do for the moment.

Clyde reappears and I gather everyone together once they finished cleaning.

'Okay, so let's get the message out there that we are open,' I say. 'Can someone contact the Twins? They'll be working down at the Safety Deposit + as usual. It's closing up time. Given they didn't help with the clean-up, get them onto the local websites and Facebook accounts and tell them to let everyone know we are back up and running. They are better at that shit than any of us. Then I want you all to call up a few of the regulars and let them know. There's football on tonight so that should bring some in.'

'Should we offer a free drink?' says Zia.

'No way,' I reply. 'This is just another night.'

Skid heads for the door.

'Where are you going?' I ask.

'Home.'

'Like hell you are. Get on that bloody phone. Call up a few of the regulars. You are here until the first punters start to arrive.'

'I need a wash.'

'Use the toilet.'

'I'm not washing in there.'

'Well, don't wash then but you're going nowhere until this place is buzzing. Now get on that phone.'

Skid slinks back to the corner and pulls out his mobile.

Jorge is sitting near the front door, sipping a coffee.

'Jorge,' I say and then in poor Spanish, '*¿Cuándo puedo volver a mi casa?*'

He shakes his head. '*No lo sé.*'

I'm not getting back in my home just yet. As much as I've told Skid to wash in the toilet I'm not up for that. But I'm slick with sweat and need a shower and a change of clothes.

I pull Zia to one side. 'Can you and Clyde hold the fort until I get back? I'm going up to Mum's old place for a shower. Jorge says we can't get back in upstairs yet and I could really do with a change of clothes as well.'

'Let me talk to him,' Zia offers.

He chats to Jorge in Spanish and comes back over.

'Tell me what you need and he'll fetch it from the bedroom. He's going to do the same for me.'

'I could do with a full change: pants, bra, the works.'

The thought of a stranger rummaging around in my smalls drawers fills me with revulsion.

'I'll live with a change of top and shorts. I don't want anyone in my underwear.'

'No one?' he smiles.

'You know what I mean,' I say with a grin.

'What top and what shorts?'

'The navy striped top, my dark blue knee-length shorts, white ankle socks and my white trainers. All of that will be lying on the bed. It's what I was going to change into tonight. Tell Jorge to touch nothing else.'

'Okay.'

Zia passes on my request and Jorge leaves, returning five minutes later with clothes for me and Zia.

'Team, I'll be back in forty-five minutes,' I say, grabbing my clothes from Jorge.

Skid eyes me as I leave. He makes a show of deliberately sniffing under his armpits to let me know he's not best pleased at him staying and me going.

I emerge into the early evening air as the sun is dipping behind the hills. Turning up the road towards the old town I stop to look at a slice of the Med that cuts through between two blocks of rentals. Storm-grey blue, it sits beneath heavy clouds. A small flicker of lightning high in the sky tells me that we are in for rain tonight. My weather app on the phone has warned me a big storm is on the cards. I'll need to figure a better solution for the pub's front door if that's the case. The lightweight dust sheet I have in place will be no protection if the coast is hit hard.

I stroll up the hill, entering a maze of mid-rise apartment blocks, some dating back fifty or so years. Squeezed between them are even older homes. There seems little rhyme or reason to the layout around me, but most of the buildings are well kept and the older ones sport traditional Spanish shutters and doors. Mum's old apartment is halfway to the centre of the old town, lying just before the roads narrow even further and traffic is all but banned. The old town is a wonderful place to wander, losing your head in the shade and the cool. I'm tempted to keep walking, maybe choose a café and order up some *vino blanco*, kick back my heels, people-watch for a while. But according to George I've been over-doing that of late and I'm also in no mood to sit and contemplate the implications of last night. I'd hoped that clearing the pub of the wreckage would empty my mind but it's now as jumbled as the pile of discarded furniture and fittings sitting outside Se Busca.

I stop in at one of the many local stores and purchase some shampoo, conditioner and shower gel. I throw in some deodorant and pass the wine aisle. The thought of a glass of wine grows in appeal and pluck a bottle of white from the shelf. One glass won't kill me. If I pop the bottle in the freezer when I get in it should be cold enough by the time I've finished showering.

A few minutes later I'm trudging up the stairs of Mum's sixties-built brutalist apartment block.

When I'd first arrived here all the rooms, save the kitchen, were in a time warp, bending back to the day Mum arrived. Dust thick in the air and thicker on the carpets, one room given over completely to junk. When Pat had sold up on the hill he had rented Mum's flat from me for a bit, and I'd had it emptied and redecorated. Pat had removed all his personal stuff when I'd kicked him out, and what's left is a white shell with neutral furniture – *let-ready,* as Zia says.

I open the front door and the faint smell of damp, stale air wafts out. The hall is hot, as is the living room. I dump the wine in the freezer in the kitchen and drop my bag next to the sofa in the living room, sitting down for a few seconds for a breath before setting about opening as many windows as I can to let some breeze flow through. Next, I strip and bag my old clothes in the plastic bag the convenience store gave me for my shopping. I'll wash them when I get back to my home. I fire up the shower but the tepid water doesn't heat up. I slap my head and return to the kitchen to turn on the gas combi boiler. When I get back to the shower the water is warm and ready. Back home I'd liked the water to be half a degree short of scalding but out here, even in the darker months, hot showers mean I'll sweat for hours. I adjust the temperature to a little above too cold and jump in.

I relax a little, the cascading fluid sluicing some of the tension from my shoulders. For ten minutes I do nothing other than spin slowly in the shower cubicle, letting the water fall over my body. Then I get to work scrubbing and cleaning to emerge, twenty minutes later, feeling a shade more human than I had when I'd entered. Back in the kitchen I open the freezer and shake the wine bottle a few times to let the cold outer liquid mix with the warmer inner layer. I put it back and slump at the breakfast table, still naked. The kitchen window is open. It looks out above the opposite apartment block to the hill beyond. I'm sure if someone in the expensive homes that dot the hill has a mind to, they could

98

probably, with the aid of a telescope, see me. I take the risk as I'm enjoying the cool wind rolling through the window.

Five minutes later I retrieve the wine bottle and dig out the corkscrew from the cutlery drawer. I uncork, pour and taste. Still a little too warm so I flick a few ice cubes into the liquid and stir them with my finger. I kick out the second chair from under the breakfast bar and place my feet up, noting that I'll need to attend to my legs at some point. My endless battle with my hirsute side is something my mother handed down to me. Mum could leave a fully-grown hedgehog in the plughole when she was finished shaving. I'm not far behind, maybe a teenaged hog's worth.

I look at my bulging tummy and consider flushing the calorie-laden wine down the sink but the need for some brain-easing alcohol outweighs the desire, for the moment, to get back to beach-body land.

I sip the wine, lean back in the chair, throw my heels higher and close my eyes. The sound of El Descaro falling towards evening surrounds me. A low buzz as the town emerges from the siesta slump. A firework explodes in the distance and reminds me that one of the many fiestas is kicking off tonight. Tomorrow will bring a big parade right past Se Busca. Zia told me that Mum always put up an outside bar for the day, to pick up trade and to stop the regulars moaning by keeping the non-regulars outside. The Twins are it for that one. I'd texted them earlier saying that missing out on the pub clean-up puts them in the frame for the outside bar. Jordan had texted back a long moan about how they both needed to be at Safety Deposit + tomorrow. I'd flicked back that that was their problem and reminded him that they own a share of the pub and have to pitch in. The reply had been curt – 'If we must'.

I adjust myself on the chair, sliding a little further down, easing my heels along the other chair and pressing the soles of my feet against the wooden back. A gust of wind runs up my legs and the wine starts to kick in. Another firework, a rocket this time, bursts in the sky with a small pop. Later, the fireworks will be far closer, far bigger and far, far louder. If the storm doesn't do for the display.

I doze.

A noise pulls me from my snooze. My head is post-sleep fuzzy as I open my eyes. I listen. Nothing. I stop breathing. Letting my mouth hang open. Straining to catch any sound. Outside. It must have been outside the flat. I was asleep. Out of it. The noise could have been on the street or in my dreams. Dreams that had barely started to form. It could have been a sleep-twitch. But something is telling me that's not the case. The sound was a click, from inside, not outside. I slide my feet off the chair, suddenly uncomfortable with my nakedness. I feel vulnerable. I feel super vulnerable. If someone is in the flat . . . The thought stops there. It needs no more formation. *If someone is in the flat.*

Carefully, quietly, gently, I slip from the chair. I need something to cover my nakedness. But apart from a slip of a tea towel that wouldn't hide my pubes there is nothing.

If someone is in the flat, I need a weapon.

A squeak from outside. A floorboard squeak. This place wasn't built to the best of specs. Most of the floorboards have worked their way loose from their nails a little. Crossing the living room is a chaotic symphony of cracks and moans. The flat above is the same and the owner, Señora Rosa, who is all but a recluse and weighs in just this side of a small camel, sends down a Mexican wave of a racket when she rises to visit the toilet.

I scan the kitchen for hiding places but none of the cupboards are big enough. The fridge-freezer would accommodate me, if I emptied it out but that would be a bit of a giveaway. I slowly press my ear against the door, conscious that if the intruder slams the door open I'll take a blow to the head. I hear nothing other than the echo of the outside world bouncing around the walls.

Okay, if the intruder is inside what are they here for? To steal. But steal what? Pat's belongings are long gone, and apart from the industrial LCD telly my mum invested in just before she died, there is nothing of value to be had. Of course, a sneak thief wouldn't know that. They would just see an imposing security door and wonder why someone in a run-down block such as this would go to the expense and trouble of installing such a thing.

Did I leave the door open?

Or were they here all along?

Hiding.

Waiting.

But if they were here, where were they hiding? I'd been in the living room, the bathroom and the kitchen but not in either of the bedrooms. Someone could easily have heard me come in and hid in one of them.

Had they been watching as I made my way to the shower?

Were they looking at me naked?

So why did they not leave while I was in the shower? I was in there twenty minutes, minimum. The roar of the water would have easily covered any noise.

Were they looking at me naked?

Is that why they stayed? Locking us both in behind a solid barrier of metal and wood. Watching as I'd entered the kitchen. Hearing the cork on the wine bottle pop. The scrape of the chairs as I'd settled in. Biding their time.

Real fear clouds the thinking and I'm right under that blanket of thick, dark fog. I should cross to the window and shout. Scream for help while I still can. But I'm five floors up and the lane beneath the kitchen window is a dead end. Only kids with cheap wine, drunks needing a piss or the odd stray cat use it. And shouting would be the starter gun to anyone in here.

I press my ear back to the door.

Still nothing.

I know there are a few tools in the bottom drawer of the cabinet, next to my legs. I lift my foot and slip my toe under the handle.

Pulling slowly, I reveal a jumble of metal crammed into the drawer. Under a few screwdrivers and a pair of pliers lies a hammer. I bend down and slide the hammer free, ultra-sensitive to scraping one tool on another.

The minutes are crawling by and there have been no more new noises. I step forward and press my ear to the door again, hammer behind my back.

Nothing.

I can't just stay here. If the intruder is a thief then surely there would be sounds. If they are here to attack me then why are they waiting? Building up courage? Me, an unexpected opportunity? Them, undecided?

Were they looking at me naked?

I listen again.

Nada.

I flick the hammer to my left hand and grab the door handle. I listen. Nothing. I take one last breath and twist.

I reach for the front-door handle and, as I take my second step into the hall, I stumble, my toes slamming into the skirting board. I fly forward, hands springing out to catch the fall. The hammer goes spinning. I face-plant the door as I try to catch both my fall and the weapon. I bounce off the oak surface and collapse to the floor. I land, instantly spinning my head around, looking for the intruder.

No one.

Nothing.

Zip.

I lie for a moment. Listening. Watching.

Both my nose and foot hurt.

I keep still.

Nothing.

I push myself up, ignoring the pain in my foot and my nose. Standing up, eyes flicking from the bedroom doors to the bath-room door to the living-room door and back, I should get outside – into the stairwell – get the hell away from here. Run. But something is telling me that whoever was here is now gone. If they had been watching me they would have attacked when I was on the floor.

Wouldn't they?

I check each room – all are empty.

I ensure the front door is secure by inserting my key to prevent anyone else coming in. I head back to the living room to retrieve my mobile. As I bend down to lift it my bare foot stands in something wet and I instantly recoil. The carpet in here is fitted above the old floorboards, a dark grey mass of deep shag that Pat wanted laid. In the half light from the window there is nothing to see at my feet. I bend down and run my fingers through the pile until I hit the damp area. The liquid is cold and thick. I lift my finger up and the smell hits me. A foul, cloying, sweet stink with a metallic note, as if someone had just switched on one of those old transformers that my friend 'Trine's brother had for his Scalextric set. My finger is coated in dark brown. I reach down and carefully trace the patch with my other hand. The stain is about the size of a dinner plate and it definitely wasn't there earlier. My handbag lies, undisturbed, a few inches from it, the sofa above. I had sat there briefly when I'd come in and my feet couldn't have missed the mess.

Like a far light through a thick mist the reality of what I'm touching dawns on me.

Blood.

11

Clean-Up

I process the implications. The blood is cold, and that means it's not fresh so the intruder didn't injure themselves in here and make a run for it. They dumped this. And it doesn't take a certifiable genius to figure whose blood it might be. *Pat Ratte's.* After all, if you really wanted to frame someone for a murder, what better than a pool of the victim's blood in the suspect's house? And if you were keen to expedite an arrest you'd call the police once you were a safe distance from the scene, informing them that you had seen something yesterday. Maybe Pat entering the building. *Officer, I heard on the news about the murder.* And even if there is no one making a phone call, and I were the Capitán, I think that the other property owned by his prime suspect might already be on the Capitán's list of 'to dos' after his crime scene team have trawled through my flat and DB's. And if the Capitán finds blood here what story will he believe? That the daughter who is pointing the finger at Pat Ratte for her mother's death killed him in this flat and dumped the body in the pub, or that some shadowy figure broke in through an almost impregnable security door and tipped a bag of Pat's blood on the carpet?

I know which one I'd pick if it was the 50/50 choice for the million quid on *Who Wants to be a Millionaire.*

And in my head a massive countdown clock starts ticking.

I jump when my mobile rings. I look at the screen and Zia's smiling face is beaming back at me. I let it trip to answer machine, my brain trying to figure out where to go with all of this. I realise that if this really is Pat's blood then I'm dealing with one sick bastard. Someone who killed Pat and then drained off his blood. Or did they tap his veins before death? Surely trying to extract blood once the heart has stopped pumping is far harder. And who thought I'd ever be thinking about something like that?

Speed is of the essence. Leaving the blood here is not an option. Sure, it might not be Pat's blood. It might not even be blood but can I take that risk? Can I hell. Bleach is my first thought – but how would that work? The carpet fibres are soaked. Would bleach clean that? And wouldn't it stain the carpet, posting a sign saying 'Blood This Way'? I return to the kitchen and the tool drawer. A bright red Stanley knife sits in the corner. I pull it out and lift a bundle of plastic shopping bags from another drawer.

Back at the stain I trace out the outline of the blood, all but invisible in the dark carpet, and lay the bags around it. But before I do anything else, I have another thought and go hunting for any other patches of blood that might have been left. A slow, painful process that has my heart thudding as I imagine the heavy beat of police footsteps on the stairwell outside. Once I'm certain there are no other stains in any rooms, I return to the plastic bags and the exposed patch of carpet. I dig the Stanley knife into the pile a few inches from the stain and rip a line through both the fibres and the hessian backing, gouging deep. I slash three more lines. A square, two feet by two feet, the blood in the centre. I need to rip along the lines a few times more with the blade to cut the square free. Once the last connection to the rest of the carpet is sliced free I lift one edge of the carpet square and slide a plastic bag under it. I repeat this all the way round and then work more bags underneath until the bloody slice of carpet is completely resting on plastic. I bundle even more bags on top of the square before sprinting back to the kitchen for some plastic bin liners. I shake my head, thinking I should have used these from the start as they are much bigger.

But who the hell thinks clearly at times like this?

I lay down a mat of black plastic bags next to the wrapped bloody slice of carpet and slide it onto it. I rip off more bags from the bin bag roll and lay them on top of the square. I then open up one more bin bag and work the edge of the offending piece of carpet into the mouth. Inch by inch, ears alive for a knock on the door, I fully insert the plastic-wrapped piece of carpet. Next I slip another bag over the open end of the first bag and repeat the operation three times on each side. I hunt for tape of some kind but the best I can find is a roll of nylon string. I tie up the bags.

Happy the stained chunk of carpet is completely sealed, I study the floor. The dark oak surface has a slight sheen in parts, where the blood must have soaked through. I fetch the bleach from under the sink and grab a pile of rag cloths and get to work, cleaning. I bundle each used rag into another bin bag and then bag all the bags twice over before tying the top of the last bag over on itself. Dragging all the bags to the hall I go to the bathroom and scrub my hands raw with the hottest water I can bear. I rinse my hands in bleach and rewash them. I return to the living room and haul the sofa over the bare patch. I'm acutely aware that the intruder could easily have sprayed a few drops of blood elsewhere. But there is bugger all I can do about that right now. Anyway, Pat lived here for a few months. His DNA is bound to be splattered around the place. Any small drops could easily be the result of a shaving nick or a cut finger.

My focus is on getting rid of the bin bags now – and I mean right now.

I dress, slip on my shoes and lift the bags. At the front door I stop. If the intruder is still hanging around or if the police are on their way up or if a neighbour pops their head out – ifs are a bastard. I turn the lock, wait a few seconds then open up. The stairwell is clear. I drop down the stairs and reach the main entrance. Another thought pops into my head. I take the stairs back to the flat, enter and hunt out a shopping trolley. A bright mauve and purple material framed thing with two large and two small plastic wheels, it can hold three or four shopping bags worth of goods, the cousin to thousands that roam the streets around here. I stuff the bin bags into it, pull the cover over the trolley's opening and descend the stairs again.

I exit the building, fully expecting flashing police lights. The road is quiet. I push the trolley away from the flat and begin to bury myself in the old town, wondering where to dump the bags. El Descaro, like most Spanish towns does not collect rubbish from the homes. Ranged across the town are brightly coloured bins that you drop your waste in. Some are massive wheelie bins. Some look like small street bins but actually sit on top of larger bins that rise like Thunderbird 1 from its swimming pool at the flick of a switch by the binmen as their specially designed trucks sidle up to the bins to suck up the contents. Any bin will do now, but not one near the house. But also not one too far away. The longer I have to walk the streets the more likely I am to be caught.

I wind my way through the pedestrianised maze of homes and shops. At the edge of the town there is a row of bins, hidden from the main street. I have four to choose from – Glass, Paper, Organic and Metal & Plastic. The Organic wheelie bin is the only one with a fully opening lid. I stand on the metal bar that lifts the lid and, with a quick look around, I sling the bags into the dumpster. It's half full of rotting veg and waste – and stinks. With a bit of luck it'll be picked up soon.

I return to the flat and there is still no sign of the police. I enter warily, thinking that if the intruder has a key they could have returned. I do yet another check of the flat and find I'm alone. My phone rings again.

It's Zia again.

This time I answer.

'Hi, lover,' says Zia. 'Where in the hell are you?'

'Sorry, pop star,' I reply. 'I showered and then sat down in the kitchen for a minute and fell asleep. I'm just leaving now.'

'Is everything all right?'

'Of course.'

'Are you sure?'

Zia can sense when things are not on an even keel with me. We've only been together for a few months but he has an ultra-sensitive radar to my moods.

'Just a bit shaken by everything,' I say. 'That's all. See you in fifteen.'

'It sounds like more than that,' he says.

'Really, Zia, there is nothing else.'

Too sharp.

'I'll see you shortly,' I say before killing the call.

I consider my next move. Head back to Se Busca as just promised or stay and see if the police arrive. I can be dumb as a dumb night after a dumb day, and I throw the second option to the wind. If the Capitán wants to search this place, let him come find me for the keys. I need to get ahead of this stuff. Figure who killed Pat. Not that the Capitán isn't fully capable of doing that but whoever is trying to place me at the end of the hangman's rope isn't for stopping. They have this well planned out and no doubt there are other evidence-laying birds that they will set free as required.

I spend ten minutes in the bathroom getting myself into as decent shape as I can when all my potions and lotions lie elsewhere. Zia frequently tells me that I don't need make-up but that's because he doesn't understand what make-up is really for. It's for me, I tell him, not for him, but he still hasn't twigged what that really means. The last thing I do before I leave the flat is to polish off the glass of wine. The ice has melted and watered it down, but it gives me a chance to take a few quieter breaths before moving on.

Outside, the streetlights are burning holes in the night. I pass a local's bar that I occasionally dip into. Brightly lit and sparsely decorated, it's busy. Although it is the aesthetic antithesis of Se Busca they do have one thing in common – there's a real buzz to the place at night. I stop and gaze in at the scene within, the night rendering me all but invisible to the patrons. The TV is showing the main Spanish news, and the bar is a line of nodding heads, all male, chewing the cud with each other. There is a table of ladies, laughing, and a card school populated by twenty-somethings is underway in the far corner. The bar is handled by a lone woman. I recognise her. Her name's Marie and she lives two floors down from Mum's flat with her kid, Felipe. Zia told me that her husband left her a year ago and she's bringing up Felipe single handed. Felipe is the furthest away of the heads at the bar. He has a book open in front of him and looks like he's trying to get some homework done. A man leaves the bar to light up a cigarette. He spots me standing across the road and, as he strikes his match, casually smiles. I smile back at him and wheel away, down the hill, senses primed for racing police cars.

As I walk, the wind in my face carries a heavy promise of rain. Frequent, distant lighting strikes confirm my earlier fears. We are in for a storm.

Se Busca has a few extra bodies in it when I arrive back. Fewer than I would have hoped for but the incoming storm will have dampened the enthusiasm of even our hardiest customers. There are still enough punters to give the impression to anyone else who arrives that we are trying to move on from last night as quickly as we can. Zia waves at me as I enter.

'We need to do something about the busted door,' he says. 'There's a storm coming.'

'I know,' I reply. 'What do you suggest?'

'I've no idea. It really needs a joiner to fix the whole thing.'

'Well, that isn't going to happen tonight.'

I run my hand up the thin dust sheet that's protecting the entrance.

'Don't we have a tarpaulin out back?' I say.

'Not that I know of,' Zia says.

'Out nearer the trees,' I add. 'Where that old abandoned VW sits. I'm sure there is one under the car. I've seen it.'

Zia nods. 'You're right. An old grey thing?'

'That's it.'

'Hell, that's been there for an age, Daniella. That VW is Saucy's car.'

'I didn't know he drove.'

'He doesn't. Back in the old days he used to drive himself here. But the police caught him once too often full to the gills. He was lucky to avoid jail so one night he drove the car out to the trees, drunk as a skunk. Said he'd get it in the morning and never picked it up again. It's lain there for a long time. The tarp used to cover the car but it was blown off one night and someone pushed it underneath to get it out of the way. It's been that way ever since.'

'Well, let's see if the tarpaulin is in fit shape to cover the door,' I say.

I push the dust sheet to one side and let Zia exit the pub in front of me. As he leaves he grabs the heavy-duty torch from its hook. Somehow it survived last night's invasion.

'Zia,' I say as we pick our way across the car park.

'Yes?'

'I need to tell you something.'

'Sounds ominous.'

'It kind of is.'

He stops and turns the torch to light up the ground between us.

'What is it?' he asks.

'We can talk as we walk,' I say. 'That storm isn't going to wait.'

I urge him to get moving again. He heads for the car but his steps are slower. I catch up to him.

'Zia,' I say. 'This Pat thing is not good. Not good at all.'

He doesn't look back.

'*Thing*, Daniella? Do you mean his murder?'

'Amongst other stuff, yes.'

He stops and turns again.

'And by *not good* you mean that someone is trying to put you in the frame for it.'

'Keep moving,' I say.

'I can't talk to you like this. If you have something to say, Daniella, just say it.'

I think about what to say next but he speaks first.

'Clyde told me about Pat's visit last week and about the note.'

It confirms that Clyde had been earwigging on my conversation with Pat in the office.

'And,' he continues, 'there's the missing key for the pub. Jorge the policeman told me that the Capitán found it on Pat.'

'Is he supposed to say things like that?'

Zia shrugs.

'Well, there's more than that,' I say. 'And it's far worse.'

'Worse?'

We are a clear fifty yards from the pub and without the torch it would be as close to pitch black as makes no difference. The VW is still a good hundred yards further on. I lower my voice. Slowly, and with a little reluctance, I tell him about the photo and then the blood in Mum's flat.

'Blood?'

'It sure looked like it.'

'Pat's blood?'

'I've no way of knowing for sure. It could have been anyone or anything's blood but it would seem likely it's Pat's if someone is trying to frame me.'

'And this intruder was in the flat when you got there?'

'Or I left the door open and they came in behind me, although I'm sure I locked it.'

'Do you have all the keys?'

'Unless Pat took copies, then the answer is yes.'

'And you saw no one?'

'No, and when I heard the noise in the flat I was in the kitchen, naked. The last thing I wanted to do was open the door for a look.'

'Smart move but why didn't you phone me?'

'My mobile was in the living room.'

'No, not then. After. When you discovered the flat was empty. Why didn't you phone me then?'

'I was too busy cleaning up the blood.'

'Too busy?'

'Cutting up and dumping the carpet.'

'Not even time for a quick call?'

His voice has an ice core of disbelief rammed through it.

'No. I was scared the police were on their way up.'

'Okay, what about after that?' he probes. 'When you got back to the flat after dumping the carpet. Why not call and tell me then?'

'I was thinking.'

'And when I called you, why not tell me about it all then? Why now?'

That is a bloody good question. And I'm not sure I have the answer so I throw a defensive left turn.

'Zia, where were you yesterday morning?'

He swings the light and plays the torchlight on the rusting old VW.

'Why?' he says without looking back. 'What has that to do with anything?'

'Does there have to be reason for me to want to know?'

'Yes. We weren't talking about me. We were talking about you and the intruder in the flat. So why suddenly ask about yesterday morning?'

'I'd like to know.'

'Why?'

'The Capitán said that Pat might have been killed elsewhere,' I say, slowly.

The implied distrust behind that statement lifts into the unsettled air.

'Are you asking if I killed Pat, Daniella?'

'No,' I lie. 'I'm only asking where you were.'

And you didn't bat an eyelid when I said he was killed else-where.

He turns around, the edge of the torchlight catching his face in a bad way, his youthful looks stripped away as if the torch is an age-penetrating X-ray. The crow's feet around his eyes are dark stripes that give him an almost scarecrow-like appearance.

He is the one that now takes a sharp right in the conversation. 'Daniella, where are you and I going?'

Zia starts to slowly move the beam of torchlight on the ground, cutting lazy circles in a figure of eight.

'This is hardly the time for that conversation, Zia.'

'I'd say this is exactly the time,' he says. 'Trust is the bolt that holds relationships together. Asking where I was yesterday morning doesn't exactly come spread with a thick layer of faith in me. After all, you are the one with blood in your mum's flat.'

'Zia, are you asking me if I trust you?'

'Do you, Daniella?'

'Do you trust me?'

'Stop turning the questions back on me, Daniella. It's whether you trust me that's more relevant.' he says. 'But now you ask, I would trust you with my open heart in your hand.'

'Zia, just tell me where you were yesterday.'

'You really don't trust me.'

He reverses the sweep of the beam as a sharp blast of wind carries a few raindrops with it – and stops talking.

'Look, let's do this later,' I say after a moment, regretting the way this is going.

'No, Daniella, let's do this now. Ever since George pulled you up about not putting a shift in you've been distant.'

'Because you agreed with George, but it took George to say it. Not you.'

'Was I wrong to keep quiet?'

'Yes.'

'Why?'

'Because you're my partner. My confidant. You should have said something. Not George.'

'Are you questioning what we have?'

'If I'm honest, yes.'

'And your conclusion?'

'I'm not sure. I think we are a fantastic pair. You make me happy. A damn sight happier than I've been in years. You're funny, smart and a thousand other things that you read in romance novels. But I also think we have our issues.'

'Such as.'

'Your unresolved desire to get more music out. Your need to lance that boil from the eighties. The one that says *what if?* What if you'd had more than one big hit? What if you'd gone your own way and not relied on that arsehole you called a manager? The boil that reminds you of what you might have been.'

'You said issues. What are the others?'

'You're not denying the music thing is a problem?'

'I've never said it wasn't.'

'This is the first time we've talked about it, Zia.'

More rain splashes down and I turn my back on it.

'Issues, plural,' he says. 'You said issues. What else?'

'Later.'

'Now, Daniella. Right now.'

'Okay, Zia, but this is a bad time to do this.'

'When is a good time? Go on anyway.'

'Look, Zia, we are great together but part of that is because we were thrown together on the back of my mum's death. One minute I'm sitting at a desk in the UK listening to liars trying to con money out of my insurance company. Next, I'm running a pub, have cash in the bank and I'm living with a man twenty years older than me.'

'Is my age a problem?'

'Not really. It's the other stuff.'

'Like what?'

'Like the stuff we don't talk about.'

'What stuff?'

'All the serious stuff in life. You know. The future. Our ambitions. What we want from life. Kids.'

He stops swinging the torch, bringing the light to rest on my toes.

'You want kids?' he says.

'I don't know if I want kids but what I do know is that I want to talk about it.'

'You've never said anything.'

'I've never said a lot of things. Because we don't talk about the serious things.'

'We talk about money and the pub and—'

I hold up my hand. 'Zia, I mean we don't talk about the serious *us* things. I'm thirty-six.'

'And I'm fifty-six.'

'Exactly. When did we ever mention that to each other out loud?'

'You just said it wasn't age that's an issue.'

'It's not. I'm just using it to show that we don't talk about the stuff that most couples grind to death. You told me, after George fronted me up on my work ethic, that maybe I have been swinging the lead out here. And when I think about it, you and George are right. Since Mum's funeral I've been on an extended working holiday. Money in my pocket. Sun on my back. Drink in my hand and no desire to talk about the serous shit in life. That's not what you go on holiday for, is it? You go on holiday to escape all that stuff. To kick back. Relax. Forget the day to day. Only I'm not on vacation. The way things are shaping up, this is my life. There is no Ryanair flight home in a week. There is no job to go back to. George thinks I'm slacking. And he's right, I am. I've been on vacation for months. And just as I wake up to the fact that I need to put in some serious work there is some bastard trying to take this new life away from me. Frame me for Pat's death. And that's making me think hard about what I really want. If someone is willing to go to the lengths they have gone to in order to frame me, is it worth staying here? Would it be easier to go home?'

'And that's why you're questioning me? To see if I'm involved? If I'm worth staying with? Staying *for*?'

'Zia, this shit has led me to question every bloody thing. Mum was a sodding institution around here. A veritable one-woman tour de force. I can't turn a corner without running smack into her shadow. And she's cast such a long one that it's proving hard to get out of it. But if you really want to know why I'm asking about yesterday, I'll tell you.'

'Why?'

'Zia, I saw you get in George's car at the same time that George claims he saw Pat at DB's. But you two didn't head to DB's when you left. You both headed up to the old town. What I can't figure is why George would lie about Pat and DB's to the Capitán. George couldn't have seen him go in to DB's. So where were you both going?'

12

The Storm

The rain is now winding up to a full hosing.

'We need to get that tarpaulin,' I say, my words whipped away by the building wind.

'You were the one that wanted to talk, Daniella,' Zia shouts.

'I do but I'd rather finish the job in hand now. See if we can fix the door and then talk.'

Zia looks confused and I know why. I'd said nothing about seeing Zia and George when George was telling his story to the Capitán. Now I've implicated Zia in George's lie, Zia's wondering why I've just pulled the handbrake on the conversation. Is he figuring my train of thought? Pat died somewhere away from here. When? Yesterday morning? Where? Who knows? But if Pat wasn't at DB's why would George say he was? Why lie? And what part is Zia playing in supporting the lie? I could probably scribe the resultant accusation on Zia's forehead and he wouldn't be surprised. If he has a good reason as to why he was with George then I'd feel a lot easier. But if he doesn't then I'm not sure where that takes all this. Other than my partner might be involved in a murder and that would mean he might also be involved in framing me. And that is way too big a thing to talk about out here.

In the dark.

Where no one can see what is going on.

Zia swings the torchlight under the car and lights up the tarpaulin, mostly hidden beneath weeds. He walks forward and bends down to grab some material and pulls. Little happens. I join him and together we pull. Again nothing happens but on the third tug the tarpaulin shifts. Rain soaks our backs as we work the tarp out from under the car.

'Let's get this back to the pub,' I shout over the roar of the storm.

Zia says nothing, grabs the tarpaulin and we start to haul it along the ground. We reach the pub entrance with the rain crashing down around us. A bolt of lightning slashes across the sky and the rip of thunder that follows makes us both jump. We leap inside the pub and stand for a few seconds as water flows from our bodies. The dust sheet blows in and a spray of water follows.

'Skid, get the hammer and some nails and make it quick,' I shout as another wave of rain flies through the dust cover.

'We'll drag up the tarp as it is, nail it to the frame of the door and let it hang,' I say to Zia.

'It's way too big.'

'I don't care. We just need to stop the water getting in the pub.'

Skid returns with the hammer and nails.

'Zia, you hold the tarpaulin up and I'll try and bang in the nails.'

We step back into the night and between us wrench the tarpaulin up to the top of the door frame. I'd guess the tarp is easily sixty feet square. It has ring holes around the edge to accommodate ropes. We wrestle one corner up above the broken door, and, reaching high, I batter a nail home through a hole. I repeat the process and work my way along the top of the door frame. All the time the rain is running in rivers down my back. Twelve nails in and I stop. We've covered the entrance. A gust hits the material but it barely moves.

Zia lifts the corner of the tarpaulin and we both clamber underneath. I stand near the door, dripping.

'I can't believe that anyone else will come out in this weather but, Skid, can you man the door for a bit? Peek out every so often just to be sure no one is trying to get in. The way that tarpaulin is nailed on it makes us look like we're closed.'

'I need to go home,' moans Skid.

'Half an hour and then you can head off,' I say. 'Anyway, you haven't got a car. If you walk to your flat in this you'll be soaked to the skin in two minutes. That heavy rain won't last. It'll ease off soon. It always does. Grab a coffee and take a seat.'

He yanks a chair from under a table, pulls it to the door and slumps into it like a kid in a huff.

'Zia,' I say, 'are we allowed back in the flat yet?'

'I've not heard anything from the Capitán.'

'Screw it, I'm going up. There's no one up there and his team have gone. I'm wringing wet and miserable as sin. Have you got the key?'

'Yes. I'll come with you.'

'Clyde, are you okay if we nip up to change?' I shout over.

Clyde looks up. 'Yes, Daniella. But I can't put a late shift in tonight. I'm up early tomorrow.'

'I'll take over when I get back down. I just need dry clothes.'

He gives me a thumbs up.

Zia and I battle the elements and sprint around the pub to climb the stairs to the flat. As we enter the living room we are treated to a full-on light show as the storm unleashes itself on the coast. Even with three panes of glass between the flat and the storm the thunder is a living thing. The flat vibrates as the sound waves pummel it.

I do a quick whizz round to see what has been disturbed by the crime scene team but with the exception of the odd smattering of black finger powder I can find no signs at all that they have been here. Even the furniture, which I'm sure I heard moving when I was below, is back where it was.

Zia uses the main bathroom to change and I take the en suite and strip. I flash shower, do my hair, re-dress and I'm sitting on the sofa facing the window well before Zia is ready. Not unusual in this house. Zia is the snappy dresser, the most often at the hairdresser, the buyer of mystic brews and remedies, the guru on a diet, the master of exercise. Me, well, I'd be happier in my own skin if I could lose the peely-wally Scottish complexion. Exposure to the Spanish sun simply colours me baboon's arse red.

I wait for Zia to emerge and wonder if I should continue the conversation from outside.

My thought is cut short by the doorbell. I rise, check the CCTV, sigh and open the door.

'Good evening, Capitán,' I say after allowing the dripping policeman in. 'And what can I do for you this fine evening?'

'I am sorry to bother you but I have another request I need to make.'

'Come on into the living room,' I say as Zia exits the bathroom.

'I do not have time, Señorita Coulstoun. I wish only to obtain your permission to search your mother's old apartment.'

'Can I ask why?'

'We have new information concerning Señor Ratte.'

'I'm getting sick of this,' I say. 'Am I a suspect or not?'

'Officially, no.'

'Unofficially?'

'Unofficially I think there are many things about this case that do not make sense, but that is normal.'

'Do you mean that bloody note, that photo, my stupid meeting with Pat and the mysterious walking keys?'

'Amongst other things.'

'And now you have reason to want to search Mum's old apartment. Looking for what?'

'I do not know.'

'And if I say no?'

'I will simply wait until the morning and get the necessary paperwork. Then you will have no choice.'

Zia speaks up. 'Daniella, I think it's time you spoke to a lawyer.'

He's right on the money with that one.

'Zia, you're not wrong,' I say while the Capitán looks on. I shake my head, dropping my hands to the side. 'Capitán, I will talk to my lawyer in the morning and if he says it's all right I will let you into my mother's apartment.'

The Capitán looks unhappy at this. 'That is up to you, Señorita Coulstoun, but it would be quicker and easier if you simply gave me the keys now.'

Get some control.

'No, Capitán,' I state, hardening my voice as best as I can. 'I've done nothing wrong here. I've spent all day trying to tidy up the wreck that is my pub and I haven't heard a single word about bringing the culprits to account. Not a word. *Nada.* Have you arrested a single person for the damage downstairs? Because it sure as hell didn't get into that state when the carnage fairies flew in.'

He opens his mouth to speak and I crash on. 'Let me finish. I know that Pat is dead. I know that is a priority. I get that. I also know that you see me as a front runner. But you know fine well that something is off-kilter here or I'd be down at the station right now, answering a shedload of questions. And yet on you plough. Searching. My pub, my house, now my mum's place. Next it'll be what? My car? My bank account? Or will you fly to the UK to interview my old work colleagues? Eh? Did Daniella ever have any violent tendencies? Was she prone to outbursts of any sort? Did she ever mention a friend of her mother's, Pat Ratte?

'Maybe I'm setting myself up for a trip to the police station by refusing to cooperate. I'm not quite sure how the Spanish system works. I have absolutely no idea what my rights are here. Can I call a lawyer if you take me in? Will I be locked up? How long for? I've not a clue to the answer to any of these questions but I've been trying to help here. I really have. But, I'll repeat, I had nothing to do with Pat Ratte's death. Nothing. But since you persist with links to me, I need advice, and forgive me if I don't take yours. I'd say that your objectives and mine are conflicted at the moment,

Capitán. Even if I give you the keys to Mum's place what are you going to find? Evidence that Pat was in the flat? Well, duh, he lived there.'

The image of the missing slice of carpet floats in front of my eyes as I say this.

'Are you finished?' the Capitán asks me.

Zia says the same thing with his body language. He's as tense as an over-strung tennis racket.

'I am,' I state. Then I add, 'For the moment.'

'Okay, Señorita Coulstoun,' the Capitán says, with an edge to his voice that suggests he's used to taking outbursts like mine in his stride. 'We *have* been looking into the damage to Se Busca, and not just because it is linked to Señor Ratte's death. But because it is not the sort of thing that people should get away with. Rest assured, Señorita Coulstoun, we do know what we are doing. But this case is complex. I am only asking for the keys to your mother's old apartment to eliminate it as a possible murder scene. Forgive me if I don't have to explain the workings of the police mind but I'm sure even you can see that, if Señor Ratte wasn't killed here, it would make sense he was killed where no one could see it happen. We are asking to search the houses of a number of people but paperwork takes time. And I too think something is, how did you say? Off-kilter? I cannot see the relevance of the keys on Señor Ratte's person is, or the point of the note if you did not write it, other than to steer us away from the real killer. Searching your mother's house would simply be another step in ruling you out.'

He's convincing. The slow-burn English and the deep Hispanic drawl works to tie his words into a very credible pattern. He is putting on a good show of being open.

I'm not bothered that they'll find the carpet in Mum's flat has a hole in it. I can simply claim no knowledge. After all, it's under the sofa. Although a whip-smart detective with an eye for the 'off-kilter' would notice that the sofa has recently been moved.

The old indentions will still be clear and a whip-smart detective will also smell bleach – fresh, recent and smack in the middle of the hole left by the cut-away carpet. And a really whip-smart detective might or might not have the resources to order a little dumpster-diving in and around town. Or maybe he's ahead of the game, and the intruder in Mum's flat followed me and has already pointed him to where I dumped the carpet and he's playing me. But if that was the case, I'd be in cuffs by now. What a whip-smart detective won't be able to do is locate the carpet if the bin lorry has already picked it up. At least not easily. And if he can't get into the flat until tomorrow then he won't be able to spot old indentions if they have risen, fibre stretching through the night, and he won't be able to smell the recent scent of bleach either. For all those reasons I now say, 'And I'll repeat, I'm going to see my lawyer in the morning and will take his advice. And if your paperwork comes through and you need the keys before then I'll be downstairs or I'll be up here. Now, I have a barman to relieve, is there anything else?'

He shakes his head. 'It is your decision, Señorita Coulstoun. I think it's a mistake to refuse me the keys. But with luck the paperwork might get here before the morning. And there is one more thing.'

'What?'

'That photo you found in the bar. The one with you and Sénor Ratte. It turns out that the CCTV in his old house is nowhere to be found. The new owner had a break in and the hard drive was stolen. It seems that Sénor Ratte left the old computer for the new owner to use for the security system. And now it is gone.'

'When?'

'A few weeks back.'

'Well, don't look at me for that. I didn't take it.'

'Maybe. But I will say *hasta pronto*, Señorita Coulstoun.'

He pulls open the door and is swallowed by the rain and wind.

'He'll get into the flat eventually,' says Zia as soon as the door is closed.

'I know that, but if it's in the morning then the smell of bleach will be gone and any signs I moved the sofa will be less. And I'm really hoping the binmen are on late-night duty.'

'Daniella, this is a mess.'

'It is and I need to sort it. And there's only one way to do that. If I can find whoever is bloody trying to hang me out to dry, then I might get on the front foot.'

'Do you mean you're going to go looking for the person trying to frame you?'

'Yes.'

'And what happens when the Capitán finds out you are looking into his case?'

'I'd hope he'd be bloody happy. Whoever is trying to put me in the dock is going to steer well clear of the Capitán. However, they *are* going to be keeping an eye on me. And that means I might get a chance to find out who they are.'

'The Capitán didn't mention anyone telling him about suspicious activity in your mum's place. He just asked for the keys.'

'He's not going to let on to everything he knows. Sure, he's making a great song and dance of sharing info, but he's way too long in the tooth to tell me anything more than he needs to. His story about wanting to check other homes is probably bollocks. I'll lay you better-than-even money that no one else has been asked to hand over keys. I'm his *it* right now, even if he does think something stinks. And that's where we might catch a break.'

'How?'

'Well, on top of the keys, photo and the note, if the Capitán *did* receive a phone call about my mum's place it doesn't make my framer the smartest cookie in the jar. If they were clever they would know that a call like that would set off the Capitán's radar.'

'Or he sees you as guilty as hell and any call just backs that up?'

I can feel the anger from our earlier conversation in that phrase. 'You don't mean that.'

'You all but accused me of the same thing earlier, Daniella.'

'Do you think I might have killed Pat?'

'Do you think I did it?'

'Zia, I only asked where you were.'

'Seems like the same thing to me.'

'Just tell me.'

'Why?'

'Because,' I shout, 'I bloody know that George lied about seeing Pat the morning of the murder and I know you were with him. That's why.'

I let the words fizz in the air.

'Daniella, can I point something out?' Zia says.

'What? Something to avoid you answering my question?'

'No. Something you should really bear in mind if you're going to throw out accusations and if you're going to look for your mysterious *framer*.'

'The framing is real, Zia.'

'I'm not saying it isn't but think on this. Just because you know someone is trying to tie you to the death of Pat doesn't mean that his death still won't all come down on you. Sit downstairs a while and listen to some of the stories of injustice that your customers talk about. Most of it is crap but every so often there is story of a completely innocent person serving hard time in a Spanish jail. A genuine story. And we have more than our fair share of such stories because we have more than our fair share of people who swim in those waters. You need to keep in mind that Se Busca isn't a club for Girl Guides. Lozano knows a lot of our clients on a deeply personal basis, and you are now tarred with the same brush as everyone that walks through Se Busca's doors. That means that any claims of innocence will be met with an industrial amount of cynicism. So just be careful.'

'And still you avoid the question.'

The lack of reply is deeply frustrating.

'We need to go downstairs,' I say when I realise he is not going to answer. 'Clyde needs away.'

'We also need to keep talking.'

'We have been talking. But you refuse to talk about what I want.'

'Not about me and if I killed Pat. That's just stupid. I'm not answering because it's so dumb. But we do need to finish the other talk you started outside.'

'Not now, Zia. I don't know why I started it out there but I'm kind of glad I did. However, once we begin that talk again, there is no *finish* to it. There never is. Never will be. At least not while there is still an us. But, Zia, until tonight we hadn't even *started* that talk and starting it was needed. It was long overdue, so let's sit down when things are a little less crazy and, at the moment, concentrate on the here and now.'

'Less crazy? Let's see, that should be in about three or four decades' time.'

'Are you going to tell me where you went yesterday?' I ask one more time.

'I'm not going there.'

'Well, then it's pub time,' I say. 'But this isn't over. Not by a country mile, Zia.'

We sprint down to the pub and I let Clyde go. The rain has eased a little and he calls a taxi. There are twelve people in the bar. I tell Skid to share a ride with Clyde and get behind the bar for the rest of the shift.

George takes up residency at the far end, whisky in hand.

'Did the Capitán get a hold of you?' he asks.

'Why? Was he in here?'

'Just asking where you were. I told him you were upstairs.'

'Yes, he found me.'

'And?'

'And what?'

'What did he want?'

'A slice of cake and a back massage. What do you think he wanted?'

He ignores my sarcasm. 'Did he have an update on Ratte's death?'

'Only that the Capitán has been over to DB's but nothing else.'

'I hear they searched your flat.'

I blank that.

'Is there anything else?'

I'm not for telling him about the request to search Mum's flat.

'Nothing else, George. But do you know what I find strange?'

'That gravity can't be switched off and on?'

I ignore the dumb attempt at humour as an elderly man with thinning white hair approaches the bar. I think his name is Ronald or maybe Richard. He orders up two beers and I pour them for him. He then asks for a whisky chaser and necks it before heading back to where he is sitting, watching the TV, with a man who I'm sure is called Walter, or maybe it's Windsor.

'George,' I say once Ronald/Richard takes his seat. 'This is a murder we are talking about. So, tell me this, what's the gossip on all this? What are people saying?'

'Not much.'

'Really. Around here. I don't buy that for a second. There are grapevines and there are grapevines and then there is the El Descaro's internal communication system. This should be gold dust to that.'

'And?'

George plays with his whisky, checking out the bar. There is no one close enough to overhear what we are saying but he sidles up towards me anyway, swapping out his seat for a nearer one.

'For crying out loud, George,' I snort. 'What is this – secret squirrel meets secret squirrel's cousin in the secret squirrel den?'

'Daniella, there is one good reason why there is no gossip,' he whispers.

He looks around again.

'George, you are killing me,' I say. 'Tell me.'

'It's simple. Stoker.'

'Stoker?'

'Stoker is one scary son of a bitch.'

'So I keep hearing. But there are other scary sons of bitches around here and that rarely prevents gossip, especially if they're up to something.'

'Except Stoker is a scary son of a bitch who everyone knows not to get on the wrong side of. A scary son of a bitch who would happily slice off your right thumb if he thought you were tittle-tattling.'

'Are you saying he's implicated in this?'

'The opposite. But if he hears otherwise you'll be minus a digit.'

'The opposite, George. Why do you say that? Do you know something?'

'No. I just don't think he's involved.'

'Who said he was?'

'I'm just saying.'

I think back to my meet with Stoker at the café. My hand is still sore 'Do you know what, George? I'm not so sure about that. Stoker seems the sort to be involved in exactly this sort of thing. Especially if Pat had crossed him.'

'Don't dare say that to *anyone*.'

'Hey, calm it down. You started this.'

'Well, he just isn't involved.'

'How can you know that? No one knows who was involved. Or if they do they are not saying. And I think that Stoker would certainly fit the bill as my framer if he was involved with Pat's death.'

'He isn't.'

'Why are you so sure.'

'Because I am.'

'One doth protest too much, George.'

'This isn't funny.'

'I agree, it's not.'

'I don't want you getting hurt.'

'Hurt? Hurt? What in the hell do you know that would get me hurt?'

'That Stoker will not take kindly to being implicated. And that's why you need to keep schtum.'

'I never mentioned him until you did. Are you telling me that's why no one is talking about this? Really? Because a man who you say definitely *isn't* involved might hear that someone says he *is* involved? That's bollocks.'

'How would you like it if you were implicated in something you didn't do?'

'In case you haven't noticed, George, that is exactly what is happening to me. I had nothing to do with Pat's death and yet I'm the one with the suspicion stick pointed at me.'

'Around here it doesn't pay to accuse Stoker.'

'No one is accusing him.'

'Good.'

I decide to poke the hornet's nest.

'But what if you are wrong, George, and he is involved? Maybe him appearing at my door and everything kicking off are connected?'

'Just leave Stoker out of it.'

'Why? What do you know?'

'Just leave him the fuck out of it.'

13

One Scary Son of a Bitch

'I need a slash,' George says and leaves me to think on Carl Stoker. Would Stoker have reason to kill Pat? Pat and Stoker both come from the same world. Criminals to the core. When George comes back I press him on Stoker again.

'Could Stoker have killed Pat?' I say.

'For fuck's sake.'

'Well, could he?'

'Okay, Daniella. Do you want to know why you need to shut the hell up?'

'I really do.'

'Because Stoker is the king in waiting around here right now and won't let anyone get in his way. And I mean no one.'

'You need to explain that one to me, George. I don't speak gibberish.'

'Pat has been the unofficial top of the crime pile around here for a long while. He had his fingers in a lot of shit and was smart. He knew how to play the game well. He might also have been all but retired and the stress of losing his house on the hill didn't play well with him, but he was still *the* man in this neck of the woods and Stoker wanted – wants – that crown. Stoker has had eyes on Pat's position for a long while.'

'You make it sound like a corporate ladder inside some big money firm. Bigwigs jockeying for position.'

'Not as far off the mark as you might think. Pat was a real player back in the day in London. But when he came out here he didn't cut all his ties. He just rearranged things a little. Handing over control to those back in the UK that he thought he could trust. Keeping the flow of cash coming his way. But it started to dry up a while back. Younger, harder men, back in the UK, moved in on Pat's turf and he was more or less kicked out. With the UK cash gone Pat turned his attention to El Descaro. He set up RatTrap Security and a few other so-called legit businesses.'

'RatTrap was a protection racket. He approached me not long after I'd taken on the pub looking for cash. He once told me that Mum paid him ten grand a year.'

'She did that.'

'And Stoker wants that game now Pat has gone?'

'Stoker's main game is gambling. He works in cash and cash only and that needs laundering – not easy around here. Not as easy as it used to be. The banks have anti-money-laundering schemes in place and if you flash too many notes someone soon notices. The days of paying for a house in thousand-euro notes are all but gone. Rumour goes that Stoker has set up some legitimate businesses but I have no idea what they are. That's where his cash will wash through.'

'And?'

'Stoker's business has been growing and Pat's has been dying. Pat's legit business interests weren't profitable. Saucy can tell you. He did accounts for Pat now and again. Then again, they didn't need to be profitable – they were just there to help Pat change shit cash into shiny, clean cash. Only Pat wasn't generating much money any more. And that made for a problem for the guys running Pat's businesses. Hard to pay the bills if no money is coming in.'

'And hard to shut down if Pat Ratte is your boss.'

'Exactly.

'And Stoker?'

'Stoker is now doing the rounds of those businesses.'

I feel like I'm on a criminal 101 learning course. 'Rounds?'

'Daniella, you need to gen up on stuff around here.'

'You told me that down at the port, but I don't know what I don't know. What are the rounds?'

'Let's assume that all of Pat's businesses are still up and running. And, let's assume that Stoker is looking for new channels to wash his cash through. The more diverse the laundering operation the less likely you are to get caught. Therefore, Stoker will be looking to Pat's businesses as a new route to run his money through a bath of Ariel now that Pat is dead.'

'And, at the same time, Stoker wants to fill Pat's shoes and become kingpin,' I say.

'Very good, Daniella. Nature hates a vacuum.'

George stops to hand me his Glencairn glass for a refill. I oblige.

'Stoker,' George says once he's half emptied the new whisky, 'will be laying the ground by contacting the people that ran Pat's businesses. Marking their cards. Probably explaining that a change of ownership is in the air. That cash will be winging its way to them soon, offering the businesses a way to get back on their feet.'

'And, because he's far too scary to mess with, he'll also threaten them into silence.'

George looks around.

'Yes,' he says, his voice barely audible. 'Hence no gossip. Stoker will have made it crystal clear he wants zip said on Ratte's death. He will be on Lozano's radar. But body parts go missing if you cross Stoker. And that's no paranoiac hype. He collects fingers. If you don't believe me have a look at Joe Royal's left hand when he next comes in. He reneged on a bet with Stoker for the grand sum of one hundred euros. Stoker took away Joe's ability to point. Check it out – Joe has no forefingers.'

'Shit.'

'Effie could deal with Stoker but I don't think you can.'

'Hang on, if Pat's businesses are legit wouldn't they pass on to whoever is in Pat's will?'

'I'm not sure what's in Pat's will, but there is a small clutch of businesses out there looking for a new owner and a vacancy at the top of the crime pile in this neck of the woods. For Stoker this is a once in a generation opportunity. If there is a way to grab that land he will, and the silence tells me he's already doing it. As they say – the king is dead, long live the king. And if I were you I'd let nature take its course. Let Stoker rise to the top of the pile and stay the fuck away from him.'

Walter this time, or is it Windsor, rolls up for more booze and he too does the whisky chaser thing before returning to his friend. As I watch him walk back to his table the tarpaulin moves.

'And wouldn't that make Stoker the number one suspect in Pat's death?' I say.

The tarp parts to reveal the Twins, as they step into the pub, waving at me.

'Hold that thought, George,' I say, leaving the bar and navigating through the few remaining tables and chairs to reach the door. The Twins are drowned cats.

One-time child models, they are still hoping for another break. But their chances are slim. Both have noses that outgrew their childhood good looks, and Jordan is sporting a gut and losing his hair at a rate of knots – soaking wet, the extent of his baldness is all too evident. But both still think there is a modelling contract out there that will transform their lives. Like many in here I think they are living in the bastard marriage of two magical lands – la-la and cloud-cuckoo.

'Why are you here?' I ask.

'You wanted us to set up the outside bar for tomorrow's parade?' says Sheryl.

'I do. But not tonight. You can't possibly do it in this storm and in the pitch black.'

'We're not,' says Jordan. 'The gear we need is stored in the cellar and we don't know if it was trashed last night.'

'Ah,' I say. 'Good thinking. Is the gear anything to do with the big metal box thing that sits against the back wall?'

'That's for the kegs of beer,' says Sheryl. 'It lets us run three beer taps outdoors.'

'Three beer taps,' repeats Jordan.

The Twins have a bad habit of repeating the last few words of each other's sentences.

'What about outside tables?' I ask. 'Where are they kept?'

'We don't have any,' replies Jordan. 'We just use four from in here and put a waterproof cloth over them. Then we stack wine and soft drinks underneath.'

'Cups?' I ask.

'There should be a pile of plastic ones behind the beer dispenser,' Jordan says. 'We've also ordered up some more from the wholesaler. They are due a drinks delivery tomorrow and said they would add the cups in.'

'Sounds like you have it all in hand.'

Sheryl looks around the bar. 'Maybe not. If we take four tables out of here that'll leave only two for everyone else. Were all the rest smashed?'

'Smashed?' says Jordan.

'Yip,' I say.

'Jordan,' Sheryl says, turning to her brother, 'will Jose be in his shop tomorrow morning?'

'He always is. He'll be baking early for all the cafés he supplies.'

'We'll breadboard it then.'

'Good idea.'

'What is breadboarding?' I ask.

'Jose at the *panadería* in the port always has a stack of large breadboards,' explains Sheryl. 'If we use a couple of trestles from the Safety Deposit + we can rig up a temporary bar. We've done it before.'

'As I said,' I say, 'it sounds like you have it all in hand.'

'Have you phoned Jeep?' Jordan asks.

'Jeep,' repeats Sheryl.

'No,' I say. 'Do we need him?'

'We sure do,' says Jordan. 'We need him as a bouncer for the drunks and to protect the cash. There will be a lot of strangers around the place and the outdoor till will be a prime target for a few.'

'I'll text him. What time tomorrow?'

'Parade starts at two o'clock,' points out Sheryl. 'We need him here about twelve.'

'Who will run the bars?'

'I'll work with Jordan out in the car park and Clyde will be in here,' says Sheryl. 'But we'll need help. It can get really busy.'

'And by busy, you mean?'

'Your mum had a saying. Some things are busy. Some things are nuts, and some things are—'

'—just as mad as a wasp's nest on fire,' I finish. 'She used that phrase all the time when I was a kid.'

Sheryl shuffles to shake off some more water. 'Well, tomorrow will be a wasp's nest day.'

They drip their way to the back cellar and I hear scraping.

I go back to talk to George, but he's slipped over to the TV to watch the football and has his back to me. Deliberately.

The rest of the night pans out in a far quieter way than I'd feared. There is no appearance of the Capitán and the storm burns itself out an hour before closing. By then we are down to Zia, me and a few last gaspers. George and the Twins have gone.

Zia washes the tables as the stragglers are pretending they can't see us shutting up shop around them. On a normal night a loud ultimatum announcing the bar's impending closure is required. Tonight, I simply tap the four bodies on their shoulders, thank them for coming out on such a bad evening, and tell them that we're closing soon. All four get up and order another drink. Which is a win. Normally when I tell everyone the pub is closing they all order two drinks.

'Zia, this place isn't secure,' I say. 'That tarpaulin won't be much of a deterrent if someone wants in.'

'True,' says Zia. 'We can make sure that there is no money in here but the local neds will be after booze. Don't underestimate the blind, stupid determination of the few.'

'And how do we deal with that?'

'Clearing the booze shelves into the cellar is a big task, but it's the only solution.'

'Sounds like a plan.'

While the last punters sup up, I start whipping down the bottles from the bar and Zia gets to work padlocking the glass-fronted fridges. I stop him. 'Zia, won't they just pan in the glass to get to the beer?'

'Probably.'

'Then let's get everything into the cellar. Soft drinks and all. The shelves could do with a clean anyway.'

'Daniella, the whole place needs a clean.'

'Have you any other suggestions?'

'Burn the place down, claim the insurance, move to the Caribbean and lie in the sun until we fry?'

'I think the insurance company might be a wee bit suspicious.'

'Well, if anyone knows how to fiddle the insurance system you do.'

We get to work shifting stock and Zia is uncomfortable. The earlier conversation seems to be weighing on his mind, and mine. In what I take as an obvious attempt to avoid opening it up again he asks, 'Daniella, did anyone ever try and pull a really big scam when you were working at the insurance firm?'

As we wheel the bottles from shelf to cellar I decide to play along and avoid the serious chat.

'I never got involved in the really big claims,' I start. 'They were handled by a different team with their own fraud squad. Our fraud detection was some tricksy software on the phone that pinpointed stress in the voice, another clever piece of software that talked to other insurers, and yours truly – the best sort of fraud detection. And we relied heavily on the call handlers for that. Almost everyone on my old team was a Zen master in the art of spotting a lie. One day, I got a call from a customer making a claim on a house fire. At first he claimed that his chip pan went up in flames.'

'They used to have TV ads back in the eighties warning about that,' says Zia as he clears the top shelf of a few dust-caked bottles of whisky.

'Well, in this century that sort of claim sets alarm bells ringing,' I say. 'There are a lot less chip pans around nowadays. Far less. Diets have changed and those that do have fryers own sealed affairs that use tiny splashes of oil. But this claimant was an exception. He said that an ancient chip pan had gone molten. I took the details and said I would send out an assessor but to be aware that, because of the policy the claimant had chosen, there was a five-k excess on it. I told him that if the assessor okayed it, we'd usually clean up, paint, replace damaged units, buy new appliances etc – but pointed out that on his policy he had estimated the whole kitchen to be worth ten thousand. And that was good news from our end.'

'Good news. Why?'

'Well, if he paid the first five thousand of the excess, my company would probably be home free because we bought goods and services at trade prices. Five k would easily fix a ten-k kitchen. Reminding the claimant of the five-k excess didn't go down well but, as I pointed out, he was the one that had agreed to the excess to dump the premium as low as possible. An hour later he phones back. Turns out that it isn't just his kitchen that's been burned. He now says it's his whole flat.'

'What?'

'Really. And my question was simple. Why did you not notice that the last time you called? His answer – *Well, the fire was still burning when I phoned you.*'

'He phoned from a burning flat?'

'No. It turned out that he set fire to the rest of his flat *after* our call. He thought to himself that if he had to pay five thousand he would try and get the whole house done on insurance. Rags soaked in meths in every room and then the fire spread out of control to his neighbour's flats. No one was killed, but quite a few people were badly burned. It made the papers. He damn near burned down twelve homes.'

'And was he arrested?'

'And some. Heavily sentenced as well.'

'Bloody hell.'

I think back on that and my mood darkens.

'I had to go and see the counsellor after that one, Zia.'

'What kind of counsellor?'

'The insurance company employed an in-house psychological counsellor. Some of the stuff you deal with in the claims game can be bad shit – from stories of abuse to heartbreaking stories of death. The counsellor was a safety net.'

'Why go in this case? No one died.'

'No they didn't, but somehow I felt responsible for the fact that after my first call the claimant had felt the need to set fire to the whole place because I'd pointed out the flaw in his claim. And because of that I felt I should have seen it coming. I know that sounds irrational but deep down I had an inkling that he was going to do something stupid when I hung up on him.'

'Sounds like he had the problem, not you.'

'He did. I asked if there would be an investigation at my end and was told no. Which helped a bit, and the counsellor worked with me, but at the end of the day six people ended up in hospital, two needing major surgery, and I still think I should have said something to someone and stopped it.'

Zia doesn't probe any further and we work on in silence.

As I stack the last bottle and check over the bar, Zia starts to put the till in the back cellar.

'Leave it where it is,' I instruct.

'Why?'

'If someone does break in and the till is gone they might go looking for it. If it's out, open – and empty – it tells them there is no money lying around.'

He manhandles the till back in place and I pick up the hammer and remaining nails.

'Help me secure this place.'

I urge the last people out and with Zia's help pull the soaking bottom of the tarp inside the pub. I use up some more nails and fix it to the wooden floor by banging in as many nails as I can. It won't stop the determined but it might put off the opportunist.

'How do we get in tomorrow?' asks Zia. 'We can go out the fire door tonight but getting in will be tough.'

'We'll rip the tarp free and I'll call the chippie to come up and put in a better fix.'

'You won't get anyone tomorrow. It's a public holiday. *El dia festivo*. Plus the last thing we need is someone trying to fix the door when this place is flying.'

'See this town and its bloody fiestas.'

'What would you rather have? Three hundred and sixty-five days of good morning Mr Sunshine, good night Mr Sunshine and Mr Monotony in between?'

He's right. Fiestas are a great thing. Great for business, great for the morale and great fun.

'Zia, just let's get this done and I'll figure out something tomorrow. I'm beat.'

I set the alarm, hoping that the tarp is secure enough not to trip the motion sensors. We both exit via the fire door in the office and climb to the flat. As we undress, Zia turns to me. 'When do you want to chat?'

'Not now.'
'When?'
'Soon.'
I'm out for the count in seconds.

14

Watched

At first I think it's the dream that wakes me. A psychedelic montage of death and storms. But it's not the dream, it's the certainty that I'm being watched. That a third person is in my bedroom. Zia is snoring gently, lying on his back next to me, the sheets pushed down around his waist. The dark in the bedroom is total. Caught in that Neverland between awake and unconscious I roll my hand across the bed, snaking it toward the bedside cabinet and the light that sits there. I feel a tiny puff of air on the back of my forearm. I reach the light and flick the switch.

There's no one there and I pull in a deep breath. The intruder up at Mum's place has me seeing ghosts. I rub my eyes and then I notice the bedroom door. When we had them fitted I'd insisted on self-closing doors being put in throughout the place. Between the hinges of the doors are two small chains that bury themselves into the door frames. A small mechanism inside the frame pulls the chains back, swinging the doors shut. The tension on the chain ensures that the door closes completely. But if you open the door and catch it just before it clicks home, the door lock will keep the door slightly open. I study the door. The door is resting on the catch. Zia could have done that if he had gone to the toilet after we retired – but I know I closed the door last night.

I err on the side of caution and tap Zia on the shoulder. He moans. I shake him. He pushes my hand away.

'Zia,' I whisper, 'I think there might be someone in the house.'

He rolls over. 'What?'

'I think someone was in our bedroom.'

He sits up, rubbing at his eyes. 'Are you sure?'

'The door isn't closed properly and I shut it. Did you go to the bathroom after you went to bed?'

'No.'

'Then someone has been at the door. I thought I heard a noise.'

'You had a rough time at your mum's house.' He's also whispering. 'Are you sure it's not your imagination? Are you certain you closed the bedroom door?'

'Yes.'

'Well, I know the front door was locked. I did it,' he adds.

'Mum's was also locked and someone got in there.'

Zia swings his feet from under the sheets and stands up. Wearing only his boxers he crosses the room to the door and listens. I can almost see myself in Mum's kitchen a few hours ago doing the same thing. He pulls open the door, slowly, and peeks out. He dips his head back and shakes it. Then he steps into the hall. I slip from the bed and join him. We both stop moving as the solid click of the front door closing rings through the house. Zia rushes forward. I'm right on his tail. He yanks the front door open. Over his shoulder I see a figure fleeing down the stairs. Zia leaps out on to the small balcony that sits atop the outside stairs and I grab his arm.

'Leave it,' I say.

'There was someone in our house.'

'You can't chase them in your pants.'

He stares into the night, me at his side.

There is something vaguely familiar about that escaping figure, but I say nothing.

This is getting way out of hand.

Neither of us sleeps well after that. Zia puts the key in the front door to prevent whoever was here getting back in. We check that nothing has been taken. Then we check that nothing has been left either. I stamp every inch of the carpet looking for a wet patch while Zia works his way methodically around the house, poking in corners, pulling out drawers, opening cupboards, searching for anything that shouldn't be there. I do likewise. We find nothing.

When the bedside alarm goes off I've done little but snooze lightly in between bursts of talk with Zia. I'm hoping that we disturbed the intruder before they could lay any more evidence linking me to Pat's death – for I'm sure that's what was going down. I'm guessing the visitor entered the flat and wanted to ensure Zia and I were in the bedroom, asleep, before they dumped more evidence. Me waking up probably scared them.

Or maybe I'm wrong and they were just a chance burglar. A chance burglar that had a set of keys to our home.

I'm a half-shut knife when I enter the shower. And the same when I get out. I usually emerge feeling like someone has thrown the on-switch on my human side. This time I climb from the cubicle with a brain fuzzier than a ball of lint.

At ten o'clock, after a light breakfast of toast and tea, Zia and I descend to the pub but not before we have a ten-minute session on how to secure the front door. I plan to get the locks changed, but, with the fiesta on, that might take a while. The twenty-four-hour locksmith who Zia knows is supposed to be working today but so far he hasn't returned any of Zia's three calls.

'Will the locksmith definitely come today?' I ask.

'He will,' replies Zia as we stand on the small balcony outside the front door. 'But not necessarily quickly. He's the only one that works on holidays. But he will come.'

'Have you got everything you need from the flat?' I ask.

'Yes.'

I pop back into the house and emerge, hammer in hand. A much newer one than the model from Mum's. I insert the key into the lock, turn it twice and then step back. I swing the hammer at the key and on the third blow the end snaps off, leaving most of the key in the lock.

'That'll stop anyone getting in,' I say.

'Including us.'

'Only till the locksmith gets here.'

When we reach the front of the pub, I expect the tarp to be open but a few tugs confirm that it's not been moved. That just makes me more convinced that the break-in last night was Pat related. The pub is a far easier target and it's been left alone. The Twins roll up behind us. Both are dressed in identical over-tight blue jeans, white T-shirts and white trainers. Sheryl looks a lot better in the gear than Jordan.

I use the claw on the hammer to loosen the nails and we are soon inside. There is no obvious sign that anyone has been inside the pub. Jordan and Sheryl get to work taking the beer dispenser outside. I noticed that a pile of breadboards have been left next to the car park fence, along with six trestle tables. The fence nearest the pub door runs for about twenty yards before turning ninety degrees and ending in a gap where the cars enter. The fence is six feet high and made of chain link. Near the pub door it runs parallel with the road along which the parade will come. Jordan and Sheryl start to set up at the point where the fence dinks towards the entrance gap, using its corner as a barrier to anyone getting behind the tables. I watch them as they work smoothly together, assembling the makeshift tables and positioning the beer dispenser before they return to fetch bottles, cans and plastic cups to set the bar up.

Inside I start to transport the products I moved less than eight hours ago back to their shelves, remembering to give the shelves a quick wipe. Jordan comes in and digs out a monumental electrical extension. Then he returns for the drop chiller that sits beneath the bar. and we manhandle it outside. Jordan powers it up by plugging the extension into an external power socket near the front door, then he and Sheryl begin to fill the chiller with tiny 20cl bottles that we'll sell for a euro each.

The wholesaler arrives an hour later with more kegs of lager than I've ever seen at one time. With practised ease they stack about twenty of them under the tables that Jordan and Sheryl have set up. The rest are piled into the cellar. Two domestic fridges appear from somewhere and are filled with white wine, soft drinks and water, and also double as a small barrier to Jordan and Sheryl's area on one side.

Half an hour later the bars are ready, inside and out.

'When will people start coming?' I ask, standing with Jordan on the doorstep.

He points to three men wandering across the car park.

'Bloody hell,' I say. There are another half dozen walking up the side street behind them.

'We told you it would be busy,' he says.

Clyde arrives just as another wave of punters rolls up. Most of them are regulars and troop in under the tarp but two are tourists and Jordan directs them to the outside bar.

By twelve o'clock, when Jeep appears, the place is already jumping.

Wasp's nest jumping.

Jeep takes up station in the shade of the pub door, having pulled a seat out from inside. His job is threefold. Try to dissuade the non-regulars from gaining entry to the pub except to use the toilets, spot trouble, and protect the outside till and stock. I'm not quite sure how he is doing the third from his seat but I let it ride.

With the first part of the parade due past at two o'clock, we are full to bursting by one-thirty. Jordan and Sheryl are doing one hell of a job serving, but they've had to rope in a young lad to stand at the beer taps and just keep pouring for those who want draft beer.

When the parade arrives, the bar quietens as people line the fence to watch it pass by. Floats towed by an assortment of pick-up trucks and four-by-fours crawl along. Each float is a work of art.

The theme for the festival is the sea and the floats all reflect this. The first is a reproduction of a shipwreck lying on the sand at the bottom of the sea. The sand is real and the ship is a beautifully carved replica of a sailing vessel, replete with a treasure chest that opens and closes as the float moves along. Five people wave to the crowd from inside the ship. All are dressed in tattered seamen's clothes, faces painted white to give the impression of death. The next float is the bow of a Titanic-liveried liner with two young lovers at the prow dressed in full evening gear. Every few minutes, to cheers from the crowd, they do the Leonardo and Kate cross, flying high above the road, while the band, marching behind, breaks into the appropriate theme song. And so it goes on. Each float a little bit more spectacular than the previous one. The last one past is a double float being towed by a small truck. On top of the two bogeys is a thirty-foot submarine. God alone knows how long it took to make but if I saw it floating in the harbour I'd have assumed it was the real thing. Twelve uniformed sailors are using the top of the submarine as a dance floor, throwing out routine after routine to the music of the brass band, made up of fifteen kids, trailing them.

As the submarine crawls up the hill, the watching hordes on our side of the fence return to the bar and more people from outside squeeze into the car park. I return to the inside bar and send Zia out to help Jordan and Sheryl. Ten minutes later Zia comes in and grabs Clyde as well.

'I've never seen it this busy,' he says as Clyde exits. 'We could easily run out of beer. But with the wholesaler shut there's not much we can do about that. We are already out of bottles. Draft only and I've had to recruit a punter to help pick up the discarded plastic cups. We are charging a euro deposit on each to encourage people to return them but they are still dropping them on the ground.'

Wasp's nest busy.

It will be Jordan who will claim he spotted the trouble first.

15

Power Play

Later, Sheryl will try and outdo Jordan and tell anyone that will listen that she knew something wasn't right about an hour before the thieves struck. Why she didn't mention this to anyone at the time is a matter of some confusion. Mainly in Sheryl's head.

I'm standing at the pub door, frankly amazed at the business we've done and are *still* doing. We've shifted almost all the spare lager kegs from the cellar to the car park, and Zia is running a book on when we will run out. Being more practical, Clyde has called a few of his student friends and has arranged for us to collect another half dozen kegs from around town if we do indeed run dry. If I smoked then this would be the moment to light up and take stock of life. Although, with the crap floating around at the moment, that could take a twenty pack.

Jeep is sitting next to me. He doesn't talk much and when he does it rarely makes sense. He has a language he uses that he thinks is cool but which I find unintelligible. Flowery, over express-ive and just downright weird. He must be in a strange place at the moment. As far as I can tell he had been working with Pat for over a decade and, now his master is dead, he must be wondering where the next buck is coming from. I wonder if Carl Stoker is in the market for more muscle. I won't be able to keep Jeep busy full time.

'Someone is thinking of dipping us big time,' he says.

'Sorry, Jeep?'

He stands up with a loud grunt that tells me how hard it is for him to get himself vertical.

'Am saying we are going to get a doing on the lolly front on the outside.'

I wish Google Translate did Jeep.

He walks across the gravel.

'I mean, right on the now,' he says and starts to lumber through the crowd.

I have no idea what is going down but, as Jeep's words coalesce and clarify, I get the gig.

Someone is thinking of dipping us big time.

He means robbed.

Someone is thinking of robbing us.

Now.

I look at the outside bar. Jordan and Sheryl are rearranging things while there's a small lull in the crowd ordering drink. The till sits next to them, perched on three beer crates. A breadboard shields it from the drinkers to stop someone trying to reach round and grab the cash. I've emptied it five times already but admittedly not for a while. It must be near full. Jeep is wading his way towards the bar and I spot two men, baseball caps pulled way down, standing at the breadboard. One has a hand wrapped around the edge of the board. The other is standing slightly to the left.

I start to move, shouting, 'Jordan, Sheryl, the till.'

The chatter in the car park covers my words but I keep shouting as I run. Jeep is a few yards from the till when the man with his hand on the board yanks it hard to one side, sending it flying towards the spot where Jordan and Sheryl are stacking. His accomplice leans over, going for the till: an old-time wooden box with a metal drawer that weighs in at a good twenty pounds. I push my way through the masses, my journey made easier by trailing in the wake of Jeep, who has ploughed a path like a bull-dozer through candyfloss. I lose sight of the bar for a second and then I break through the crowd in time to see Jeep rugby tackle the man with his hands on the till. The man, till clutched to his chest, is barrelled over the breadboard tables into the space beyond. As he flies back he lets go of the till and by luck, more than design, it bangs down on the crates it came from. The second man leaps forward and seizes the box. With Jeep on the ground, pinning the first thief to the dirt, I have no choice but to try and repeat what Jeep just did with the other man. But I'm a quarter of the weight and although I'm moving slightly faster than Jeep, and force is after all a combination of mass and acceleration, I'm lacking on the former. Instead of sending the second thief flying I glance off him. It's enough to send him stumbling to one side but not enough to knock him off his feet. I crash onto the tables sending a slew of lager-filled cups into the air. I end up, tit over arse, spread-eagled on the ground. I scrabble to stand up.

'Jordan,' I scream as I get back on my feet.

He's already ahead of me and is leaping over the table. The man clutching the till launches himself into the crowd. Someone tries to grab him but he shakes them off. Then he's swallowed by the masses. I hurtle after him, Jordan ahead of me. I catch sight of the thief's baseball cap, bobbing and weaving through the mob. An hour ago and his progress would have been severely restricted by the numbers but things have calmed down somewhat and there's space between the bodies to weave through.

The thief has two choices. Try and escape via the car park entrance or run into the woods where Saucy's old VW stands. The baseball cap swings towards the entrance and then flicks towards the trees as a car chooses that moment to use the entrance for a three-point turn, blocking it.

The trees beyond the VW range up the hill towards the town's most expensive homes. Each a bespoke build. The higher up the slope the more exclusive the home. There's maybe two hundred yards of trees before the first home. The man in the baseball cap breaks from the crowd; a few seconds later so do Jordan and I.

We both hit the slope and my lack of fitness shows immediately, as does Jordan's. In contrast the thief is gazelle-like, despite the weight of the till. As we slide into the woods the noise from the car park vanishes and there's nothing to hear but the buzz of insects, the crashing of brush as we push through and my breathing. For a second I lose sight of the thief and then he reappears, much further up the hill than I would have thought possible. He stops and looks back.

I'm down to a walk and I look back to see Jordan on his haunches. I push on, leaving him behind, my mind fixed on nothing but getting the cash back. I've not been up here before although technically this is my land. The brutal building restrictions on it prevents it from being a sea of homes and flats by now. I'm not even sure if it's fenced in all the way around. I keep climbing and the slope steepens again. My hands are pushing down on my knees to help me move forward. Head down, checking for my footing, I lift my eyes for a second and the baseball cap is impossibly far away. Again the thief checks if he is being followed. Then he vanishes.

I keep going and a few minutes later, air rushing in and out of my lungs like someone trying to blow up a burst tyre, I reach the top edge of the woods. A wall of concrete lies across my way. It's the boundary to the first of the homes up here. There is no gate in the wall. It stretches out of sight to my left and on my right it stops a few yards away. It's an easy ten feet tall and unless gazelle man can leap like Superman he has to have gone right.

I want to stop for breath but somehow I find enough energy to get moving once more. I reach the gap and stare up an even steeper slope, riddled with rocks and low-level plants. The thief is at the top, scrabbling up an almost vertical bank. Who in the hell is this guy? Super-Fitness Magazine's Man of the Year?

I trudge up the hill beginning to wonder if this is worth it. If Jeep has the other thief then surely we'll find out who this one is. He might have had his baseball cap pulled down tight but there would have been dozens of witnesses who will ID him when he's caught.

I use the garden wall on my left to help me up the slope. I reach the bank that the thief scrabbled up and sigh. It's near on vertical. A car slides by above me, which means the bank is topped off by a road. I dig my foot into the dirt and push up. The soil is wet and slick from the rain but it holds and I swing up my other foot, digging my hands into the bank. A few steps up and my shoes are caked in mud, as are my hands. I look up but there is no sign of the thief, or anyone to help me. Eventually I crest the bank and slump onto the mud that edges the road. Another car purrs past, a few feet from my head, and I lie, gasping for air.

After a few seconds I lift my head and study the road. It's a two-way concrete strip, curving gently up to my right and down to my left. I can see a number of garden walls, gates and driveways on either side, but no sign of the thief. I stand up and look both ways for any indication of where he went. He could have gone up or down but he's probably not in any of the surrounding gardens. Most have high, security-protected walls and gates. I'd be inclined to head up rather than down if I were him. I'm sure this road is the one that ends up passing the pub entrance and it would be too risky to head back that way. He's probably headed up and will drop down at a later point into the old town and vanish into the rat's maze of streets.

I stand up, thinking on my situation. Do I keep up the chase? Do I really want to catch this guy on my own? Hell, he must be desperate to raid a till in full view of such a large crowd. High on something? Wouldn't you have to be, or desperately want to be, to try a stunt like that? I yank my mobile from my pocket and see four missed calls, all from Zia. My phone is on silent. I must have flipped it to that last night before bed. I call him back.

'*Are you okay, Daniella?*'

'I'm fine. Pissed off, knackered and filthy – but otherwise fine.'

'*Where are you?*'

'Through the woods behind the pub and up on the first road you come to.'

'And the thief?'

'No sign. What about his partner?'

'Jeep is babysitting him. The police are here already.'

'We'll be their favourite bloody people at the moment.'

'This isn't down to us. And they know it.'

'Do we know who the thieves are?'

'Out of towners, I'd guess. The one here is saying nothing and so far no one recognises him.'

'How much was in the till?'

'You'll like this.'

'What?'

'Next to nothing.'

'You're kidding.'

'Sheryl was getting nervous about how much cash was in it. Said she thought that the two guys in baseball caps were acting funny. She'd just cleaned it out. Being careful to do it out of sight of everyone. She'd bagged the cash and hid it in an empty bottle crate. She was about to carry it to the pub when the thieves struck. There was maybe fifty euros in coins and small notes in the till. At the most.'

'Why didn't she say something to someone about her suspicions rather than act on her own?'

'Come on, Daniella, she just saved you a couple of grand. Don't get on her case.'

Another car drives by, the driver giving my dirt-ridden state the once-over.

'Fair enough. I'll walk back down on the road,' I say. 'It shouldn't take long. Can you let the police know where I am and that I lost the other thief? They might want to drive up and have a scout around.'

'I'll come up for you. If the thief is still there he might not be too happy when he opens the till and finds it's no more than loose change. I'll walk up and meet you.'

'Zia, there's no need—' But he's gone.

I hear rocks hitting rocks and a filthy hand rises over the bank. I jump back, fearing it's the thief, only to see Jordan rise from the dead, his white T-shirt and shoes now mud brown. He lifts his hand as if to wave but turns his palm over and stretches out his forefinger, pointing to something behind me. I spin round and take a blow to the head. My vision explodes and I tumble to the ground. The till lands next to my head, thrown at me with some force. There's the briefest of pauses and then I hear Jordan scream, a sound that fades to a moan. With my face planted in the dirt a trainer clad foot appears. It's caked in mud.

'Message for you, Daniella Coulstoun,' says a voice from above.

I try to lift my head and the trainer rises and pins my head to the ground, grinding my ear.

'Time to move on,' the voice says. 'There's a new man in town. *The* new man. Pack up and leave . . . or else.'

The trainer twists and I scream as it tears at my ear. Then the pressure is lifted and I'm about to turn over when I'm kicked hard in the ribs. I yell and curl up.

'Leave,' says the voice. 'Just leave.'

The trainer lifts and vanishes from view. I hear the soft tap-tap of someone running away and push myself up to see the retreating figure of the thief hightailing it up the road. There is no sign of Jordan but I can hear a sound from over the bank and haul myself upright, clutching at my ribs. I think the bastard might have broken something inside. Hobbling to the edge of the bank, careful not to get too close, I look down. Jordan is lying in a heap a few yards below.

'Jordan,' I shout. 'Are you okay?'

'He pushed me over the edge,' replies Jordan, shoving his hands down to get up. 'The bastard just ran up and shoved me over.'

'Can you get back up here?'

He looks up. 'Give me a moment.'

I decide to sit down, to avoid falling down. The till is lying next to me, sprung open. Coins are scattered over the ground. I hear scrabbling as Jordan pulls himself back up the bank; a few minutes later he rolls over the top and lies next to me.

'Who was that bastard?' he asks, spacing out each word as he tries to catch his breath.

'I've no idea. I called Zia just before he attacked me and he thinks the two of them might be from out of town. Did you recognise him?'

'No. He spoke to you. Did he have an accent?'

I realise that the accent was British. 'Maybe London?'

'Why attack you?' Jordan asks. 'He came running down the hill at you. Why didn't he just run off?'

I wonder if Jordan heard the threats.

'Did you hear what he said?'

'I heard nothing,' he replies. 'He hit you and I was about to run over when he shoulder-charged me over the bank. Why, what did he say?'

I've no reason not to tell Jordan of the warning but I decide not to.

Time to move on.

'I'm not sure. It was all a bit confused.'

I try to stand back up and gasp.

'Are you okay?' asks Jordan.

'The thief kicked me in the ribs. It bloody hurts.'

'Do you want me to look at it?'

I lift the edge of my top until it reaches my bra strap.

'Ouch,' says Jordan. 'There's a massive red mark. That's going to leave a bruise. Does it hurt to breathe?'

I take a deep one. 'No.'

'That's good. When I was young I fell on a tree root. I smashed three ribs. One poked into my lung. It hurt like hell when I breathed.'

'I still think something might be broken.'

'Do you want me to go and get help?' Then he stops and thinks. 'Although, what if that nutter comes back? I don't want to leave you here on your own.'

'I don't think he's coming back, Jordan.'

In fact I'll be surprised if I ever see him again. He's delivered his message. What I don't understand is why he did it the way he did. Stealing the cash seems an odd way to get me on my own for any message. How could he know I'd give chase and why risk being caught in the first place? Although when I think about it he had checked at least twice that he was being followed.

Another thought floats in the air. Didn't Pat say that the forged note telling him I wanted to see him was delivered by a lad in a baseball cap?

I sigh.

'Jordan, I think I can walk,' I say. 'It's all downhill from here. Plus Zia said he's coming up to meet us. Let's get the hell out of here.'

Jordan pulls on my hand to help me up and I wince.

'Sorry,' he says.

'Not your fault.'

With his help I get up and, as we set off, I notice that Jordan is limping.

'Are you hurt?' I ask.

'Might have sprained my ankle. It nips like a good one.'

Holding on to each other we start the journey down, me thinking about the attack and Jordan interrupting my thinking with questions on the theft. I'm looking at one person for all this now. And it's not Brost. This is all too smart for him. This has Stoker written all over it. Based on what George said about Stoker filling Pat's shoes I'm of the mind that Stoker is moving quickly to seal the deal. There may be others who have spotted the opportunity left by Pat's demise and if I were in Stoker's shoes I'd be laying down the new law as quickly and as hard as

I could. Getting me out of town would all but hand him Se Busca.

We round a corner and Zia appears, head down, trudging up the hill. He spots us, waves and breaks into a small run when he sees Jordan is limping and I'm clinging to him.

'What the hell . . . ?' he gasps as he arrives.

I give him the low-down on what had happened.

'The till is still up there,' I point out.

'We can get it later,' Zia says. 'Jordan, let me take Daniella. Do you need my shoulder to lean on?'

'No, thanks.' he replies. 'I think I can manage.'

Zia starts to ask more questions about the attack as we walk down the hill. I'd rather wait until Jordan is gone before getting into all this so I say, 'Zia I think it was just opportunistic thieves. They saw how much money we were taking and took a chance.'

'But why come back and attack you?' Zia asks.

'As you said on the phone, he was probably pissed off to find out the till was all but empty. He was lashing out. He threw the thing at me.'

'Well,' says Zia, 'we'll see what's what when the police talk to his mate.'

The Capitán will love this.

'Did the police wrap up the party?' I ask.

'Yes. They took statements from those who thought they saw something and asked Sheryl to shut down the bar. A few people moved indoors but the rest were finishing up and moving on when I left.'

I stumble and Zia catches me. I look back up the hill and the nose of a black car has just popped into view. It sits for a second and then backs out of sight. I recognise the grill. A BMW grill. A black bonnet with a BMW grille. Stoker drives a black BMW. I double up, clutching my chest, not through pain but to give me a second to see if the car reappears.

'Daniella, are you okay?' asks Zia.

I nod, wait and decide to move on – the BMW is staying out of sight. I know there must be other black BMWs out there but the Occam's razor answer is that Stoker is trailing us. Why else back out of sight? As to whether he meant to be seen or not is a good question. If I hadn't tripped I'd not have seen the car.

The pub heaves into sight and not a moment too soon. I need a seat. There's still a smattering of people clustered around the temporary bar. A lone Policía Local car blocks the entrance.

'What are you going to say to the police?' asks Zia.

'The truth,' I reply.

Well, maybe not the whole truth.

There's a new man in town. The new man . . . Time to move on.

We hirple into the car park, skirting the police car, and Zia takes over when an officer approaches us. The officer doesn't speak English. A young man with bright blue eyes, he listens as Zia chats and is equally patient as Zia asks me for clarification on a couple of points.

It goes like this . . .

POLICE: 'Did you recognise him?'

ME: 'No.'

POLICE: 'Would you recognise him again?'

ME: 'Yes.'

POLICE: 'Why do you think he came back to attack you?'

ME: 'Hacked off at finding the till all but empty.'

POLICE: 'The till was not well protected.'

ME: 'As far as I know we've done it that way for years.'

POLICE: 'Do you think Señorita or Señor Norman might have been involved?'

ME: 'Why do you ask that?'

POLICE: 'Do they often stuff money in a plastic bag and hide it in the empty bottle crates?'

ME: 'Sheryl thought we were going to be robbed. Anyway, if they were in on the theft why not leave the till full and let the thief take it?'

POLICE: 'How do you know that all the money taken at the bar is accounted for.'

ME: 'I don't. But I trust them.'

ME: 'Are you saying there is a link between the Twins and the thieves?'

POLICE: 'I am just asking questions at the moment.'

I'm dismissed with a promise that someone will be in touch.

'Zia, where is the Capitán?' I say as we are walking to his car. I'm going up to the local Centro de Salud for a check-up. They have a small emergency section that can assess me.

'I've no idea,' he says. 'This is a Policia Local matter – not Guardia Civil.'

'I know but shouldn't Lozano have appeared with the warrant for Mum's apartment by now?'

'Maybe he didn't get it.'

'Or never applied for it.'

We get into Zia's car, me whining at the pain from the beating, Zia holding the door open and offering me a hand in. He starts the car up, but I hold up a hand for him to wait and we sit for a minute letting the air conditioning kick in.

'Stoker,' I say.

'Stoker what?'

'Was Stoker behind the theft?'

'What makes you say that?'

'The black BMW that followed us down the hill.'

'A what?'

'When I tripped, I saw a black BMW.'

'It could have been anyone.'

'I've not seen another black BMW around here for a while.'

'Daniella, there are loads.'

'Really?'

'Really. Now can we get to the health centre?' Zia says and starts to roll the car up the hill.

I think about telling him what the thief told me.

There's a new man in town. The new man . . . Time to move on.

But I don't say anything. I just sit as we are swallowed up by the buildings. I look at Zia. The crow's feet that stood out so heavily last night are less pronounced in the soft afternoon light. And I know I'm feeling more than I thought I would for this man. A warm glow at being around him. A level of comfort in his presence that makes me feel I could talk to him about anything and everything. But that slipped a little yesterday when he kept dodging the question on where he was the day before.

I've never had a real confidant in my life. Mum was not one when I was young. And for the last twenty years she wasn't there at all. My one long-term friend, 'Trine, is in the UK and I'd expected her to come out here by now but she hasn't. We've Zoomed a few times and phoned a few more but I'm reluctant to talk about anything around Se Busca and that cuts the conversation to a minimum, me dodging question after question. 'Trine hasn't been in touch for nearly a month. Of the people out here the only other one that I have any sort of rapport with is Clyde. I think he fancies me but is too respectful of Zia to take that any further. On occasions he brushes past me or lingers a little closer than is socially acceptable. I'm flattered. Clyde is a good-looking guy with a lot going for him. Kind, open, warm and helpful I'd be a liar to say that the odd image of him and me hadn't strayed across my mind.

I shake out that thought as Zia reaches for a lower gear, the hill biting. I touch him gently on the arm, my feelings for him at the fore.

'Now that Jordan's gone there's something else I need to tell you about what else happened up on the hill.'

He waits for me to speak again.

'When I was on the ground the thief told me to get out of town.'

'What exactly did he say?' asks Zia in his usual interrogative manner.

'He said *Message for you, Daniella Coulstoun. Time to move on. There's a new man in town.* The *new man. Pack up and leave or else.* Then he said *Leave. Just leave.*'

'Anything else?'

'No. Isn't that enough?'

'What do you think it means?'

'That Stoker is moving in on us.'

'If it is Stoker.'

'I talked to George today. He told me he thinks Stoker is trying to take over from Pat.'

'And do you think he's right?'

'The thief confirmed it for me.'

'It's a bloody strange way to hand out a warning, Daniella. All a bit elaborate and hit or miss. You might never have chased the thief.'

Zia swings the car into the main square and pulls up outside the health centre.

'He kept checking I was following. If I hadn't chased the thief I'd have probably got the message a little later,' I suggest. 'But I'm sure it would have come.'

'I wouldn't go accusing Stoker.'

'Why?'

'Not someone to cross.'

'And that's not new news, Zia. George is of the same opinion.'

Zia helps me out of the car.

The doctor is an older man with a close-cropped, greying beard. He gently prods me while asking questions. His English makes life easy for me but it also serves to tell me how much I just need to dig in and learn Spanish. The doctor doesn't think anything is broken, although he would like to send me to the main hospital for a check-up. I ask what they will do if I have any broken ribs and he tells me that there is little they can do. Strap me up and let them heal. He lets me know that this late in the day we could wait a while to be seen. That I might be better going tomorrow but, with tomorrow being a Saturday, he warns I could also wait a while even then. He makes me promise that if the pain increases I'll go straight to the hospital as an emergency.

The doctor wraps bandages around the bottom of my ribcage and when we exit Zia expresses his own displeasure. 'Why not go to the hospital now?'

'You heard the doctor. We could be there for hours.'

'They'll still see you eventually. I just want you checked out.'

'I know you do and thanks for that. I promise that if anything changes I'll go tonight. Anyway, I have this bloody feeling that Stoker wants me out of the way and that's a good reason not to be.'

Zia helps me back into the car. 'Why? What do you think he's going to do?'

'Who knows, given his track record?' I say, then add, 'did you get in touch with the locksmith?'

'He's coming at six and is bloody expensive.'

'Better that than someone else getting into the house. And we need to fix the pub's front door.'

'Saucy has a mate, a joiner. Saucy texted to say that his mate can come out and look, so I said yes. He's due about the same time as the locksmith. He's doing us a big favour coming today. So is it back to the grind, my lover?'

'Pop star, take me away from here. Ravish me in a white linen tent set upon lush sands where the waves of an azure lagoon brush gently at the shore. Feed me grapes peeled by twenty-year-old athletic men, honed to within an inch of their lives, and drip

16

Lenny's

Suddenly I can't be arsed with the pub. It's a soul-sucking monster at the moment, the problems outweighing the upsides everywhere I look. Today should have been a good day. We sluiced cash through the tills at the outside bar. Until the thieves struck, the place had been humming with an energy that makes the pub game worth it. But when I see the Capitán standing in the car park, I say to Zia, 'Get us the hell away from here. We can get back in time for the locksmith and chippie but let's take some time out.'

He sees the Capitán as well, takes the next right and heads for the shore. I pull my mobile out and kill it.

'Give me yours.'

Zia wrestles it from his front left pocket and hands it to me. I switch it off as well.

'What now?' he asks.

'I've no idea. I just want some me-time.'

His brow creases.

'I mean *we*-time,' I correct. 'Not long. But I just need a small break from it all.'

'Where?'

'Will Lenny's be open?'

'I can't see why not.'

'Then let's go there.'

Lenny's, real name Leo Henri's, is a small bar perched on the edge of the cliffs that border the southern edge of the El Descaro bay. Lenny is half Spanish, half British and acquired the name Lenny as the anglification of Leo when at school, his school friends noting that Leo Henri was as close to the comedian Lenny Henry as made no odds – it was an easy leap for kids looking to take the piss. Lenny's bar is tiny but the view is gorgeous. At the height of summer you need to book a seat, even if you're just out for a drink. He has a miniscule range of overpriced, pre-cooked tapas, made in his home half a mile away, and charges through the nose for booze. But all is forgiven when you gaze down on the rocks below and out at the horizon. The view is worth paying for alone.

The land around the bar is his, or rather will be when his nonagenarian father passes on. It would make stunning building land but Lenny has told me that his father is having none of that 'building shite' as he calls it. Lenny's dad is the English side of Lenny's parental equation. Come the day God remembers that Lenny's dad is still around and takes him away, Lenny will wait a suitable time and then sell the land for a mint. In the meantime, he's more than happy to overcharge his customers in whatever way he can creatively think of. At this time of the day and the year the bar will be quiet.

Zia and I drive in silence. I shred the thoughts of the death and the pub in my head and scatter them with an imaginary fan. I close my eyes, shutting out the world. I pull up my mental jukebox and look for a song for the moment. Zia beats me to it by flicking on the radio. The 1975 join us and are singing about a change of heart. I sing along, badly. Zia sings along, well. He has a great voice and it hurts me to know that his attempts to resurrect his career have never amounted to much.

We top out the climb from the valley and Zia takes us off the road onto a small dirt track. It winds between some houses before opening up on a rock-strewn plateau. We pass a couple, hand in hand, equipped with backpacks and hiking boots.

Lenny's place has a small car park and there are a couple of cars in it. From the rear the bar looks abandoned. Wood stripped of its colour, rusting pipes, cracked panes of glass and missing tiles on the roof, all talk of neglect. Lenny tells everyone that he is going for derelict chic. I call it cheapskate lunacy. We pull in next to a green BMW and the car marque takes my head back to Stoker and the incident with the thief. I instantly try and shake that thought loose.

We exit the car and take the path to the front of the building. There is still little sign that this place is occupied. The path is only kept under control by the thousands of feet that transit it. Either side is a knotted mass of plants and discarded rubbish. The track hugs the building before pulling its party trick. As we reach the corner of the wooden hut the view snaps into place like a magician doing a reveal.

The cliff edge drops away less than twenty feet from the edge of the building. A hundred and forty feet, straight down. The view takes in the whole of the El Descaro bay and is not for those who have an aversion to heights. There are plenty of stories of people reaching this very point and then either running screaming or freezing in fear. Well, there are such stories if you listen to Lenny. Between us and the edge of the cliff is a concrete platform dotted with a mishmash of chairs and tables. None match. The canopy above them is a faded ripped sea of brown cotton and provides no protection from sun or rain. The bar front is open to the elements and there is no space inside for seating. When bad weather hits, you get wet or you leave.

There are five people in total in sight. All seated in the chairs nearest the edge of the cliff. All have drinks in front of them. None have food. Lenny discourages eating at this time of year. Too much hassle. Lenny is behind the bar, on his mobile, and doesn't see us appear. He's a small man given to wearing jeans that are too blue and shirts that are too stained. His hair is tied back in a bun and the service here, when Lenny is on his own, is slower than a week in jail. I pick a table away from the other people and Zia walks up to Lenny.

I know that Lenny is obsessed with a mobile game called 'Marshmallow World'. He plays it endlessly on his battered old iPhone, rarely lifting his head. He's been playing it for nearly five years according to Zia and still hasn't killed the Marshmallow King, whatever in the hell that means. George's nephew nailed the whole game in one day and said it's one of those phone games that is devoid of fresh ideas.

Zia brings me a glass of wine and he hugs a Coke. Table service is optional here. I swing my legs towards the view, as does Zia, the vista a magnet to the eyes.

We sit. Saying nothing. The gentle chat of the other customers caught on the late afternoon breeze drifts over us. I don't recognise any of the punters and none of them look at us, lost in the world between each other and the view. The wine is average and that's hard to do around here. Good comes as standard. I've rarely met an establishment that tries so hard to fail and fails to fail.

A few late season boats are skipping the waves in the bay and the dark clouds of last night have been replaced with flakes of white lit by a warm, dipping sun.

Lenny has paused his game and is talking on the phone, head turned away from us. He looks at Zia and I before hanging up and returning to his game.

'Are we going to talk?' asks Zia.

'Not about us. Not yet but I do have one question.'

'Shoot.'

'Don't jump down my throat.'

'Okay.'

'But you didn't answer my question from yesterday.'

'Which was?'

'Where were you on the morning that Pat was killed? I saw you get in George's car and vanish up to town. Yet George told the

Capitán he saw Pat go into DB's at about that time. He couldn't have been there unless you drove into town and doubled back. Did you?'

'Are you asking me if I was involved in Pat's death?'

'No. I'm just asking where you were.'

Zia takes another look-see at the view.

'I was doing what you wanted me to,' he finally says.

'Me? What did I want you to do?'

'When George told you that you weren't cutting it and he'd take the pub if you didn't shape up, I told you I'd talk to him. Well, that's what I was doing. He was going to a meet and I blagged the ride in the car with him to chat.'

'What did he say?'

'That he was serious.'

'Anything else?

'No. I pressed him on why now. What had changed lately and he went quiet on me.'

'He gave no reason?'

Lenny lets out a yell and we turn as he slams his phone onto the bar.

'He probably got killed in the game again,' Zia speculates, watching Lenny shuffle a few dirty glasses around.

'Back to George,' I say. 'He didn't tell you anything else?'

'Other than you and the pub needed sorting soon. That's why I haven't said anything as there was nothing to tell. He was heading for Saucy's place and dropped me off halfway up Saucy's road and I walked back.'

'Why would I, or the pub, need sorted soon? The place is hardly on its uppers and I think today's take will put us ahead of last year. What in the hell does he want from me?'

'It's hard to tell.'

'But you're one of them. The Ex-Patriots. Surely George has talked about this to you all.'

'If he has I've not been present. But that's to be expected. You're still an outsider in these parts and I told you before – I'm now tarred with your brush.'

'They're cold-shouldering you?'

'A bit. At first I thought it was because your mum was gone. She was the glue that kept us together but I've begun to realise that it's not that. I've been sidelined. George, the Twins, Saucy and Skid are still friendly enough to me, or as friendly as they used to be. But I know there are meetings I'm not privy to and Saucy threw a small party for his wedding anniversary. I wasn't on the invite list.'

'I never knew I was having that impact, Zia. They are your friends. Am I killing that for you?'

'I've thought on that a lot, Daniella. Moving in with you kind of placed a small nail in my coffin lid with them.'

'They really don't trust me that much?'

'They like what they had with your mum. And now they are finding their own feet and you're not a natural replacement. Put me with you and I was always going to be the soor ploom to their bar of chocolate. But I'm cool with it.'

His words say one thing. His tone another. It's not that I hadn't considered my impact on Zia's relationships. After all, he's been here twenty years. But I assumed he was handling it and the reason he was seeing less of the Ex-Patriots was because he was seeing more of me.

'Is that why you've been ducking the serious conversation about us?' I ask.

'Probably. I'm burning a few bridges here and I'll be straight with you, Daniella. I've no idea if the land on this side of the river is more fertile – but, and this is a *real* but, I've been scared to ask you about anything more momentous than what we are eating tonight.'

'Why? In case I tell you that we are not a long-term thing?'

'Kind of.'

'Zia, you're an idiot sometimes.'

His face falls.

'The only way either of us is going to know how we feel is if we talk.'

'I know that,' he says, the hurt hard in his voice. 'But you've been so good for me I didn't want to run the risk of asking about us and you telling me what I didn't want to hear.'

'God, I so didn't want to do this conversation here.'

His face collapses further. 'You're going to dump me.'

It's my turn to let my face fall. 'What? No. Don't be so stupid. We need to talk because I don't know how you really feel. I'm not bloody psychic. You aren't the only one in the dark over where this relationship is going. There are two in it, in case that missed your attention.'

'You are worried about me leaving.'

'Are you?'

'What?'

'Going to leave?' I ask.

He surprises me and laughs. A high-pitched noise. The other customers turn to look. Lenny ignores him, lost back in his game.

'Daniella, we are a bloody pair. I wasn't talking to you because I was afraid of what you might say and because I wasn't talking you thought I was having second thoughts.'

'And you weren't?'

'Were you?'

'No.'

'Neither was I.'

'We are a sodding duo,' I say. 'Okay, let me make this as clear as I can. I like being with you. Life is good. You make me feel happy and you make me feel secure. I don't know where this is going and I'm happy about that. It's running at its own speed and that suits me at the moment, but every so often a girl needs reassurance. Like now, when you told me how dumb we both are. I need honesty and I haven't been getting that.'

'And every so often a guy needs the same.'

'We are both idiots.'

'And some.'

'Then things are good.'

Only they're not. Not really. As I say the words I know there is something off. He's just lied to me about George and the reason he was in his car. I don't know why but I know he's lying – and as far as I know Zia hasn't lied to me before. It may be nothing or it may not. But I know he has just lied.

'Zia,' I say, 'we are as good as it can be but this conversation isn't finished. It'll never be finished. But at least it's started so let's not get to this point again.'

'Do you want to put in a date for our next session?'

'Sure, let me get the diaries out.'

I reach for my bag and the look on Zia's face is a Kodak moment. I put my bag down and laugh. 'Of course I don't want to diarise the bloody thing. I just want us to talk when we feel we need to talk.'

'Agreed.'

He leans over and kisses my lips and a warm glow wraps itself around me, despite the kernel of reservation growing inside.

'We have time for another drink,' I say when he pulls away.

'I'll get it.'

'No, let me, I need to use the toilet.'

I rise and Zia slides his hand along my forearm making me smile.

'Lenny, can I have the toilet key?' I say, rousing him from his game.

Lenny keeps the toilets locked to stop non-customers using them. He reaches behind him when I approach, eyes stuck firmly to the phone screen, lifts a key, attached by a chain to a rolling pin, from its hook and hands it to me. The rolling pin makes the thing almost unusable but it's his way of ensuring that people bring it back.

The toilets sit out back and unlike the rest of the fading glory the facilities are fresh, clean and well kept. Even Lenny knows that there is no quicker way to lose custom than dirty toilets. Especially with the women. Once inside the cubicle the small light above flickers a few times before settling to a bright glow. The smell of lemon bleach is strong and reminds me of the carpet back in Mum's old place and that makes me wonder if the Capitán was back at Se Busca to ask for the keys or if he was following up on the till theft. Either way I'm glad I gave the pub a wide berth and turned my phone off.

When I'm done, I wash my hands and hear a car crunch up to the car park. The small rear window of the toilet is frosted and sits slightly open to aid with circulation of air. I push it open a little more and watch as a dusty, dark-grey Land Cruiser pulls up. Two men get out. A tall, fair-haired bloke wearing a black hoodie is follwed by a smaller man, stomach pushing at a bright gold golf jumper. The smaller man has two cauliflower ears and a badly smashed nose. I've seen both of them around town. And one of them not that long ago.

My anger starts to bubble again.

I exit the toilet and, as I reach the bar to hand the keys back, I stop. The two men are standing at our table, tight around Zia. It doesn't look friendly. I watch for a few seconds. The tall one is talking to Zia and from here Zia looks scared. To my right, Lenny has stopped playing his game and is watching the men. I back up a little, putting Lenny between me and the patio. Zia tries to stand up and Cauliflower Ears pushes him back down.

I step out and drop the key with a bang next to Lenny.

'Call your mates did you, Lenny?' I spit as I pass him.

'Eh,' is the sum total of his reply.

'Earlier, Lenny. I saw you on the phone. Did you call in those bozos?'

'I—'

'You shit.' I dismiss him and stride towards Zia and the men.

'Can I help here?' I say as I approach. I say it loud enough to attract everybody in the bar's attention.

Cauliflower Ears moves away from Zia and Fair Hair turns to look at me.

'Just having a word with your boyfriend,' says Fair Hair. He has a small lisp and his hands fidget as he talks.

'Well, we're having a private moment if you don't mind,' I say, pushing past him to my seat, but I don't sit.

'And I need a private moment with you both,' Fair Hair says.

Cauliflower Ears says nothing.

'Make an appointment then,' I reply. 'You know where I live. *Don't you.*'

Again, I say this loudly. Again, making sure everyone can hear.

'Are you taking the piss?' says Fair Hair.

'No, but you are. Malky Robertson isn't it?'

'And?'

'Has Capitán Lozano talked to you about the raid on my pub?' I say, keeping the volume up.

'What the fuck has that to do with you?'

I laugh.

'So he has been in touch. Zia, tell me, I might be wrong here but wasn't there a tall skinny one and a wee fat one as part of the team that wrecked Se Busca the other night?' I say this for the benefit of the crowd. 'I'm sure George described a couple like that.'

'We weren't near your place,' says Cauliflower Ear.

'The fingerprints they found might disagree with that,' I offer.

'You don't get fingerprints when you wear gloves,' he says.

'Who said anyone was wearing gloves?' I say.

He stumbles over his next words. '. . . no one would do what they did without gloves. That's what I meant.'

'And what is it they did? Since you seem to know,' I ask Cauliflower Ears.

Malky Robertson glares at him.

'I don't know,' is Cauliflower Ears' weak reply.

'You weren't the idiot wearing the welder's mask, were you?' I say to Cauliflower Ears, taking a wild stab in the dark.

His eyes flick to Malky. My wild stab isn't so wild.

'What a dick that guy was,' I say. Volume still on loud. 'I mean, the rest were idiots for what they did but what kind of tosser wears a welding mask to raid a pub. You'd have to be seriously fucked in the head to do that.'

Cauliflower Ears rolls forward on the balls of his feet. I've struck a real chord with this one.

'Don't you think so,' I say to the rest of the customers. 'I mean. Come on. Who in the hell would wear a welder's helmet in the pitch black to break into a pub? That's a real Facebook moment – or maybe a *You've Been Framed* two hundred and fifty-quid banker.'

Cauliflower Ears teeters on the edge of jumping at me. He's got a hair trigger of a temper.

'I think we have it all on the CCTV, Zia,' I continue. 'We could post it up on YouTube. What would we call the footage? Wanker in a Welder's Mask? That would rack up the hits.'

Cauliflower Ears loses it and flies forward but he may as well have signalled his attack in last week's *Daily Mail*. I have more than enough time to step out of the way and he careers past me towards the cliff edge. He slams on the brakes, but almost too late. Lenny has been told fifty ways from here to the North Pole to fence off the cliff edge, but his only concession is a small, crumbling two-foot high wall that surrounds the concrete patio. Cauliflower Ears trips on the wall as he tries to stop himself flying into space and tumbles forward. He finishes face down, inches from the cliff edge.

Malky closes in on me. 'Think you're the smart cow?'

'Smart enough to know that whatever you came here to say would have been better said away from others. Not in a public

173

café. So, yes, maybe I am smarter than some people around here.'

He drops his voice to a whisper. 'And your time is up, Coulstoun. You just don't know it yet.'

'I've been told that already today,' I growl. 'Your dumb fucking boss uses the worst delivery men in history. Don't you talk to each other?'

'Get over here,' Malky shouts to Cauliflower Ears – who has risen and looks like he's getting ready for a second run at me. 'We are going.'

'See you later, Mr Welder,' I say as Cauliflower Ears walks towards Malky. 'Wear your mask next time you come to visit. It suits you.'

Malky has to grab Cauliflower Ears by the shoulder to stop him charging again. 'Leave it,' he says.

They both walk away and before Zia can say anything, I make for Lenny, who is now deep in his game again.

'And you, Leo Henri, I'll not miss when I tell people about this little incident. Thanks for grassing us up. We told no one we were coming here. I've a Capitán who will be more than a little interested in what just happened.'

'I never called anyone,' he says.

'Bollocks. Hand over your phone and we'll see.'

'Will I hell? Who do you think you are? You're no Effie Coulstoun, that's for sure.'

'Oh, that soooo hurts,' I spit back. 'And you're a stingy old bastard waiting and hoping your dad dies so you can cash in.'

As soon as I say that I regret it. But I'm rock solid sure that Lenny called Stoker who, in turn, sent in Malky – and that has pressed my anger button. Malky has to be working for Stoker.

'How dare you?' he shouts.

I zip my mouth. There's nothing I can say here that works. I'm too mad to say sorry and too worked up not to say something worse. I whirl away.

'Zia, pay the man. We're out of here.'

I leave Zia sitting at the table and depart like a diva. I reach the car but Zia has the key and I stand, fizzing, waiting on him. When he appears, it's crystal clear he's not happy but before he can speak I put my hand up.

'There's only so much of this shit you can take,' I say. 'And I'm not taking much more.'

'Why did you say that to Lenny?'

'I'm certain he phoned Stoker who, in turn, called those two. And I only said what everyone knows about Lenny wanting to sell up.'

'Come on, Daniella. You do know that his dad has only days to live.'

'What?'

'He was taken into hospital the day before yesterday. The news isn't good.'

'I wasn't aware. So why is Lenny here and not at the hospital?'

'Because he can't go.'

'Can't or won't.'

'Both. He can't face it and won't face it.'

'Well, that's just wrong.'

'Daniella, it is what it is. He knows fine well what everyone thinks about this place. But you didn't need to rip into him about it.'

'He phoned Stoker, and that moron Robertson appeared. How else would they know we were here? I'm not having that.'

'Okay, say you're right and he did phone Stoker, Stoker is a hard man to say no to. If Stoker said to Lenny to call if we appeared then call is what Lenny had to do.'

'Lenny could have just blanked us.'

'He could and then, when Stoker found out we were up here, Lenny would have been in for a right kicking. If I was in Lenny's place I'd have phoned.'

'Well, I wouldn't.'

'Only because you still think that normal rules apply around here. But they don't and never will. Yes, Lenny is a bastard for phoning but there's hardly a person in his position that wouldn't.'

'You don't know his position, Zia.'

'Oh, get real, Daniella. If you were in touch with what is going on around here the way you should be you'd know exactly why Lenny has to kowtow to Stoker.'

'Why?'

'This is the last real high-price chunk of land of any size around here that has no buildings on it. Virgin development land is rare. And it'll have a high dollar value once built on. Millions, we're talking. Pat Ratte had Lenny well in his pocket. He was in for a share, come pay day. Everyone knew that. And now Pat's gone, Stoker is moving in.'

'Stoker can't cut in on Lenny's land.'

'He can and he will. You'd be amazed what you can be made to sign if the right pressure is applied. Lenny's Marshmallow King days would be over if he lost his thumbs. And it's not as if Lenny won't end up a rich man. Just not as rich as he might have liked. So please leave the whole Stoker thing alone.'

'Why? Why do you keep telling me that? Why does George? Stoker sure as hell doesn't seem to want to leave me alone. He sent those goons up here. And I'll tell you something else – that was Malky that was up at our house last night. I thought I recognised the lanky git.'

'Do you know all that for sure?'

'Yes.'

'How?'

I walk away from the car, knowing that I can't be certain. 'Zia, how in the hell can you stand this place? Twenty years you've been here and you talk as if all of this is bloody normal.'

'That's because it *is* normal,' he shouts after me. 'And, Daniella, do you want to know the secret to how you survive and thrive around here?'

I stop. 'Don't tell me. Be as bent as the next man.'

'No. You need to look to Kenny Rogers, that's the secret.'

I have no idea what that means and simply stare at him.

'His best song is "The Gambler",' says Zia.

I wait on the connection to the conversation.

'Daniella, you do know the song?'

I nod.

'Knowing when to hold, when to fold and when to walk away,' he says. 'The words could have been written for El Descaro, and you need to step up your understanding of when to do which.'

'This is so tiring. Why in the hell can't this just be a place of sun, sea and sod all else?'

'It never was, it isn't now and it never will be. And you need to stop acting like a kid and face up to it.'

'A kid?'

'Life's not fair and around here it's even truer. Just get used to it.'

'Are you telling me to walk away.'

'I'm telling you to do what's needed. And what's needed is to leave Stoker alone. And also get a grip on yourself. That's not you Daniella. Talking like that to Lenny. It's just not you.'

My shoulders drop, the tension unsustainable.

'Okay, I was out of line with the comment about Lenny and his dad,' I admit. 'But those other two idiots needed a telling.'

'No they didn't, Daniella. You should have just let them have their say and then worked out what to do. That would have been a better plan. They're not Stoker. If he did send them then they are just his mouthpiece. There's no gain to be had in rattling their cages. They're not in charge. All that'll happen is that they'll tell Stoker what you said.'

I pride myself on keeping cool. But I know that when I lose it, I lose it. Mum was the same. An on and off switch for emotions. No one-to-ten dial. With Mum you were in the firing line or you weren't. No grey. And I have some of that in me. Actually, I have a lot of that.

'Okay, okay,' I say. 'I pissed them off but there was a point to it.'

'Which was?'

'I might be the newbie around here. But one thing I do know is that in this place it's the survival of the fittest. You just said it yourself in as many words. If I just roll with the blows each time I'm screwed, we are both screwed. Stoker and his kind live for weakness. They seek it out and stick a bloody big knife in it. I need to let this bastard know I'm not a soft touch. He's racking this whole thing up and I can't let him. Mum managed to control him so there must be a way.'

'She did it with Pat's help.'

'Pat was an old man playing at gangsters. How did he help Mum?'

'Pat might have been past his muscle sell-by date but he knew stuff.'

'Like what?'

'Like stuff that keeps others at bay.'

He lets that hang for a moment.

'Others.'

'Others, Daniella. It's not all about beating the crap out of people to get your way. It's also about having the gen on your enemies, and that can be just as effective as an army of nutters doing your bidding. Pat had a lot of dirt on a lot of people. It's how you stay on top.'

'And that's how he controlled Stoker.'

'That's how you always control guys like Stoker. Outsmart them, don't outmuscle them – the latter isn't winnable. Not with someone like Stoker – unless you have a squad of Ninjas.'

My anger is rolling away. I shake my head and walk back to the cliff edge.

'Where are you going?' Zia asks.

'I'm going to apologise to Lenny. I was out of order with what

I said. He deserved to be put in his place for making the phone call but he didn't deserve to be accused of wanting his dad dead.'

'He won't listen.'

'I don't need him to listen. I just need to say the words in front of him. Then you and I can head back to the bear pit.'

17

What-less

Zia was right, Lenny didn't listen to what I had to say. Or, at least, he gave a good impression of throwing me a deafy. He just stared at the screen while I talked. He didn't even acknowledge my presence. I said my piece but it didn't make me feel any better.

Zia is now driving me back to Se Busca with his mouth zipped closed. At this moment in time I feel like I shat on his living-room carpet in front of the minister and his six cousins.

I watch the buildings slide by, and not for the first time wonder if this place really is for me. Even if Stoker, Pat, and all the crap that's trailing in behind them vanish, I'm wondering if my computer screen and a life of second-guessing insurance claimants wouldn't be a little more straightforward. I have the money in the bank to ensure a comfortable life and, if I sell up here, I might not even have to work back home.

My head is spinning with thoughts as we round a hairpin curve, when the world lurches. I'm thrown hard against my seat belt and the car snaps to the left. Zia shouts and saws at the steering wheel as we slide across the road, heading towards the cliff edge. Beyond it the land drops off towards the rocks below. I scream as the car's tyres howl and the engine wails. We slam to a halt with barely two feet between us and fresh air. We've spun one eighty and the car that's just tried to drive us off the edge of the cliff is reversing up the road. A familiar dirt-grey Land Cruiser. I watch it stop and then it leaps forward.

'Zia,' I yell. 'They're going to hit us again.'

Zia has no time to react and we brace ourselves as the attacking car rams us square on. We jerk back. Zia has his foot hard on the brake and we stop inches from going over the cliff. The Land Cruiser reverses again, to take another run and Zia thumps his foot on the clutch, throwing the car into gear. He plants his foot and shoots us towards the reversing car. At the last second he flicks the wheel to the right and we catch the corner of the Land Cruiser, ploughing it to our right. Zia puts his foot down and accelerates up the hill. I spin round and am distraught to see the other car is already turning to chase us.

'Zia, they're trying to kill us.'

He says nothing, his eyes locked on the road, hands tight on the steering wheel, foot on the floor. The car is underpowered and the slope is killing it. We're not so much accelerating with meaning as drifting upwards at a sedate pace.

'Get the hell off this road,' I say.

With a near vertical drop on one side and a curving line of villas on the other my instructions are all but useless. There is nowhere to go but up. I look back and the other car is gaining. Zia spots a gap between two homes which I've missed. A strip of wasteland maybe ten feet wide, hemmed in between the walls of the gardens. He points us at the gap and we go off road. The ground is soft from the rain and we splash through puddles and sling mud up in our wake. Our rear screen is instantly covered in sludge and there's no wiper to clear it. I look at the wing mirrors but they are just as filthy as the back window. A smack up the tail tells me that the chase car is not for giving in. We slew to one side, and Zia manages to catch the skid and keep us from scraping a wall.

We lumber from the gap onto another road. To the left the road climbs, to the right it dips, and Zia chooses down. We start to gain speed and, at the last possible second, as we cross a junction, Zia drags the car sharp left. As we slide across the road I glimpse the chasing car as it overshoots the junction. Zia repeats the move fifty yards later, doubling back, and then he runs us up onto a pristine white gravel driveway, sliding us in front of a grand statement of a home, throwing loose stones in a wave as he stops.

He kills the engine and I look up at the house. All the *persianas* are shut tight and there's no sign of any life. With the rear window of the car covered in mud and a wall between us and the road, there's no way to see if we have shaken off the chasing car. I push open the door, jump out and scrabble around until I can see the entrance to the driveway. I stand, hidden from immediate view, but if a car goes past I'll see its rear as it heads away.

For over a minute I wait, ears open for the slightest noise. I slip back to Zia's car and knock on the window.

'Zia, take the car round to the side of the house, out of sight. If they start searching this road house by house they'll see us.'

'Daniella, this is insane.'

'I know, but let's not chat about it here.'

Zia slowly drives the car into the shade of the house. I walk back to the entrance and look back to where Zia has parked. Our car can't be seen. I turn to watch the road and give it another few minutes before heading back to Zia.

'Zia, get out,' I say to him through the car window.

He slides from the car.

'They obviously waited for us,' he says.

'They may wait again,' I reply. 'I think you were right when you said I should have just let them mouth off. It's the wee man with cauliflower ears who's driving. My crack about the welder's mask must have tipped him over the edge. But I don't believe they would be stupid enough to be seen with us at Lenny's if their intention had been to kill us. I've a feeling that Cauliflower Ears has gone off-piste on this one.'

The sound of a rattling car limps by. I risk a quick glance and spot the mud-covered tail of the grey four-by-four vanishing along the road.

'They are looking for us, Zia, and your car is too slow to get away. And, as far as I know, the only way out of here is down the cliff road. I don't fancy our chances if they have another go there.'

'What do you suggest?'

'I saw a lane at the last corner. It looks like it heads into the woods that line the cliff top.'

'Then where do we go after that?'

'Back to Lenny's. It's the only place open around here. We'll be safer up there. Then we can figure what to do.'

Zia walks round the car. 'Look at the state of it. They've wrecked it.'

'At least we're alive, Zia. Vehicles can get fixed. Do you need anything from the car?'

'No, but I hope the homeowners are away for a while. I'm not sure what they'll make of this if they find my car in their driveway.'

'Come on, let's go before those two nutters get a chance to circle round and find us. We can pick your car up later.'

The gravel sounds unnaturally loud underfoot. Both of us are shaken by the ferocity of the attack. If we had gone over the edge of the cliff we would have been dead for sure. I hope I'm right and it was an aberration by Cauliflower Ears and not Stoker's orders that sent him gaga with the car. Otherwise Stoker has upped the game considerably.

The lane I'd spotted lies about forty yards away. Zia and I scan the road.

'We just have to run for it,' I say. 'The less time we are out in the open the better.'

'Agreed.'

'On three.'

'Okay.'

'Three.'

Coast still clear.

'Two.'

No movement.

'One.'

Run.

We jink down the road, heads up, scanning for the car. This is a flat-out sprint and I hit the lane a second after Zia. We plunge up into the shade of the trees before barrelling to a stop and turning to look back. There is no sign of the four-by-four.

'Let's keep walking,' I say.

The wood is a mix of old olive and citrus trees interspersed with the odd rubber sapling. They are spaced out, making it easy to walk between them, and thick enough on the ground to cast shade and keep the sun off. The cicadas are in full buzz, a million tiny chainsaws all cutting away at the same time. With no clear idea where Lenny's place lies, we head up the slope and soon hit the edge of the cliff. We look down on the El Descaro bay and can clearly see the cliff edge road that Cauliflower Ears had tried to push us over. The Land Cruiser is sitting, waiting. If we had tried to leave they would have had a clean second shot at us. We duck back into the cover of the trees and work our way up to the top.

'What do we do when we get up to Lenny's?' asks Zia, dodging an exposed root.

'I'm tempted to call the Capitán.'

'You're kidding?'

'I'm not. Those two idiots are down there. Waiting on us.'

'We could call a taxi.'

'And if they see it go up what will they think?'

'Someone has ordered a taxi.'

'And do you think that would stop them trying to push it over the cliff if they see us in it? But I doubt even they would have a go at a police vehicle.'

'They won't wait there all day.'

'Are you sure, Zia? How long will they wait? Ten minutes? An hour? All night?'

'You said it was just the wee man throwing a fit.'

'I could be wrong.'

We keep climbing, occasionally glimpsing the sea below as the trees part. We reach the rear of Lenny's fifteen minutes later.

'Hold there,' Zia says to me. 'Let me just check that the coast is clear.'

He dips behind the toilet and vanishes from view for a few seconds before reappearing.

'There are four customers plus Lenny and two cars in the car park.'

'Lenny's not going to be happy to see me again so soon,' I point out.

'He'll get over it.'

Zia leads me out of the wood and I take his hand. We pass the toilet and I hear the door open behind me.

'Well, if it isn't Daniella Coulstoun herself.'

I spin and find myself looking at Carl Stoker.

'And the boyfriend,' he adds.

Dressed from tip to toe in black he looks for all the world to have walked out of some horror flick, emerging from slaying his victim in the backwoods toilet.

'On your own, Mr Stoker,' I say.

'Why wouldn't I be? I prefer my own company. If that's not too vain a thing to admit.'

Because no other bugger will give you the time of day, I want to say.

'Malky Robertson and his little sidekick are still down the road.'

'Robertson? Skinny, fair-haired bloke?'

'Are you saying you don't know him?'

Stoker ignores me and walks to the bar, then he turns and says, 'I have a coffee waiting for me.'

I look at Zia. 'What the hell?'

Zia hasn't anything to add. He simply shakes his head. He looks nervous as hell as Stoker sits down. He must have seen Stoker's car in the car park but said nothing.

'Can you go and see what Stoker's up to?' I ask Zia.

'And you?'

'I need to use the bathroom.'

Ten minutes later I emerge and find Zia sitting with Stoker. Zia looks massively uncomfortable while Stoker looks as cool as an ice cube on a ski slope. I'm somewhere in between.

'What brings you up here?' I ask as I sit down next to them both.

'The view,' Stoker replies with half a smile.

'Not Robertson?'

'No idea what you are talking about. Why would you think I know anything about him and his whereabouts?'

'A hunch.'

'I hear you had a little trouble at the parade this afternoon.'

'Did you?'

'Yes. Theft around here can be a pain. You know I can help with things like that?'

'Like what?'

'Like providing a little security when it's needed.'

'You're into protection now, Stoker, are you? Taking over from Pat. You didn't mention that when we last met.'

He sweeps his hair back with the back of his hand and his eye is drawn to the view.

'Not protection,' he corrects. 'Security. And there are many things that I did not mention at our meeting. I also see that you haven't updated the El Descaro Classic website for this year yet. Why not?'

He says that in the same way a bloody teacher would shut down a five-year-old who hadn't wiped his hands after pissing.

'I still haven't decided if I'm doing it yet,' I say. 'That's why. It was my mum's thing, not mine.'

His eyes harden, his mouth sets and his jaw clamps. He has on his Tony Soprano face. His *hard* face.

'I think you misunderstood our last little conversation,' he says.

'No, I don't think I bloody did,' I reply. 'I know exactly what you want me to do but I never agreed to anything and, since our tête à tête, I've had other issues to deal with.'

'Ah, the sad death of your mother's old friend, Mr Ratte. That was unexpected. But he was a man with a reputation, and such men have to be careful. Such reputations attract the most unsavoury of characters to your table. Have the police made any progress?'

'They haven't been in touch with you yet?'

'Why would they talk to me? I had no connection to Mr Ratte and was out of town on the day that he died.'

'Where were you?'

'On business.'

'Out of town?'

'Out of town.'

If there is a chink in this guy's armour it's not obvious. He's dodged the question on Robertson, brought up the theft at the parade, the death of Ratte and threatened me with protection with nary a blink. Cool as cool does.

'It seems you are trailing trouble behind you, Daniella,' he points out. 'And, in my experience, someone who attracts such trouble rarely stops dragging it around. The bad attracts the bad.'

'You would know.'

Zia lets out a small gasp.

'I just say it as I see it,' he says, brushing off the jibe. 'You attract trouble.'

'Really, and how would you suggest that such trouble is avoided in one's future?' I say, mimicking the half-arsed 'polite speak' he flips in and out of.

'Answering that would constitute advice on my part, Daniella, and I charge for that. But in this case I'll make a small exception.'

Lenny shouts out. Killed by a marshmallow warrior no doubt. Everyone looks up and Stoker sweeps his hair once more, then, for good measure, smooths down his polo neck.

'If I were you, Daniella,' he says, 'I would listen to what you are being advised to do.'

'By whom?'

'By those that are doing the telling. Even the people that may not look worthy of listening to. Those that may seem a little tangential to your life or, as you might say, rough around the edges – but their message can be just as valid as messages from those you know and trust.'

'Jesus. Do you mean the halfwit that tried to steal my till or that dick Robertson?'

'I mean many people.'

'Stoker,' I say.

'Carl, please, Daniella.'

'Stoker,' I repeat. 'Have you ever considered taking part in *Mastermind*?'

'I know of the show but—'

'You see, they have a specialist round. The one where the contestants choose the subject they think they know well. Well, you have a subject that you would excel at.'

'And that would be?'

'Obscuration.'

'And that means?'

'You know what it means. And that is exactly what *I* mean.'

'You have lost me.'

'Look, I'm sorry to be the bearer of bad news, *Mr* Stoker, but you are not sodding Samuel L Jackson in *Pulp Fiction* or Brad Pitt in *Once Upon a Time in Hollywood*. You're not working to a Tarantino script or lines from a Guy Ritchie movie. You're a wannabe. A small-time bully getting others to spread your grubby little messages because you think you're being super smart. Directing others to do your bidding. Whereas I think you're hiding in the dark with your trousers around your ankles pulling hard on whatever it is you keep in your, no doubt, black boxers. Too scared to do your own dirty work because you might get caught.

So if you want to play fucking games feel free. But where I come from if someone has something to say, they are brave enough to say it to your face. And they don't behave like a shitty little coward.'

Zia draws another breath. The sound can probably be heard back at Se Busca. Stoker's face doesn't change one iota. Which wasn't what I was expecting. He pushes his coffee to one side and stands up. He drops a five euro note on the table and walks away. Not a word uttered.

'Shit,' says Zia when Stoker has gone. 'Why didn't you just insult his grandmother while you were at it?'

'I have to admit,' I say, my heart racing, 'that his reaction wasn't quite what I was hoping for.'

'What were you hoping for? A punch in the face? A knife in the stomach? Or maybe you'd like him to burn down the pub and our house.'

'He'll not do that?'

'He will, all three and more. I already told you. He's not to be messed with. This isn't a game.'

'No, Zia, it's not. And even if it was, I'm no expert in it. I get that. I'm just someone who is being royally screwed from all sides and trying to figure out how to stop it.'

'And you think that poking Stoker will help.'

'If he is behind all this, do you think me calling him a few names is going to make much difference? Anyway, in my mind he's in the frame for Pat's death.'

'Why?'

'Because Stoker has a host of reasons and it's all upside and no downside for him if Pat is dead.'

'He said he was out of town.'

'And you believe that? I'd be out of town if I knew that Pat was entering his last days. What better alibi than not being here? But that doesn't mean he's not involved. He's got slaves to spare, it seems. The likes of Robertson and Cauliflower Ears or the thieves at the fiesta. And I'd bet money he was behind the raid on the pub and the blood in Mum's flat.'

'And, knowing all that, you still felt like winding him up?'

'I need to do something.'

'And what if you have it all wrong?'

'Do I? Is that what you think?'

'Daniella, I have no idea what to think other than the crap just seems to keep coming at the moment. And poking Stoker with a shitty stick doesn't seem to make much sense to me.'

'Zia, are you trying to defend him?'

'No. I'm just pointing out what you don't want to see.'

'What? And if you tell me he's one scary son of a bitch I'll scream.'

A voice cuts through our conversation.

'Señorita Coulstoun, how may I help you?'

The Capitán approaches our table. Zia does a double take before looking at me. 'Daniella, did you call him?'

'Hi, Capitán,' I say, blanking Zia. 'Thank you for coming so quickly.'

I hope he didn't hear what Zia and I were just talking about. For a moment I'd forgotten I'd called him when I was in the toilet.

'It is no problem,' the Capitán, says. 'I was looking for you anyway, Señorita Coulstoun. I tried your premises but you were not there. But I'm also here because you said that you had been attacked.'

'Please sit down, Capitán. Zia, can you get the Capitán a coffee?'

Zia obliges and while Lenny reluctantly coaxes coffee from the machine, one wary eye on the Capitán, I relay what had gone down with Malky Robertson and his sidekick. I omit the bit where I was told to get out of town, and lay on the attempted murder thick.

As I finish I say, 'I can take you down to our car and show you the damage. I'm fairly sure there will be bits of vehicles on the road where they tried to ram us off the cliff.'

'This is a serious allegation, Señorita Coulstoun. You say that one of the men is this Malky Robertson but you do not know the other?'

'No, but I have seen him around.'

'And what was the reason for this attack?'

'I've no idea. I don't even know how they found Zia and me up here, but they were clearly here, to see us.'

I glance at Lenny but his head is so buried in the phone that his nose is almost through the glass.

'And you also think they were involved in the raid on your bar?' the Capitán asks.

'I don't know for sure but when I accused them they acted as guilty as hell.'

'And why would you accuse them in the first place?'

'Call it a hunch. But I'll tell you this, the wee man took it badly.'

'Wee man?'

'The small man with Malky.'

'And you say he was the driver?'

'Yes.'

Zia plonks down the Capitán's coffee and sits next to me.

'And why were you looking for me otherwise?' I ask the Capitán.

'I have the documents necessary to search your mother's apartment. Did you talk to your lawyer?'

'No. Not yet.'

I reach into my bag and pull out the keys. 'Be my guest.'

He takes them.

'You do not want to see the paperwork?' he asks.

'No. I'm sure it's all in order.'

He drinks some coffee and is content enough to kick back a little in the chair.

'Was that Señor Carl Stoker I saw when I arrived?' he says.

'You know him?'

'I know of him. Were you talking to him?'

'When we came out of the woods he was here.'

'So you do know him?'

'No. But like you, I know of him.'

'But you did not answer my question. Were you talking to him?'

'Yes.'

'What about?'

I'm fairly sure that we weren't overheard.

'He has an interest in me running a thing called the El Descaro Classic.'

'The vintage car rally?'

'Yes. Mum used to set it up.'

'It is a big event for the town.'

'So everyone tells me.'

'And he came up here to talk to you about it?'

'I've no idea. As I said, we walked up through the woods after abandoning the car and he was here.'

'And did you talk about anything else?'

'I asked if he knew this guy Malky and his sidekick.'

'And did he?'

'He denied it.'

'And why would you ask him that?'

'I hear that Mr Stoker is a *not-a-nice* person. Since a *not-nice-thing* had just happened to us – and lo and behold Mr Stoker was here – I put two and two together and maybe I got five.'

'And what did he say to this accusation?'

'Not a lot. He walked off.'

The Capitán takes his phone from his pocket and dials.

'*Tengo las llaves del apartamento de la madre de la Señorita Coulstoun. Te veo allí en media hora.*'

He finishes the coffee. 'Señor MacFarlane, can you take me to where your car is?'

'Sure,' Zia replies.

As we leave, Lenny has a face like a pig on downers. Not happy, and I don't think it's to do with my earlier accusations. Having Stoker on site would have been bad enough if Stoker really does have his claws into him, but having a senior capitán of the Guardia Civil here will rattle every cage he has. I throw him a small smile as we leave, and his eyes avoid me.

We get into the Capitán's car. A Fiat 500 loaded with discarded food wrappers and soft drink cans. I sit in the front; Zia squeezes into the back.

'I would have thought a time-served police officer would drive a slightly grander car,' I remark.

'Señorita Coulstoun, it gets me to where I need to go and is cheap to run. And around here it is hard to keep scrapes and scratches off your car. If I bash this a little, I do not care.'

We bump along the dirt track until we hit tarmac, and Zia guides the Capitán to the house where his car is hidden. We take a few wrong turns before we find it.

'Here,' says Zia. 'This is the house.'

The Capitán pulls the car over and we all get out. As soon as we walk up to the entrance I know there's something wrong. The gravel driveway had been pristine when we arrived earlier and, when we'd pulled in, Zia's car had ploughed a lone track. Only, now, there is a second track. I walk up the driveway and head for the side of the house.

There is no car.

'Our car is gone,' I say, turning to the Capitán.

'Gone?'

'It was here. Look you can see the tracks leading in and another set where someone has taken it back out.'

'Did you leave the keys in the car?'

'No,' replies Zia.

'A spare, maybe?'

'Back at the house. I'm not stupid enough to leave it in the car.'

'And you are sure the keys are at the house?'

We both say yes at the same time.

The Capitán walks into the space that was occupied by the car. 'And why would someone take your car, Señor MacFarlane?'

193

'That's a bloody good question, Capitán,' he says.

'The second track suggests to me that whoever took it drove it out and didn't tow it,' I observe.

I join the Capitán in the space where the car was. 'I'm telling you, Capitán, the car was here.'

I spot something glinting in the late afternoon light.

'Look,' I say, bending down.

I lift up a piece of opaque Perspex.

'See,' I say.

The Capitán takes the piece of plastic from me. He examines it. 'It could be from your car but it could also be from any car.'

'Why would we make up such a crazy story?' says Zia, edging towards the back of the house, as if hoping that somehow the car has slid around the rear.

'I hear many crazy stories, Señor MacFarlane. You'd be surprised what lies people tell me.'

'Well, I'm not telling any lies,' Zia states. 'My car was right here – not an hour ago. And someone has taken it.'

'Do you wish to report it stolen?' asks the Capitán.

'Of course I do, but aren't you a bit curious as to why someone would steal my car in the first place?'

The Capitán picks up a piece of gravel and turns it over in his hand. 'An opportunist thief, perhaps. Maybe the owner of the house had it moved?'

'Look at the house,' Zia says. 'It's locked up tight as a drum, and why would a sneak thief take a battered old Accord?'

The Capitán flicks the stone into the air. 'Because it was a battered old Accord and easy to get into. Or maybe there's another reason that, for the moment, escapes me. Or maybe there was no car here in the first place?' The Capitán moves. 'You said that Mr Robertson and his friend tried to push you off the road.'

'They did,' I say.

'Well, let us go and look at where this took place. Maybe that can throw some light on the mystery of this missing car.'

When you're a kid there's a tone of voice that you learn. The one that a parent uses when they know fine well you're lying. It has roots in sarcasm but is cleverer than that. Delivered with a flat, disbelieving repetition of the facts, it's designed by nature, or more likely by nurture, to put you on the back foot. The power of the adult over the child, the paternal and maternal over the brood. People in authority learn it as well. Their positions allowing them the luxury of refutation without the need to defend their inference. The Capitán's words are loaded with that tone.

'I'm not making this up,' Zia splutters, half an octave higher than normal and rising.

'I am not saying you are, Señor MacFarlane. All I am doing is looking at the facts. Certainly, there are two tracks in the gravel. Certainly, that could mean a car came and went, but it could be anyone's car and at any time in the past few weeks.'

'Why in the hell would we bother to bring you here if it wasn't Zia's car?' I say.

'I have no idea, Señorita Coulstoun. Absolutely no idea at all. I am only here because I need your keys for your mother's flat and you genuinely sounded distressed when you called me. A missing car is not a matter for the Guardia Civil.'

'But if someone is trying to kill us? That would be a Guardia Civil matter?'

'If that is the case then yes you are correct, I am the right person. So, let us go to the place where you claim you were rammed. I told my officer I would be with him in thirty minutes and I am now wondering if all of this is not just a convenient diversion to slow me down from searching your mother's old apartment, Señorita Coulstoun.'

I'm flabbergasted. 'Diversion? I called you. If I'd wanted a bloody diversion I'd have just pissed off.'

'Exactly, and where to? To somewhere like Leo Henri's maybe?'

My head is spinning.

'Zia, let's show the Capitán the road where we were rammed. There has to be plastic, glass, paint, tyre marks – something on the road.'

'My car,' pleads Zia.

'We've reported it to the police, have we not, Capitán?' I say.

'You have. Although a formal report will need to be made to the Policía Local. Now, can we go?'

He moves off to his car at a brisk pace. I have to pull Zia along by the hand to catch up with the Capitán.

We get back in the old Fiat and, after another wrong turn, we emerge onto the cliff-top road and find the spot where we were smashed into. There's no sign of the Land Cruiser. The Capitán pulls up against a garden wall and we all get out again.

'There,' I say, triumphantly, pointing at the road. 'Skid marks.'

Two black lines are scrawled from the centre of the road to the edge, stopping at the dirt border, just where we came to a halt after the first hit.

The Capitán, checking for traffic, crosses to the spot and looks down.

'Tyre tracks,' he admits. 'Although there would be no way of knowing what made them.'

'I told you,' I say. 'We were rammed.'

'And where is the debris?'

I look around for signs, as does Zia. There are some small flakes of paint and a few specks of plastic but nothing larger than a quarter of a cocktail stick. I walk up the hill to the point where we pushed past the four-by-four. Again, there are tiny fragments of plastic and paint on the ground, but nothing that says there was a major shunt here. I shuffle over to the cliff top and look down. I scan the scrub below.

'There,' I say. 'Down there. I can see plastic in the bushes.'

The Capitán joins me. 'I see it too. Plastic water bottles? Cellophane wrappers perhaps. It is a long way down.'

'It isn't either of those. The stuff is scattered all over the cliff. Someone has swept the debris off the edge.'

'And what do you want me to do? Abseil down and recover whatever is there?'

'You wanted proof.'

'I've had enough of this, Señorita Coulstoun. I am going down to meet my officers. I will do you the courtesy of giving you a lift while I consider what to do next.'

With this he checks for traffic once more before crossing the road, leaving Zia and I staring down at the cliff. I wonder if any of the debris got caught further up. There's a lip about ten feet down and there could be fragments hiding under that but what in the hell would that do for me? Who would be able, or willing, to examine it and declare it part of Zia's car? A car that, at the moment, we do not have.

The Capitán starts his Fiat up.

'I'm taking the lift,' I say to Zia. 'We have to secure the pub and get into our home.'

'But my car? The ramming?'

'I know, Zia, but standing here won't help. You heard what the Capitán said. He thinks we're making all of this up.'

I wave my hands in the direction of the Fiat and cross the road. Zia pauses, then, reluctantly, follows. We get back into the car and the Capitán moves off.

'Capitán Lozano,' I say, 'our story is true.'

'So you say, but with no car and no evidence of any crime I have more important things to attend to.'

And that kills the conversation all the way back to Mum's apartment, except when I ask to be dropped off at the pub. My request is met with silence and no deviation. We are emptied onto the street next to the entrance to Mum's place. Outside there are two police cars and a forensic van waiting.

'Should I wait?' I say to the Capitán.

'If you wish.'

'And if I don't wish?'

'Do not go far.'

He leaves.

I pull Zia to one side. 'Let's go to Se Busca. If we are quick we might just catch the locksmith and the chippie. Were they not due about six?'

'That's when they said.'

As soon as we are out of earshot I say, 'Do you think Stoker took your car and cleaned up the road?'

'I don't know.'

'More likely it was the two idiots that tried to kill us. Lozano thinks we are a pair of nutters.'

And when he finds the square of the missing square of carpet in Mum's apartment, things aren't going to get any better.

'What do we do about my car?' moans Zia.

'Zia, we report it, but we do that tomorrow. However, right now I want my pub secure and I want in my home. Then I want a bloody large drink and something a little less bogging than Lenny's crap wine.'

'This is no time to get drunk, Daniella.'

I speed up my walking, using the down slope to its best advantage.

'Zia, this is the perfect time to get drunk. Maybe in a drunken haze I'll be able to see clearer.'

But I know this is the wrong time to fall into a bottle. Much as the idea of oblivion appeals to me.

'They'll find the hole in the carpet,' says Zia.

'I bloody know that,' I reply.

'Then what?'

I stop, waiting for Zia to catch up.

'Do you know what?' I exclaim as he stops next to me. 'Do you know what?'

'What?'

'I don't know *what*. I have no bloody idea what *what* is or where *what* bloody is. I don't know if *what* even fucking exists. I am clueless on *what*. Absolutely clueless. My head is so fucked over with all this that I probably can't even spell *what* never mind work out what *what* it is. I'm *what-less*, Zia. Fucking *what-less*. I don't want to be. I really don't want to be but I bloody am. For all I know, the answer to all this shit lies in the bottom of a bag or maybe I can phone an astrology hotline and ask for advice. Or what about a psychic? What about trying to contact Mum? Eh, Zia, would that work? Would she know what to do? Would she?'

He stands, taking the onslaught. His head down. Feet shuffling.

'And I'm not bloody happy that you're lying to me, Zia.'

'What?'

'You heard me. Lying.'

'About what?'

'About where you were with George Laidlaw on the morning Pat was killed.'

'I told you we went up to Saucy's and he dropped me off.'

'At Saucy's?'

'Near his.'

'And you walked back.'

'Yes.'

'Okay, I saw you leave Se Busca with George at just after ten, correct?'

'About then.'

'And when did you get back?'

'I don't know. Eleven thirty. You were out. When did you leave?'

'I went up to get my hair done at eleven.'

'Half eleven is probably right then.'

'Really?'

He takes a small step back, his Adam's apple bobbing as he swallows dry. He knows something is wrong.

'You walked back from Saucy's to the town and then to the pub?' I say. 'Is that what you are telling me?'

'Yes.'

'Zia, why are you lying?'

'I'm not.'

'You bloody are. I saw George's car sitting near Mum's apartment – which is not two hundred yards from my hairdresser's. I saw it ten minutes before my hair appointment.'

'And?'

'And there were others in the car. I couldn't see who, but it looked full.'

'You would need to ask George about that.'

'Why?'

'Why not?'

'Because I'm asking you. Saucy lives five miles away, a mile and a half up a one-track road. It's the only road to his house, up or down. There is no way George Laidlaw could have dropped you off at Saucy's and you get get back in town for ten to eleven without a lift. And if you were dropped near Saucy's then George would have drive right past you on the way back. Right past you, Zia! If, that is, you were ever out at Saucy's, which I very much doubt.'

'You never mentioned seeing George's car before now.'

I have an urge to swat him round the head. A real slap to the skull. A wake-up slap.

'I never mentioned it because I was waiting for you to 'fess up. Because I thought you must have had a good reason not to tell me what really happened and, also, because deep down I have another fear.'

'Like what?'

'Zia, I said earlier we needed to talk. And this is talking. Not the laugh and tickle conversation we had earlier. This is exactly the sort of talk I want. This is the moment you say, *Hey, Daniella I've got a little story for you. A little confession. Nothing major. Nothing to worry about. Just a wee thing that I should have mentioned.* Like normal couples do, if there is any such thing as normal in this world. *Daniella, I know you asked earlier about where I was the day Pat died, and I kind of dodged the question a wee bit, and maybe I said I was at Saucy's but that wasn't quite true. No biggie, Daniella. Just a little lie because I didn't want you to worry about stuff you didn't have to.* That's what I'm waiting on, Zia.'

If Zia feels now is the time to jump in and unburden himself, he's showing none of the usual signs. He can be a man-child at times. Desperate for approval, the pop star in him wanting appreciation and admiration. Always hunting for that reaffirmation of his actions. And that makes him quick to confession. Normally. But not today. He has moved away from me a few feet. Subconsciously or consciously looking for some safety in distance. A sign that all is not well in the house of Zia.

'Zia, what the hell is up? You've been skitty and off colour since they found Pat. I get that that wasn't a nice thing but there is something else. What?'

He looks smaller, standing on the edge of the pavement, hands crossed in front of him, head bowed, as if in prayer. Praying for some intervention to stop my questioning.

'Come on, Zia, out with it. What is it that you need to tell me?'

'I can't.'

'Can't what?'

'Can't tell you.'

'Can't tell me what?'

'I promised.'

'Promised who? Promised what?'

He doesn't reply, preferring to swing his clenched hands back and forth across his body. A pendulum counting off the seconds.

'You know you can't leave it there, Zia,' I say. 'Do you think I'm going to let this go? You may as well tell me whatever it is you're hiding.'

His eyes scan the pavement.

'It's all so out of hand now,' he whispers. 'I didn't know what to do. George took control. He convinced us all that it was better this way. To say nothing.'

I'm not sure that he knows he's leaking information without realising it. Small bits dribbling out as he tries to justify keeping me out of the loop.

'So, George made you promise to say nothing about whatever this is?'

'I said we should have told you,' he whines. 'I said it didn't make sense and, as things have gone on, it makes even less sense. But George kept saying that we didn't need to let you know. That things would work out. But they're not working out. They are getting worse.'

He's now dancing from foot to foot. Agitated. I've never seen him like this. Nervous, yes, but not so on edge.

'Zia, I need you to talk. I need you to talk right now. Whatever it is you have to say, we are strong enough to take it.'

I'm not sure that's true, and the way he reacts to that statement, swinging his arms at a quicker pace, suggests he's not sure either.

'Zia please just let me know what it is that George told you to keep quiet.'

'It all seems so wrong,' he replies. 'Even at the time it seemed like the wrong thing to do. You have to believe me, Daniella. But George was insistent it was only until we figured stuff out. And then that stupid raid took place by DB's and that changed everything. George wouldn't shift. Even then. He rolled out that dumb story to the Capitán about how the afternoon seemed so normal.'

'So George lied to the Capitán about the events in the pub the afternoon of the raid?'

'Daniella, it . . . I . . . Can we—'

'For crying out loud, Zia, just bloody tell me what happened.'

His arms stop swinging and he raises his head, looking me in the eyes. His shoulders are high, tense.

'Okay,' he whispers. 'And believe me, Daniella, I only kept quiet because George said it was best.'

'Okay. Get past that. Just tell me whatever it is you need to tell me. I'm not mad at you about George.'

I bloody am.

'Well, when George gave me a lift we did go to Saucy's that morning. But only to pick him up. We stopped on the way back to pick Skid up as well. When you saw the car there were four of us in it. I didn't know you had seen us. I'd forgotten you were going to that particular hairdresser's, or I'd have told George to pick up Skid elsewhere.'

'And you all went to Se Busca?'

'Yes. And the Twins.'

'Why?'

'To talk.'

'About?'

'Exactly what you wanted me to talk to George about. The pub. The future.'

'And did George call this meet or did you?'

'He did. He wanted to know where we all stood if he stepped in and took action to grab the pub.'

'Action like what? To kick me out?'

His hands link up and his arms start swinging again.

'That's why I wanted to attend the meet,' he says. 'The others had met a few times before without me. But after our chat I wanted to make it clear that I wasn't going to be a party to any attempt to remove you. So I insisted I was at the next meeting.'

'And you told George where you stood?'

'No.'

'Why not?'

'Because when we got back to the pub we never got the opportunity to talk about you or the pub.'

'What did you talk about?'

'George will kill me if I say.'

'Come on Zia, just tell me.'

'We . . .'

He stops.

'We,' he says again, 'we spent the rest of the morning talking about Pat.'

'Pat? What about Pat?'

He waits until a van, rumbling up the hill, grinds past us both. His arms stop swinging again and he double flexes his fingers on both hands.

'When we all got to the pub things changed,' he says.

'What changed?'

'Pat was there.'

'And what did he want? What did he say?'

'He didn't say anything.'

'Why?'

We wait on another vehicle to slide by.

'Why, Zia?' I say again, once the car is gone. 'What do you mean, he said nothing?'

Zia tilts his head to one side and drops his arms to his side. 'Pat couldn't say anything, Daniella, because Pat was dead.'

18

Antonio

'Dead?' I exclaim.

The word rattles off the surrounding buildings. A bullet ricocheting. Looking for a place to settle but unable to do so.

'What do you mean dead, Zia?'

'In the cellar. When we all met at Se Busca that morning. He was in the cellar. Dead.'

'No, Zia. He was brought in by the DB's guys when they broke in later that night.'

'That's not true. When we all arrived at the pub when you were up at the hairdressers, Jordan was given the job of getting us all drinks. We sat down near the pool table and Jordan shouted over that we were out of coffee. I told him there were more packets in the cellar, and the next thing I hear is Jordan yelling. We all shouted out, asking him what was wrong, but he just kept yelling. We hadn't a clue why, so George got up and went into the cellar to see what was wrong. Then George came back through and told us all to come over. So we did.'

Zia takes another involuntary step away from me.

'And?'

'And,' he says, 'there was Pat, lying on the cellar floor.'

'Dead?'

'Dead.'

'He was there that morning,' I gasp. 'That means he lay in the cellar all day?'

'Yes.'

'And no one said anything? Everyone knew there was a dead body in the cellar and no one did or said anything?'

It's hard to hide the incredulity in my voice and I fail completely.

'I know how it sounds but it wasn't my idea,' he pleads.

'Who exactly was there at the time?'

'George, Saucy, Jordan, Sheryl, Skid and myself.'

'What about Clyde?'

'He didn't arrive till later.'

'And what did he say when he saw the body?'

'Nothing,' Zia says. 'Pat was well hidden behind all the kegs. Clyde never saw the body until after the raid.'

'George said he saw Pat's foot sticking out after the raid finished. Clyde would have seen that at some point.'

'George moved Pat when he went in to check on Busca, pulled him out a bit.'

'Why?'

'To make it look like DB's had left him? Clyde had been in and out all day and never saw him. If Pat had really been where he was when the police arrived, Clyde would've seen him at some point. But since he didn't . . .'

'. . . it made it look like DB's left Pat there.' I finish for him.

He nods.

'Zia, it sounds zipped-up insane. You left Pat, dead as a dodo, lying in our cellar for an entire day and said and did absolutely nothing. Why in the hell didn't you call the police?'

'We couldn't.'

'Why not?'

'I can't do this here,' he blurts. 'I really can't. Can we do the rest of this back in the house? I'm just not comfortable talking about it out here.'

'What difference does it make where we do this? Is there much more?'

I shake my head as I say this. Of course there is. I mean how can you leave a dead body lying in a cellar while the clientele sip lager and watch the goggle box? How can you sit in a pub knowing there is a corpse decomposing in the cellar, and chew the cud? I mean *how? How?*

'Yes,' he replies. 'There is more.'

'Then talk as we walk.'

'I'd rather talk in the house.'

We are less than fifteen minute's walk from the pub and our place – so I reluctantly agree as Zia is for saying no more right now.

Neither of us says a word as we walk. My head is, if possible, more of a mess than it was after discovering that Zia's car had been removed and the crash scene cleaned up. Zia, walking slightly behind me, is lost in thought. I look back and his eyes are fixed on some random spot in the distance. He trips on a crack in the pavement through lack of attention.

A lone cyclist, up out of the saddle, swaying from side to side as she pushes hard on each pedal, grinds her way up the hill towards us. Dressed in black Lycra, black tights and wearing black cycling shoes she could be Stoker's sister. Her head is bowed, eyes focused on a tiny sliver of ground just in front of the bike's front wheel. With each downward press of the pedals she exhales, a noisy whoosh of air as it's forced up her throat. The hill is at its steepest here. No big deal if you're in a car or walking but for a cyclist the slope bites hard.

As the rider draws level I catch a glimpse of her face, a gnarled, sun-wrinkled phizog that speaks to many hours of riding without sufficient protection from the Mediterranean sun. Her eyes are hidden by stylish sunglasses filled with bright blue lenses that reflect the streetlight in a wash of dancing patterns. A car crawls up behind her, and she is forced to ride over a drain as the car passes. The bike wobbles and her lips almost vanish with the effort of staying upright, thighs straining as the bike veers towards the kerb. For a couple of heartbeats, she looks like she's about to go down. Then she catches the fall, keeps the bike upright and, with an extra loud hiss of breath, she toils on.

'Zia, does what happened with Pat involve Stoker?'

He says nothing.

'Does it?'

He still doesn't reply and that's as good a reply as I need.

'Is that why you keep warning me off him? Did he kill Pat?'

Still *nada*.

'Zia, you need to talk.'

He stops and looks away.

Screw this.

'Okay, Zia,' I shout, 'I've changed my bloody mind.'

He exits the vow of silence, 'About what?'

'I want to know what else happened in the pub. And I want to know now.'

'I can't. I've said too much already. George will kill me.'

'Who cares about George? I've had enough of the lies. Enough. Talk. And talk right now.'

'I can't, Daniella, I really can't. Please don't ask.'

'Don't ask? You just told me that Pat Ratte lay in our pub, dead, all day and you say don't ask.'

'I'm . . .'

He begins to walk away.

'Where are you going?'

'The pub.'

'Tell me one thing, Zia. Was Stoker involved in Pat's death?'

'I can't say.'

'Well that settles it. I'm not going back to the pub.'

'What are you going to do?'

'I'm going to find that bastard Stoker.'

He stops walking. 'Don't be so stupid. You can't.'

'Why not? You're not going to tell me what happened to Pat. Are you?'

It was the woman on the bike that had altered my thinking, her sheer effort at staying upright reflecting on my situation. The drain she hit was an obstacle to be overcome just like I need to overcome Stoker. Just like I need to stop this crap. Unexpected, unavoidable, and there, right in front of me. No way round. Either ride over or fall off. And that's what I need to do with Stoker. Somehow find a way to roll right over him. He's used to people running scared and he's even more used to getting his own way. And I can't allow that. Not in my case.

'I know Stoker's a bastard, Zia, but he's not going to stop, is he? And you're not going to tell me any more about Pat. Are you?'

'No,' he whispers. 'I can't. I really can't.'

'So that doesn't leave me much choice, does it? I need to find a way out of all of this, and Stoker is the key. Knobble him, and I stand a chance. Let him throw us to the lions, and I'm screwed.'

'And you're going to find him now. *Right now?*'

'I am. I have to. If he was involved in Pat's death and you won't talk, then I need to fix it. Stoker is in every bit of this thing and he needs sorted, and sorted before I end up in jail. You've just thrown the bloody straw on that sodding camel's back. 'But,' I continue, 'when I get back I want it all. The A to Z of Pat's death and what happened after. But now all I want you to do is to go to the pub. Get the place secure. Get our door locks changed and new ones put in. I don't care how much it costs. I want both the pub door and our door a model of paranoid security.'

'I can't let you go and see Stoker on your own.'

'Why? Because he killed Pat?'

'I just can't—'

'You can and you will. I'm not stupid. I simply need to find a way to put him on the back foot and I can't do that by just waiting for him to pull his next bloody stunt.'

'What are you going to do?'

'I don't know. Where does he live? Where does he hang out?'

'It's too dangerous.'

'Where?'

'I'm not telling you.'

'Where is he?'

'You shouldn't go.'

He starts to walk away, backwards.

'Why not, Zia? I'll find out where he lives. That idiot Malky Robertson and his sidekick will know. As I'm sure will a slew of people at DB's if I go and ask.'

'Daniella, you don't want to do that. Please. If you start asking questions in DB's, Stoker will hear and Stoker doesn't like people prying into his affairs.'

'Why are you so keen for me to avoid him? Is he threatening you?'

Nothing.

'Look, Zia, I don't like someone fucking up my life.'

'You're really going to do this?'

'Yes.'

'Then I'm coming with you.'

I rush forward and grab his hand, pulling him in close. 'No, Zia, you're not, and before you start some macho *me-Tarzan-you-Jane* crap I'll tell you why. On my own I'm a lot fleeter of foot. Sneaking around in pairs is hard. Also, I'm not intending to meet him. I just need to get some gen. Something I might be able to use. But there is another reason.'

'What?'

'I can't trust you. Not after today. You know more than you are saying and won't talk.'

'I just can't.'

'Stop fucking saying the word can't. We are so done here, Zia MacFarlane. I've no more desire to cross Stoker than you do. I'm not

210

underestimating him but Stoker will keep finding ways to throw me under his bus. He's determined and resourceful. He moved the car and cleared the crash scene in less than an hour. He had Robertson break into our house and probably into Mum's place. He planted the pub keys on Pat, wrote that stupid note that Pat had *and* happily drained Pat of blood and dumped it on the carpet. And then, casually, dismissed all of it when we talked to him up at Lenny's.'

'You don't know he did all that.'

'I fucking do. Or is there some secret figure lurking in the woods? A Machiavellian stranger putting me through the wringer? Tell me differently.'

He pulls his hand from mine. Head down. He says nothing.

'Okay,' I say. 'If you won't talk, I'm assuming Stoker is behind all of this, and letting him have free rein isn't working out well for either of us. I'm going to see what's what and you are going to the pub. I need to go now. I have a feeling that Stoker has planted some other sodding surprise in Mum's place for Lozano to find. I've been saying it for a while now but I really do need to get out in front of all of this, and I can't do that while Stoker roams free.'

'I don't—'

'What, Zia? You don't like it? I get that but it's the way it's going to be. Unless whatever you have still to say on Pat's death makes me change my mind.'

He must know I'm playing a game to get him to talk but, whatever it is he knows, even the threat of me going rogue and hunting down Stoker isn't shifting him.

'Daniella, you don't understand.'

'Zia, I think I understand only too well. Go fix the house and the pub.'

I give him one more minute to talk. He says nothing.

It hurts to turn away from him. Deep down hurts. My actions are impulsive. I know that. And if I stop and think on this I could find another way to deal with it all. But Stoker needs addressing and Zia staying schtum has pushed me into action.

Zia shouts after me as I walk. 'He has membership at the Muir-end Club out past Cala Negra. You'll need a taxi, it's a fair walk.'

He doesn't wait for me to reply before he walks off. Which just deepens my disquiet.

I stand for a second and then move away. The nearest taxi rank is down by the port. I remember my mobile is switched off and turn it on. A few messages appear. Nothing urgent. I decide not to call a taxi; I want the walk to straighten out my head. Something that I seem to be doing far too frequently of late. I consider turning around and catching up with Zia. I won't. Can't. I've chucked those dice on the floor, hard. I'm not sure what I'm looking for when I find Stoker. All I know is that I'm going to find him. I just need something. Some info. Some insight. Anything that can give me a little leverage. And Zia can go fly for all I care at the moment.

My mobile rings ten minutes later.

'Where are you?' asks George without even saying hello.

'Out for a walk.'

'I need you to get back to the pub right away.'

'Why?'

'Zia has just walked in.'

'I know. I left him a few minutes ago. He's there to see that the doors in the pub and the flat get fixed.'

'And you two have been talking.'

'Fantastic observation, George. It's what human beings do on a regular basis. It's called conversation. You know, like we are having now.'

'This isn't a time to be flip.'

'Who's being flip? I'm not your bloody lackey, George Laidlaw. You may not think I'm your boss but you sure as hell aren't the boss either.'

'Who said anything about bosses?'

'You did. When you were relaying that fantasy tale to the Capitán about how the day of Pat's death panned out. You told him that I wasn't your boss. Well, from where I stand, someone has to be the boss. Because, from what I hear from Zia, this is a bloody mess and a half.'

Silence.

'George?'

Nothing.

'George.'

He's gone. I pull up his number and dial him back. It trips to answer machine. I try again with the same result.

My mouth was ahead of my brain there. Needing to stick the needle in for no good reason.

I let the thoughts about Zia and George go for a second and try to work out what I'm going to do next. I've never been to the Muirend Club, although I've heard of it. A private member's affair that allows people to join through a secret ballot. At one time it had a sister club in Glasgow but that building burned down in a fire years back and never reopened. I'm uncertain as to how many members the Muirend Club has. Notionally, it is open to all, but from what I know, most, if not all the members, are British expats and male. It's owned by a Liverpudlian called Ray something.

I reach the taxi rank and get in the first car. '*Vamos a Cala Negra, por favor.*'

I can't risk going straight to the club. I wouldn't be allowed in and I've no idea if Stoker will be there. It's also out in the boondocks. If the taxi dropped me there I'd stand out like a lemon in a bowl of strawberries. There's a small strip of bars and cafés that lies about a half mile from where the club is. On the strip there's a café run by a local I know. His name is Antonio and he's the third-generation owner. He's also a bit of a gossip. He'll know someone in the club who can tell me if Stoker is in attendance and, if Stoker isn't, Antonio'll probably know someone who will be able to tell me where his house is. He also might be able to give me some heads-up on the man. Of course, such information will come at a price. Antonio might be one for the grapevine but if you want to tap it he likes to have his palm well greased. I'll need to be prepared, so while the taxi takes me to Cala Negra I make a call, and after five moments of negotiation ask for confirmation of our agreement by email. A few minutes later there's a ping on my phone and I check the confirmation is as agreed. I'm not sure if it will be enough. It will all depend on Antonio's mood.

The light is fading outside and in this neck of the woods twilight is a short-lived entity. God has a light switch this far south, not a dimmer. I study the email confirmation again and wonder if I'm sliding inevitably into becoming my mum. A year ago the most outrageous thing I would have considered doing was wearing a skirt too short for company regulations. Now I'm on my way to scope out a violent criminal while happily arranging to bribe someone into helping me find him.

All too soon the taxi driver parks out front of Antonio's café. Lights shine down on a small clutch of aluminium chairs and tables. Two are occupied, one by a couple chatting over drinks, the other by an older man chowing down on a plate of *albóndigas*. Through the café's plate-glass window I can see another half a dozen people inside. Antonio is talking to a wild-haired woman. I pay the fare and get out, pausing on the pavement for a few moments, looking up and down the row of businesses. The crowd is thin. A few well-wrapped souls out for an early evening stroll. We are still quite a few degrees below that required to deliver the hordes that are the lifeblood of the cafés and restaurants. A chill wind has blown up along the coast, and I realise that Antonio's outside patrons are hardy souls. All three have café-supplied blankets draped across their knees and above them red bar heaters glow. I take one last look around and step into the café.

Brightly lit, the interior is a clinical mix of doctor's waiting room and hospital cafeteria. Neon-white strip lighting banishes shadows completely and every table is topped off with disinfected surgical white plastic. The bar is lined with the familiar glass-domed structure that protects a range of tapas. Antonio's wife, the wild-haired woman, is called Carmen and is at the range, cooking. When Antonio spots me he stops talking to her and waves. The seats at the rear of the café are free and I pick one in the corner, as far away as I can get from prying ears. Antonio comes over.

'Daniella, where have you been hiding?'

His accent is wafer thin and if you didn't know his origins you would struggle to nail him as Spanish.

'Working, Antonio. Just working,' I reply.

'Ah, the curse of the food and drink trade. All the hours that God gives you and a few more that he doesn't know about.'

Antonio is a stick-thin individual who looks on the verge of anorexia. All bones and sinew, he was once a long-distance runner. I say once. He still is, but in the past he has knocked on the door of running for his country. Now he just endures the pain for fun. He has an ever-present face fuzz and a ponytail that is permanently tied back. I think he looks a little like Frances Rossi from Status Quo.

'Antonio, do you have a moment?'

'For you, Daniella, always. But let me serve my customers first.'

I've not known Antonio that long. Maybe three months. Zia had introduced Antonio to me, and we'd hit it off. When we have the time Zia and I eat here, and we've been to Antonio and Carmen's house, and they to ours, a couple of times for meals.

Antonio busses the tables, dropping off food and drink while simultaneously clearing plates and glasses. A few minutes later he slumps into the chair across from me and hands me a glass of *vino blanco*. I smile and take the drink. He is a very good host.

'What can I do you for?' he says, rubbing at an invisible spot of dirt on the table with his ever-present cloth.

'It's a bit of an ask, Antonio, but I'm looking for some info on someone.'

'Who?'

I lean in. 'A man called Carl Stoker.'

Antonio lets out a small whistle. 'Daniella, I wouldn't be asking after Mr Stoker if I was you. People have been hurt for less.'

'Let's park that chat, Antonio. I know of his reputation but I have good reason to ask. I think he hangs out at the Muirend Club.'

'He does,' Antonio replies, and can't help but look over his shoulder to check if anyone is listening. His face has a rolling wave of nervousness crossing it. 'What is it you want to know?'

'Where is he right now?'

'Why would I know? What do you want with him?'

'It's better if you don't know.'

'Daniella, this is a bad idea.'

'Antonio, everyone seems to tell me the same thing.'

He scrubs at another point on the table, avoiding my eyes. 'And does that not tell you something?'

'It does, and I still want to find out where he is.'

'I can't help.'

'Yes, you can.'

'I can't.'

Another *can't* person.

'Please, Antonio. It's important. I just need to know where he is.'

He looks at me and sighs. 'Okay, but you will need to excuse me for a moment, Daniella.'

With that he disappears into the rear.

I'm left to sip at my wine. He remerges, a full fifteen minutes later, just when I was thinking he's done a runner. He looks even more nervous than before.

'I think it would be better if you left.'

'Look,' I say. 'I know that Stoker isn't someone you want to be messing with, but I just need to know where he is. I'm not asking you to do this for free. I've a little gift for you.'

I reach into my pocket, pull out my phone and hit the *on* button.

'You should go,' he says as I fiddle with the phone. 'Please, go now.'

'Hang on,' I say.

I find the confirmation email from earlier and push the phone over to him. He glances down at it. His eyes light up a little, then fade.

About five miles from here lies a whale of a building, a shambles of a place that sits beneath a giant neon sign that flashes through the night. Set just off the main coastal road it's called Desnudo Desnuda. At any time of the day you can find a range of cars and trucks parked up outside. Inside you will find a chocolate-box assortment of people, men and women, in various stages of undress. Antonio likes the private dance booths. But Carmen monitors Antonio's spending money like a hawk. He rarely has more than twenty euros on him, and his credit and debit cards are controlled by Carmen. The confirmation I have on my phone gives him a hundred and fifty euros credit at Desnudo Desnuda. If I feel any guilt at my bribe it's mitigated to a major extent by the simple fact that I know Carmen attends a similar establishment a few miles in the other direction. I'm also fairly sure that they both know what the other is up to – what's good for the goose and all that. Although, as Zia tells it, Antonio likes the boys and Carmen likes the girls. Each to their own.

'Antonio, what in the hell is up? Did I do wrong with this?' I say, pointing to the phone. Carmen is now looking at the two of us. She can tell something is wrong but is holding back from interfering for the moment.

'I'm sorry, Antonio,' I say pulling the phone away. 'I thought I was just rewarding you for a little info.'

'No, Daniella it's just that—'

A voice comes from behind me. 'It's just that he was wondering why you had chosen to come all the way over here when your own establishment needs your attention.'

The voice sends ice water streaming through my veins. I spin around and Carl Stoker, the man in black, is standing in the doorway. He is sporting a shit-eating grin that would scare a blind man. There are three customers left in the café. Two get up to leave as soon as they see Stoker enter. The remaining man stops mid bite and watches Stoker stroll across the space between the door and my table.

'I'm sorry, Daniella,' says Antonio.

'Quite the little spy in my camp you have, Antonio,' says Stoker sitting down across from me. 'Héctor is the little chatterbox.' He taps me on the back of the hand. 'Héctor,' he explains, 'is Antonio's cousin. He's been working at my club for a good year now. Good worker but a little too loud when he talks on the phone. Antonio, can you get me one of your excellent *cafés con leche* please?'

Antonio's face is creased with fear. 'Daniella, I really am sorry.' His skin colour is bleached white as his blood runs for cover. He moves away.

'I understand that you are looking for me, Daniella,' Stoker says.

Stoker has ditched the black roll-neck jumper he had on earlier for a black, long-sleeved shirt and a black tie.

'I wasn't looking for you,' I say.

'You weren't? Then why ask poor Antonio here where I was?'

'I didn't. Antonio got the wrong end of the stick. I was telling him about our meeting earlier and said that I didn't know where you usually hung out.'

'And he called his nephew to answer that question?'

'My fault, not his. He was just trying to help. He said you were a member at the club and, before I could stop him, he zipped off. He must have thought I wanted to know.'

The excuse is as weak as watered-down paint.

'He's a good soul,' I say. 'But we've not known each other long and I tend to ramble on and he misread me.'

'Really?'

'Really.'

'So you are not looking for me?'

'No. But I am a little curious after our meeting.'

'That would be the meeting where you called me a shitty little coward.'

I can almost hear Zia taking another deep breath all the way back at Se Busca. My pulse ticks up as Stoker pulls the Tony Soprano face again.

'Well, Daniella. This shitty little coward doesn't take well to people sticking their noses into his business.'

'And, Mr Stoker, this girl doesn't take well to that either. But let's not dance around that handbag again. Why don't we cut to the chase? I'm sure that there's a drink waiting on you up at the Muirend Club. We wouldn't want it getting warm.'

'I'm sure that my club will serve me a fresh one. After all, I own the place.'

'You own it? I thought some guy called Ray owned it.'

'Ray Doyle. He did until a short while ago but he sold it to me.'

I wonder how much cash Ray got. Or if a healthy set of hands was all the persuasion he needed to sign it over.

'That's nice,' I say.

'It is, actually.'

Antonio brings the coffee over and his hand is shaking so much that he spills the froth into the saucer.

'Thank you, Antonio,' says Stoker. 'When I'm finished here I'd like a word.'

If there is a paler shade of white left on the colour palate, Antonio's face finds it.

'Certainly, Mr Stoker,' he mutters.

I reach over and pull Stoker's coffee towards me, lift the cup and take a sip. 'Nice coffee, Antonio.'

Antonio nearly chokes at my action. Stoker's face doesn't flinch. A hard, hard man to get a rise out of.

'I'll have another,' Stoker says to Antonio.

Antonio slinks away.

'Daniella,' Stoker says. 'You like trying to boil my blood a little.'

'I told you earlier, I don't like bullies,' I say, my mouth dry despite the coffee. I'm flying on fumes here.

'Has Capitán Lozano been in touch since he searched your mother's old apartment?'

I wonder how he knows about that and then realise that this man knows a lot about every bloody thing around here.

'No. Why? Should he have been?'

'Well, you never know what people leave lying around their property.'

I slam my hand on the table. 'Oh, for fuck's sake,' I say. 'For fuck, fuck's sake. For fuck, fuck, fuck's sake. For more fucks than I've ever said in my life's sake.'

The last customer gets up, drops cash on the table and leaves in a hurry. It's now Stoker, Antonio, Carmen and me.

'Antonio,' Stoker says. 'Why don't you and your lovely wife go for a little walk? Grab some fresh air.'

Antonio looks at me and I nod. 'Go on, Antonio, this has nothing to do with you.'

'But don't go far, Antonio,' Stoker adds. 'I still want to have a few words with you.'

Neither Carmen nor Antonio moves.

Stoker sighs. 'Okay, Antonio. Either take a stroll along the front or I'll have a few words with Héctor instead.'

'Antonio,' I say. 'Please go. I'll be fine.'

With the threat to his nephew in plain sight, Carmen and Antonio both lift their coats and reluctantly leave.

'Is this the bit where you cut off my fingers?' I say. 'Or do you peel back my eyelids and drop salt in them? Do you know that George Laidlaw once threatened to have thirty-one of my bones broken? When I asked why thirty-one he said he just liked the number.'

'Daniella, you think you're a smart little witch, don't you?'

The voice has taken on that deeply threatening tone.

'No, I don't,' I reply, my heart racing. 'I just want to stop all this idiocy. I had nothing to do with Pat Ratte's death. Nothing at all, and you know that.'

'True.'

'Yet you are trying to hang it on me.'

'Am I?'

'Of course you are.'

'And why would I do that?'

'To get your hands on Se Busca now that Pat is gone.'

'You think this is all about your little hovel in the woods?'

'Isn't it?'

He reaches into his trouser pocket and my heartbeat finds a new level but all he extracts is his mobile.

'Daniella, I don't give a rat's tit about your pub. But did it ever occur to you that I might be doing you a favour?'

'A favour,' I exclaim. 'What kind of fucking favour could you possibly be doing me?'

'What about keeping your loved one from spending the rest of his life in prison?'

He fiddles with his mobile and pushes it across the table. I look down and what saliva I have left in my mouth vanishes. I pick up the phone and stare at the photo on the screen. I gasp.

'You see, Daniella,' he says, 'I'm not the bad guy around here.'

The photo is taken in the cellar of Se Busca. There are six people in it. Each is dressed in a white overall, hoods dangling behind. The sort of white suits that the forensic guys were wearing when they went digging around in my flat. The same suits that I saw at the pub on the morning after Pat died and the same suits that were waiting outside my mum's old flat when the Capitán dropped me off earlier.

But *these* people are no Spanish forensic officers.

The six in the photo are clustered together in a line. Arms linked, their expressions fixed, ghoulish grins on their faces. From left to right we have Saucy, the Twins, George, Skid, and at the end, Zia. Zia is holding something. A knife. The fancy carving knife that he bought a few months back on the Internet at a ridiculous price. It has a ribbed metal handle with a razor-sharp serrated blade that he was convinced would improve his culinary skills. Three hundred euros. He is holding it out in front of him. Its reflective blade dulled at one end by a deep stain.

My breathing has ceased.

Beneath all six, lying on the floor, stretched out like some animal trophy on an African safari is a body. The body's feet lie at Saucy's toes and the head rests at the knife-wielding feet of Zia.

The body's head is turned towards the camera. Set in a grimace. Eyes open but unseeing.

I stare at the face.

Pat Ratte lies beneath the Ex-Patriots.

Tyvek suits, knife, body – one for the murder album.

The six Ex-Pats smiling for the camera.

Six wounds, the Capitán had said.

That's what had killed Pat.

Six of them.

Six wounds.

19

Fourteen Eyes

Stoker is talking but he may as well be speaking in ancient Martian. I'm lost in the photograph. My eyes transfixed on the moment in time. Transfixed on Zia and the knife. He has it grasped by the handle, pointing it up, the tip of the blood-covered blade level with his eyes. His face, so familiar, yet now so alien, is partly obscured by the blade but not enough to hide his smile. Not one of joy or pleasure. More forced. The sort of smile that you put on when asked. *Pose for the camera guys.* Twelve eyes staring straight ahead. All are saying the same thing. Pat is dead and we are happy about it. Pat is dead and we did it.

'So?'

Stoker's word cuts through the fug that's clouding my brain.

The timer on the phone kicks in and the photo vanishes. I gaze at the blank screen. Stoker reaches out and takes the phone from my hand.

'What say you that I pass this along to the good Capitán, Daniella?'

I look up. Head swimming, wondering if the photo is real. That Zia and the rest of the Ex-Patriots killed Pat and *then* posed for a photo. No wonder Zia wouldn't tell me any more about Pat's death. I grasp at the glass of wine and, in one swift gulp, it's gone.

Oh my God, the killing of Pat Ratte – Zia – part of it – responsible for it – did he do it all himself – the others watching – egging on – holding Pat – Zia, knife in hand – how many stabs – how long did it all take – or did they all take part – passing Zia the knife at the end – him the leader – did he make the last stab – the sixth one – the one that killed Pat Ratte?

'Well, Daniella?' Stoker says.

I rise, pushing down with my hands on the chair arms, too weak to stand using my legs alone. The chair scrapes across the tiled floor. The sound loud in my ears. I lean on the table, for balance.

'Where are you going, Daniella?'

I raise one hand to signal for Stoker to stop talking. I take a step back, using the back of my knee to push the chair out of the way.

I let go of the table and stand still. Testing if my legs will hold me up. I rub at my temple, trying to stop the maelstrom in my head. Stoker is watching me with wry amusement, smugness oozing from him like sauce.

I move away from the table by taking a single step.

'What are you going to do, Daniella? Tell me?'

I put my hand up again and take a second step. Stoker makes no move to stop me. He just watches, that smug smile flicking on and off. Another step and I'm moving towards the door. Moving away from that photo. The *killing* photo.

Six wounds.

'This isn't going away,' says Stoker.

I throw my hand up for a third time, palm out towards him, silencing him. My focus is now on the door. I need fresh air. I need out of here. I need out of here – *right now.*

'I'll be in touch, then,' Stoker shouts as I push open the door. Cool air rushes over me but gives no relief. No sense of cleansing. I walk out and let the door close behind me. I stand, unsure which way to turn. I can hear the sea in front of me, but it's hidden – the lights of the bars and cafés too weak to reach the shoreline. I hear the waves lapping on the rocks. And a new thought rises up. Don't turn left. Don't turn right. Just walk straight on. And keep walk-ing. Let the sea swallow this problem.

The thought lasts for only a second but it's there. Like the knife in Zia's hands. Too obvious to ignore but too scary to be real. I *could* just walk into the sea. A man, out with his dog, throws me a sideways glance. I turn left, for no other reason than straight on is wrong and right is away from Se Busca.

I look up and, in the distance, I see Antonio and Carmen walk-ing towards me. They spot me and stop. I turn around and walk the other way. Away from them. Hunting space to think. Hunting answers. Hunting peace.

The sea whispers to me as I walk.

I'm not as cold as you think.

I shiver at the thought and speed up.

At the end of the strip of buildings there is a small car park. In the summer you can wait for hours for a space to come free. Now it's empty. I cross in the dark to its exit and start to walk back along the feeder road that runs along the rear of the bars and cafés. On the other side of the road lie trees and scrub. If I walk a little further this will be replaced by the high-rise apart-ment blocks that dominate this end of the bay. It's a four-mile hike back to Se Busca and I wish it was ten times that. The photo is a life-changer. Zia, a murderer. Me, the all-time number one patsy. The Ex-Patriots, the accomplices. Those three phrases spin through my head, a baby's mobile in full flow. Each one too much to take in. Each one opening a floodgate of questions. Too many to even start to answer. More questions pile in and there is no rhyme or reason to the order. No wonder Zia didn't want to discuss what really went on that day. That they had all waited until I left the pub and sneaked back to kill Pat. How could he ever tell me that? Me waffling on about how couples *talk* to each other. How that fixes things. And him knowing all the time that no amount of talk was going to fix what they, what *he* had done.

I slide into the built-up area, streetlights taking over but providing me with no illumination or way forward in my head.

What else don't I know? Why kill Pat in the first place? Was it a fight that got out of hand? A fight where Zia wore a Tyvek suit? That suggests preparedness. Premeditation. Cold murder. Or was it a *Murder on the Orient Express* moment? All of them in on it. They were all wearing the white suits in the photo. Someone had to go out and buy those. Buy those knowing what they were for. Or does Zia keep a stash for just such occasions?

Six wounds.

And that raises more questions. Is this the first time? Has Zia done it before? Have they all done it before? A one-off? Or more? Any in the last few months? What other lies are there? What don't I know? A lot. That's what. A huge stinking pile of shit. That's what I don't know.

My feet slap the pavement, the rhythm a counterpoint to my thinking. A ripping of reality, footstep by footstep. Goodbye life in the sun. Hello what? Who knows? At this moment in time it's hard to see a few seconds into the future. Everything has changed with that photograph. Every plan I've never made. Every project that hasn't been formed. Every conversation that hasn't been had. All are gone. I feel betrayed. Utterly betrayed. And I feel dirty. Deep down dirty. An uncleanliness that will never be gone. I think of that photo and I see nothing but a world of misery.

I hit a small down slope and pick up a quicker beat. I slip my phone from my bag. After the call to the strip club I'd killed it. I risk firing it back up. Within a few seconds the screen is flashing, telling me that I have messages. I switch it off. I'm not ready for contact with the outside world. I feel I'll never be ready for that.

So staged. So bizarre. So . . .

Who took the photo?

The thought pops into my head and, for a second, manages to push everything else into one corner. Who took the photo? There were George, the Twins, Saucy, Skid and Zia (holding that knife).

Who's left? None of the Ex-Patriots. They are all accounted for. Clyde? Had they dragged him in on the deed? Much as it pains me I can see the Ex-Patriots in this together, but Clyde is too nice. Too gentle. Or maybe I have him wrong as well. I never had any of the Ex-Patriots down as murderers and yet that's what the photo says.

Does it matter? Of course it does. It matters a lot. Does someone else know about this? Someone beyond the Ex-Patriots and Stoker? Or did Stoker take the photo? If not, then who? Not six in the room – seven. Not twelve eyes that saw Pat killed. Fourteen. Fourteen eyes witnessed his murder. The six in the photo. George, Saucy, the Twins, Skid, my Zia and one other – the photographer.

Six wounds and fourteen eyes.

I walk into the beach area of the bay and decide to wander away from the seafront. My feet take me deep into the backwaters of El Descaro – cutting through holiday lets to the orange groves that range from here, up the valley and beyond. I've occasionally walked these back lanes and roads that weave through this part of the world. They are rarely used. They a place to escape and think but I'd normally avoid them at night. Not that there is any real danger.

Not that my partner is a real killer.

But at night there are no street lights here and when the moon is a sliver, as it is now, it's hard to see more than a few feet in front of me. I leave the built-up area behind and I'm swallowed by the black of the countryside. I turn a corner, and the last of the street-lighting from the beach area vanishes.

I pick a spot a few hundred yards further along, an old brick wall. I sit on the rough surface, my feet on the road. Behind me a lonely hut sits in a few acres of orange trees. The trees are bereft of fruit. They were picked clean a while back but a few late wind-falls lie on the ground. I pick one up and examine it. Un-bruised, peel the skin from it and take a bite. Cool, sweet, juicy. The oranges around here are to die for.

Time slides by, lost to the whirling questions in my head. All questions and no answers. I stretch out on the wall. Feet up, head lying on the bare surface, my brain looking for a moment's respite.

A passing car's headlights sweep over me. If the driver sees me, he doesn't stop to check if I'm okay.

I stare up at the sky. The clouds are parting. Dark sky and stars patch the grey. The chilling wind has dropped. Protected by the surrounding orange groves, I don't feel cold. Just weary.

At some point I stand up and rub my thighs. Start walking again. I pick up the pace. I pull my head up.

Fourteen eyes.

Six wounds.

One death.

This needs finished and I don't care how. Whatever way this goes down, Zia is going to talk and, after that, who the hell knows?

20

Ultra-Fucked

I expect to see the Capitán's car or a police car outside Se Busca but the car park is empty. The front door is still covered in the tarp. I take one hell of a breath and lift the edge.

The bar is busier than I expected. Maybe twenty people. Clyde is serving, and I look around for Zia, but he's not in sight. Neither are any of the Ex-Patriots.

'Clyde,' I say as I approach him. 'Where is everyone?'

'Upstairs.'

'Who is?'

'Saucy, the Twins, Skid, George, Zia – all of them.'

'I thought the door was getting fixed.'

'The joiner is coming back tomorrow. It's a bigger job than he first thought.'

'Any other news?'

'The police are looking for you.'

'Who?'

'The Capitán.'

'When?'

'He's been in twice tonight. The last time was an hour ago. You've to call him.'

'Thanks, Clyde.'

I turn to leave as Clyde places a few glasses on the shelf. He pauses. Then, 'Daniella?'

'What?' I turn back to face him.

'What is going on?'

Clyde's face says it all. He looks his age and younger. When Mum was here I think she saw him as a surrogate son. Replacing her errant daughter of twenty years. Clyde is staring at me, wearing his heart on a selfie stick – thrust in my direction.

'Clyde, I don't know. I really don't. I need to talk to Zia.'

'People are saying that you killed Pat.'

The words squeeze from his lips like out-of-date silicone sealant trying to exit the tube. I don't answer right away. Instead, I walk around the bar and approach him. He backs up a little and I take his hand. I can feel him shivering, a wee boy again. I pull his hand toward me, bringing him nearer to me. He's a good six inches taller but he's hunched up, nose inches from mine. To anyone in the bar this will look like some romantic moment.

'Clyde,' I whisper, 'listen to me.'

God, his eyes are so sad. So afraid.

'Clyde, just listen. I did not kill anyone. I don't have it in me to do such a thing. I could never do such a thing. You knew my mum and she told you about me. Okay, it might have been stories about me as a teenager but at any point did she suggest that I was violent? And in the time that I've been here have you seen any sign that I could do something as evil?'

'I don't know what to think, Daniella.'

'Just look at me. That's all I ask. Just stare into my eyes and you'll know. I didn't kill Pat.'

His head slides forward an inch, and I truly believe that he is going to kiss me, that his pent-up feelings for me are about to be released, and I don't move. Don't back away. I should. I know I should. Zia is upstairs. *Zia the killer.* I close my eyes. Wondering what in the hell I'm doing.

'I need to go,' he says, and I open my eyes to find him pulling away. I think he knows what was going to happen and I think he wants it but something stopped him. I turn my head and, standing at the door, is Zia. I don't move. I just study him, anger building at the thought of him in that photo, knife in hand, Pat at his feet. I reach for Clyde and try to pull him back but he resists. I want to kiss him. A crude and destructive action designed to hurt Zia. The red mist that is falling around me throws common sense and restraint to the wind. I pull at Clyde and his eyes widen.

'Daniella, you're hurting me.'

I let go.

Hurting.

'Oh God, Clyde. I didn't mean to. I was . . .'

Have you seen any sign that I could do something as evil?

'I'm so . . .'

And then I'm crying. I turn away and walk into the cellar. A few seconds later Zia enters.

'Daniella?'

My sobs stop me replying. I just stand there. Zia wraps me in his arms. Hugging me tight.

'Zia,' I burble. 'Zia, I saw the photograph.'

'I knew you would,' he says without hesitation. 'When you went chasing Stoker I knew you would.'

'You killed Pat.'

'No, Daniella. I didn't.'

'I saw it. The knife. The white suits. The smiles.'

'It's a lie.'

I look up. 'How can it be a lie?'

'It just is. Look, you wanted to talk. Now's the time. Come upstairs.'

'And that will make things all right?'

'I doubt it. I'm not sure anything can make this right but you need to know the whole story.'

He puts pressure on my waist to move and I oblige, reluctantly, but I let him lead me. We drift through the bar, my eyes on a confused and uncertain Clyde. We go out through the tarp and we skirt the pub, nipping through the gate that leads to the path, up the stairs to the door of my home. Not house. Not flat. *Home*. Safety. Security. Sanctuary.

No sanctuary now. Not with Zia, the killer.

Zia inserts a key into a shining new lock and pushes the door open, letting me enter first.

I can hear voices in the living room. I push through and the talking stops. Everyone turns to look at me. Saucy, glass in hand. Sheryl, gazing out of the window. Jordan, playing with the music system. George, sitting in the La-Z-Boy that Zia loves. I do a U-turn and make for the toilet. If there is talking to be done I want my eyes clear, not red. I throw water on my face. My make-up regime this morning was ultra-light. Soft touches. I spend a few minutes sorting the damage. And then I spend a few more minutes sitting on the pan. Collecting myself. Dragging back up the Daniella Coulstoun that is needed now. Breathing deep.

When I return to the room, no one has moved.

'Okay,' I say, 'this is going to be bloody simple. I want every person in this room to focus on one simple question and one question only. And I want it answered truthfully. No bullshit. Anything else and I'm history. Gone. UK bound. The hell out of here.'

Zia visibly shudders at my words. George opens his mouth to speak and I throw my hand up. 'No, George. I ask one question and then we go from there.'

He closes his mouth.

'Right, all of you. One question. One simple question. Who killed Pat Ratte?'

I drop onto the sofa. And wait.

'The Capitán is looking for you,' says Skid.

'That's not an answer to my question,' I say.

'Where have you been?' asks George.

'Still not an answer to my question,' I say.

'We heard you were up at Lenny's,' says Sheryl.

'Not an answer.'

'You were also at Antonio's,' states Jordan.

'Not an answer.'

'Have you any more drink in this place?' pleads Saucy.

'No answer there, either.'

Silence.

'Who killed Pat Ratte? I'll give you all ten seconds.'

'Ten, nine . . .'

No one stirs a muscle.

'Eight, seven . . .'

George shifts his arse on the chair.

'Six, five . . .'

Jordan coughs.

'Four, three . . .'

Saucy sips the last of his liquid.

'Two, one . . .'

Zia bends at the knees, tilting his head to one side.

'Zero . . . I'm out of here.'

I stand up and walk with purpose to the door. I grab the handle and pull.

'None of us,' says Zia.

I stop.

'None of us killed Pat Ratte,' he says.

I swivel on the spot. 'That's still not an answer.'

'Stoker,' slurs Saucy. 'Stoker did it.'

Everyone looks at Saucy, including me. George slams a hand on the chair. 'Saucy, what the hell?'

'Well, he did,' barks Saucy. 'We all know it.'

'Stoker killed Ratte?' I say. 'Saucy, are you drunk and talking shit?'

'I'm drunk but I ain't spouting piss. Stoker killed Ratte.'

'Zia?' I say. 'Is Saucy telling the truth?'

Zia doesn't speak. Instead he just nods his head, a tiny movement.

'For fuck's sake,' explodes George. 'We all agreed to say nothing.'

'And the photo, Zia,' I say, pushing George's outburst to one side. 'What about the photo?'

'He made us do it,' says Jordan.

'Jordan, shut up,' shouts George.

'Why should he, George?' intervenes Sheryl. 'Stoker's trying to lay it all on Daniella, and you know she had nothing to do with it. And now Lozano is after her.'

I walk back to the chair. 'Is that why he was here again tonight? To arrest me?'

'I think so,' says Zia. 'He didn't say as much but his body language was clear. He wants to find you and quick. Something has changed.'

I wonder if he found something at Mum's apartment when he searched it. I wonder what Stoker has planted.

I sit down. 'Jordan, what do you mean Stoker *made* you do it? Made you pose for that photo? Is that what you mean?'

'Yes.'

'Made you. How?'

'Malky Robertson was with him. He had a gun.'

'Stoker made you all dress up in Tyvek suits?'

Jordan shrugs. 'We had no choice. Robertson had a gun. Stoker made it clear what would happen if we didn't do what he wanted.'

'So you all put on suits,' I say. 'Then you take up positions, grin, and he runs off a ream of glossies for his album?'

'What would you have done?' says Saucy. 'Ratte was already dead on the floor and Robertson has history with guns. A bad one. Would you have braved up and said no?'

'But it's stupid,' I say. 'All you have to do is go to Lozano and tell him what happened. At worst, it's your words against Stoker, and Lozano knows who wanted Pat dead most. He'd never believe that you all decided to incriminate yourselves with that dumb picture.'

'What do you know?' says George. 'Do you think it's that easy? Oh, hey guys, we missed a trick here,' he half shouts to the others. 'Daniella's got it all figured out. We're soooo dumb. I mean why didn't we think of that?'

'Okay, George, tell me why, if you really did nothing, you can't just 'fess up?'

George throws his head back and flaps his arms around like some demented clown.

'Oh, Daniella,' he growls. 'What did we do without you?'

Zia, standing behind him takes a single step forward, lifts his hand and slaps George across the back of the head. Hard. George yells. 'What the fuck?'

'Shut it, George,' Zia snaps. 'Just shut it. It's listening to you that's got us in this mess.'

'I'll cane your fucking arse,' barks George, standing up.

Saucy rises, unsteadily. 'Give it a rest, George. Zia's right. We should have gone straight to the police with this.'

'What the fuck would you know, Saucy?' George spits. 'Why in the hell would we listen to you?'

'Because,' says Jordan, 'Saucy's right and you are just plain wrong. I've been shitting myself for two days.'

'Two days,' repeats Sheryl. 'Cacking myself for two days.'

I look at Skid to see if he's going to chip in but he's looking away. Staying out of it.

'Did you see Stoker kill Pat?' I ask them.

'No,' says Saucy. 'But Jordan walked in on him when he went to get coffee for the machine that morning. Caught him with the knife and Pat on the floor, didn't you son?

Jordan nods.

'He must have heard you all coming in? Didn't he try to run?'

'Stoker doesn't run,' says Saucy. 'He's a cocky bastard. When he saw it was us he must have thought that his wish fairy had dropped by.'

'Why?'

'Fuck the why,' says Skid. 'We should have gone to the police.'

'And if we'd gone to the police, Skid?' George says, spinning his head to look at him. 'What then? Are you clean in all this? Are any of us really clean in this?'

'What does that mean, George?' I ask.

'It means that he'd rather kowtow to Stoker than go to the police,' says Saucy.

'You're not making sense, George,' I say.

Zia chirps at George, 'What now, George? Eh? What now? Stoker will use that photo to rip the piss out of our lives. He's a bastard and doesn't care about people. What then, George?'

I have a thought. 'Why would you lot turning up be a good thing for Stoker?'

'Because of the other stuff,' says Zia.

'Shut the fuck up, Zia,' George shouts. 'Shut the fuck, right up.'

'What other stuff?' I interject.

We're back to quiet.

'What other stuff?'

Zia moves and George glares at him.

'Zia, what other stuff?'

'Sit down, Daniella,' Zia says. 'Please sit down.'

I do as he says. 'What, Zia? What?'

'Look,' he starts.

'Don't you dare,' nips George.

'I'm not going to talk about anyone but me. Okay?' he replies. 'Just me.'

George looks fit to burst. His face is a deep crimson. Eyes on stalks.

'Daniella,' Zia says, 'you've not been here long enough to know everything you need to know. There are other things that made us stay away from the police on this.'

'Things? Things that trump a dead body?'

'It's the Se Busca way. More layers than an onion. More secrets than a brothel.'

'And what is it I don't know that you want to tell me?'

He sits down next to me, laying a hand on my lap. 'Everyone around here carries a few life lessons that they wish they'd never had to learn. More than most, Se Busca kind of attracts the slightly shop-soiled individuals of this world. And we are . . . ,' he pauses, '. . . okay, not *we*, I am a little dirtier than some.'

'Very poetic,' says George.

Zia continues. 'Anyway, we all have a few skeletons that we wish would stay buried. But those bones don't like to settle. And Pat knew that better than anyone.'

'Pat?' I say.

'Pat was the man around here for years before you came,' Zia goes on. 'Your mum ran him a close second. But in truth Pat was a hard nut and, unlike your mum, was well used to meting out punishment. *Well used* to it when he needed to be. And that's what put him top of the pile. But that wasn't his only weapon of choice. Pat ran with some bad people in London and learned, the difficult way, that the real power comes from a combination of violence and knowledge. Know your enemies – and your friends' – weaknesses. That was what he was good at. I tried to tell you this earlier.'

'Go on,' I urge Zia.

George is fidgeting. He'll burst more than a blood vessel if he doesn't calm down. The red in his face is not dissipating.

'Zia, I'd shut the fuck up if I was you,' he spits.

'Well, George, I'm glad you're not me,' Zia says. 'Because I'm not for shutting up.'

'Anyway, Zia?' I say, blanking George.

'Anyway,' Zia continues, 'Pat gathered a lot of information on a lot of people, on everyone and anyone that he thought might prove useful, and he'd use it when he needed to. He'd threaten to reveal the hidden in people's lives when he wanted something. And he wasn't afraid to reveal shit if he didn't get his way. There's no end of stories of Pat ruining lives by throwing out bad stuff that the individuals couldn't refute.'

'And he had bad stuff on you.'

'Yes.'

'Really bad stuff?'

He pauses. Even in full flow there's a small dam in there. A last barrier to be breached.

'Really bad stuff,' he finally says.

'And do you want to tell me what that is?'

'No. But it is bad enough that Pat had a hold over me.'

'And a hold over everyone else in here,' I say.

'That's for them to say,' Zia replies but the mood in the room suggests that Pat had something on them all – there isn't an eye looking at me.

'What's this got to do with Pat's death, Zia?' I ask.

'Stoker now knows what Pat knew,' he says.

'About you? He knows things about you? What does he know?'

'Things. Stoker has the same info Pat had. He got it when Pat died. I don't know how but he has it.'

'And he's holding this info over you? Is that why none of you can take the risk of telling Lozano the truth about Pat's death? Stoker has an ace up his sleeve with every one of you?'

'Ask them but in my case Stoker made that crystal clear,' says Zia.

'But whatever he knows can't be as bad as being framed for murder,' I say.

Silence.

If there was tumbleweed it would be rolling through my living room right now.

'Tell me it isn't that bad.'

More tumbleweed.

'It *is* that bad,' I gasp. 'Really. As bad as murder? What's as bad as murder?'

The tumbleweed makes a third trip.

'What can Stoker have on you that would make you all dress up and pose for that photo?' I say.

Fourth trip.

I change tack. 'Who took that photo? Was it Stoker?'

'Yes,' says Saucy.

George can't help himself. 'Look,' he says, 'don't you think we've talked this through till the fucking cows got lost? Stoker has the photo. Stoker has gen. Stoker can let fly as and when he wants, and we all sink. We had to go along with this.'

'And when will *this* end, George?' I ask. 'Do you think a man like Stoker will ever let this end? He has you on the hook for life with that photo unless you go to the police. He told me that he didn't want this pub but that's bollocks. He wants it because he can't have it. He's that sort of person. And he's neatly buggered every one of you and is now after me. If I'm out of the picture he'll move right in. Zia was right.'

Zia's eyes flash, 'I was?'

'You said he was shaping up to be the new king around here, and he can't be king if this place is not his. We, and I mean *we* are a big barrier to him controlling the dark side around here. And Stoker is systematically eliminating all threats.'

'And he's done a bloody good job of it,' rumbles Saucy. 'We're all fucked.'

'Saucy, that doesn't help,' I say.

'It's true, we're all fucked.'

'Okay, Daniella. Tell Saucy why he's wrong,' says George.

'Fucked, fuckety, fuckety, fuckety fucked,' says Saucy.

'Saucy, shut up,' says Zia.

He doesn't. 'We are so fucked even the word fucked isn't good enough to say how fucked we are,' Saucy rabbits on. 'Ultra-fucked. That's what we are. Ultra-fucked.'

'Saucy, can it,' shouts Sheryl. 'Daniella, what do we do?'

'I'm not sure but we haven't much time,' I say. 'The Capitán will come back for me. Of that I'm sure. Therefore, I have one request.'

I have their undivided attention.

'I'm going into the spare room and I'm going to set up some chairs. And one by one I want you to come in. Zia first and the others wait their turn.'

'Why?' asks Zia.

'The Daniella Coulstoun confessional is opening for business.'

21

The Blonde Woman

I'm sitting on the chair that usually tucks under my dressing table. Opposite me are two chairs from the kitchen. I've set them up to face me. Next to me is our double bed; behind me is the small window that looks out on the road below.

There's a knock on the door.

'Come in,' I say.

Zia slinks in. Head low. Uncertain what's ahead.

'Sit down,' I order.

He takes the seat on the left.

'What's this about?' he asks, feet crossed at his ankles, hands lying on his crotch.

'I need to know what it is that Pat had over you. I need to know what Pat had over all of you. I need to know because Stoker knows it. And I'm going to talk to each of you in private so the others don't find out what he has on anyone else. That photo is for shit and I need to know if I can neutralise whatever it is that you did in the past. That's the real money shot in sterilising Stoker. It's my best bet at finding a way out of this. So I need you to talk.'

'Daniella, this can't be fixed.'

'Everything can be fixed, Zia. It's just that some things are a little more difficult than others. I want you to tell me what Pat had on you. I want to know what's so bad that you'd rather be in the frame for murder than 'fess up.'

'Daniella—'

'Now, Zia. Right now. Talk. The Capitán will be here soon to arrest me and if I'm in prison there's nothing I can do. So just bloody talk.'

He uncrosses his feet, sighs, leans in and speaks, slowly. 'It was a couple of years ago. I was at a party at Pat's place. A bit odd as he wasn't one to throw many parties and certainly wasn't keen on me. But he'd invited me to come up, and you didn't say no to Pat. I wish the hell I had. Anyway, the party was pretty dull. There was no one there I knew and I spent most of my time gazing at the view from his front room.'

Pat's house had sat at the top of the hill that overlooks El Descaro. It was a monumental affair with a view to die for.

Zia goes on. 'It was maybe eleven o'clock and I was thinking of leaving when all hell kicked off between a couple. Out of the blue this woman stood up, screaming something about the man cheating on her, and lays into him with a vase, smashing it over his head. He responded by punching her. A full-on blow. He followed up with a couple more punches before anyone could intervene. Then Pat leapt in and rushed the girl to his bedroom, returned a few minutes later and asked if I could sit with her. I obliged and when I got to the room I found her sitting on the bed, head in her hands. Pat appeared and told me not to let her back into the living room until he had sorted out the man. He was really insistent that she didn't leave the room and that I was not to leave her alone.

'She was in some state, Daniella. Blood all over her face. Her eye already turning black. She was crying. Moaning really. I didn't know what to do or to say. I tried to talk to her but she ignored me and put her head in her hands again. She started rocking back and forth. Then she spoke. Asked if she could have a glass of water. That put me on the spot. Pat had told me not to leave her alone. There was no water to be had without going to the kitchen. I stood up, wondering what to do. She pleaded with me to get some water. I couldn't refuse her. I walked to the door and as soon as I opened it she leapt from the bed and ran at me. Grabbing me by the neck. Screaming that she wanted out. She could have just escaped but she chose to hang on to me and was strangling me. Her nails drawing blood. She was strong. I tried to push her away but she was like a limpet. And she was choking me hard. I mean hard.'

He stops and leans back in the chair. His head is back in the moment and I let him play it out a few times before saying, 'What happened next?'

'She wouldn't let go and I was beginning to panic. She really had a grip of my throat and I was struggling to breathe. We must have staggered around the room a bit because suddenly we were next to the wardrobe and I could see spots dancing in my vision. I gave one almighty shove and she let go, crashing back onto the dresser. I fell onto the bed and lay for a bit trying to recover.'

'And the woman?'

'She was lying on the ground. Not moving. Pat rushed in and jumped across the room to where she lay. He bent down and then he stood up, looked at me and said . . .'

'He said what?'

Zia shakes his head.

'What did he say, Zia?'

'He said that she was dead.' Zia's entire body slumps. 'Dead.'

'She died? How?'

'She must have hit her head on the dresser. That's what Pat said.'

'And what did you do?'

'I told Pat what had gone down. How she had gone wild and that she had grabbed me. I told him it was an accident. That we should call the police. But Pat told me there was no way we could call the police. He said she and her partner were wanted by the police for drug trafficking and if she was found in Pat's house there would be hell to pay for him and some of the other guests. He told me to leave it with him and he would sort it.'

'How can you sort something like that?'

'I had no idea and I kept arguing we should call the police, but Pat wasn't for moving. I said I would call the police if he didn't. Pat got angry and told me that if I did he'd tell them that he saw me throw her against the dresser deliberately. He said that he'd tell them that I'd seen an opportunity to rape the woman while in the bedroom.'

'Jesus.'

'I had no choice, Daniella. You have to believe me. Pat said my DNA would be on the woman. Skin under her fingernails. And he was right. She'd badly scratched my neck. Pat shoved me out of the door telling me to say nothing.'

Zia shivers and then tears flow. An unburdening of the soul. I reach over to touch his hand but stop. The man I knew and cared for has somehow slipped away. Zia, the fun-loving, eighties pop star with a gentle manner, is now implicated in two deaths. Not just implicated but maybe culpable. *Two* deaths. My Zia.

'Zia, what did Pat do next?'

'I've no idea,' he burbles. 'I've no idea.'

'But you heard nothing more?'

'Nothing. I thought about surfing the net for information. You know the sort of thing: looking for a body turning up in the sea or a random car accident but I was too scared to search. The police can track your internet history and if she was found I didn't want them to find that sort of thing on my machine.'

'And did Pat ever mention it?'

He nods his head. 'A few times. Normally when he wanted something. Favours usually. Favours that I would normally have been unwilling to do.'

'Like what?'

'He had me carry a few packages for him.'

'What sort of packages?'

'I don't know.'

'And where did you take these packages?'

'Mostly Spain.'

'Mostly?'

'Madrid a few times, but London once.'

'By plane?'

'No, by car.'

I push the chair back and stand up. 'And Stoker now knows all about this.'

'Yes. He took me to one side the day after the murder and told me.'

'And Stoker has something similar on the others.'

'I don't know what he has on the others and they don't know what he has on me. You're the first person I've told. I'm scared to my core that Pat buried the body and Stoker knows where it is. My DNA will be on it.'

I'm not sure what to say. If things had really panned out as Zia has just said, and if the body is still around, then I'm fairly sure that the forensics team might be able to tie Zia to the death.

'What do I do, Daniella?' he says, eyes wide.

I look at my phone. I have more questions I could ask but time is humming.

'Let me think on it. Can you send in the Twins?'

'That's it?'

'For the moment.'

He rises, a leaden movement of huge effort.

When he's gone I push open the window to grab a few lungfuls of the fresh stuff. There is a knock at the door.

'Come in.'

Sheryl and Jordan enter.

'Look, this has to be quick,' I say as they drop into the chairs. 'I need to know what Pat had on you both.'

'Do you know what he had on Zia?' asks Sheryl.

'On Zia,' repeats Jordan.

'Forget Zia. Did Pat have something on both of you?'

'We're not sure we can tell you,' says Jordan.

'Look, either you tell me or you don't. At the moment I can't see a way out of this mess, but if I know what Pat had on you then I at least have the whole picture.'

'Did Zia tell you what Pat had on him?' says Jordan

'I said forget about Zia.'

'We don't want to know what it is he had on Zia,' says Sheryl. 'We just want to know that you know.'

'That you know,' says Jordan

'I know what he has on Zia,' I say. 'Tell me what he has on you two.'

They look at each other.

I can't wait. 'Sheryl, you talk. Jordan, can you just let Sheryl tell it? I'm waiting on a knock on the door from the Capitán – so please don't interrupt.'

Jordan agrees, a little too quickly for Sheryl's liking.

'Okay,' she says. 'A while back Pat came into Safety Deposit + to rent a box. He already had a few but needed another. He said he was in a hurry as he had two friends in his car and they were heading for the airport. I handed him the paperwork, and when he'd signed up I did the stuff you need to do on the computer and gave him a key. Jordan was back of shop. Pat had a small holdall with him and he opened his new box, took out the internal box and went into the small cubicle we have for privacy. For someone in a hurry he took his time. Ten minutes at least, and then the shop door opened and a woman walked in. She had blood pouring from her nose and a black eye.'

'And what happened next?'

'Pat bursts from the booth and sees the woman. She starts wailing that her partner has beat up on her. Pat turns to me and says can I keep an eye on her as he needs to sort out the partner.'

'And insists that you don't let her out of the shop,' I say.

'Yes. How did you know?' she asks.

'A guess. Go on.'

'Pat leaves and I'm left not knowing what to do.'

'What to do,' adds Jordan and I glare at him.

'Well, I was there as well,' he adds.

'Sheryl, what happened next?' I ask.

'The woman wanted to sit down. So I guided her behind the counter. We're not supposed to let anyone do that but it's the only bit of the shop with chairs. I told Jordan to flip the sign to *cerrado* and lock the door. I didn't want a customer seeing what was going on. If word got back to the owner we'd probably be fired. The woman sat down, and Jordan shut the top that covers the gap between the front of the shop and behind the counter. I offered the woman some water and she said yes. I poured some from the cooler and handed it to her. And then she went nuts. She leaped up, grabbed me by the hand and Jordan by the collar of his T-shirt. She wouldn't let go.'

'And she scratched you both.'

'She did that – and kept scratching. Jordan and I were caught between her. I pushed at her and, well, she just let go of both of us and flew backwards, hitting her head on the desk. Next thing I know, Pat is banging on the door demanding to be let in. Jordan opened it up for him and Pat ran in and straight to the woman.'

'And said she was dead.'

That stops Sheryl in her tracks. 'How did you know?'

What did she look like?'

'Five feet six, slim, blonde, nice clothes.'

I hadn't thought to ask Zia for a description of his woman but I have a feeling I know the answer.

'Give me one minute, you two.'

I get up from the bed and rush through to the living room. George and Saucy are sitting next to each other, Skid is at the window and Zia is folded double on the armchair.

'Okay,' I say, 'George, Saucy and Skid, tell me this. Does your Pat secret have something to do with a five foot six slim blonde woman, a fight, scratching and a death?'

The looks on all three of their faces are akin to the ones I would expect if I'd walked in naked with a fan stuck up my arse.

'I'll take that as a yes,' I say.

I shout through the open door, 'Sheryl, Jordan, come out here.'

When they enter I sit on the edge of Zia's armchair.

'Blonde, slim,' I say to him.

He nods.

'I don't need to hear any more,' I say. 'Other than to say that there is no dead blonde woman. Does that make you all feel better?'

'But—' says Zia.

'I know,' I say. 'You all saw a blonde woman die, am I right?'

Nothing.

'Well, you've all been set up,' I say. 'A scam. A bloody clever one. Pat set each one of you up. Saucy, George, Skid, I don't know the circumstances for all of you but the MO will be that Pat gets you on your own – a man and a woman fight – woman is put in your charge – woman goes nuts – woman scratches – you defend yourself – woman dies. Pat then lords it over you. Threatens to tell all if you don't help him now and again. Am I right?'

Everyone looks at each other.

'It's all a scam,' I say. 'He did the same thing to all of you. Your blonde woman, who probably isn't even blonde, is a con artist and is probably back in the UK sipping champagne on the money she got from Pat for the act.'

There is a wave of relief around the room that is palpable.

'A con?' says Saucy.

'All a con,' I say. 'If I'm right about what I just said. Tell me I am.

More relief as a few heads nod.

'Are you sure?' asks George. 'Are you really sure?'

'Positive. Did none of you suspect?'

'I saw her die,' says Skid. 'Pat let me check her pulse. She was dead.'

'Skid,' I say, 'have you a blind clue how to check a pulse?'

'I watch *Grey's Anatomy*, of course I do.'

I almost laugh. 'Skid, trust me, it was a con. An out-and-out scam. A hell of a scam but one that worked. He had you all wrapped right around his finger. Bloody smart. And none of you said a word to each other? Did Pat tell you to say nothing to anyone? I bet he did. I bet he made that real clear.'

George answers, 'I was convinced it was on the up and up. Pat had a video.'

'Video?'

'From his CCTV in his house.'

'Me too,' says Zia.

'It looked real enough,' George continues. 'When he played it back it looked very real, and there's no way I could take a risk and call him out.'

'And no doubt,' I say, 'Pat had used it as leverage ever since with all of you?'

'Now and again,' says Saucy.

'A couple of times,' says Jordan and Sheryl.

'Once,' says George.

'All the bloody time,' says Skid. 'All the bloody time. He had me polish all his shoes once. Sixty-seven pairs. SIXTY-SEVEN.'

With relief in the air, that actually gets a few smiles.

'His shoes, Skid?' says Saucy.

'And his laundry most weeks.'

A few giggles.

'And washing his sodding car,' Skid adds.

A laugh from Sheryl.

'Are you really sure it's a con, Daniella?' she says.

'What do you all think?'

The sense of unburdening is thick.

'And he even had me clean out his whole swimming pool once,' Skid says.

The dam bursts and the pent-up anxiety transforms into gales of laughter. George creases up on the sofa and Saucy starts to howl. Jordan and Sheryl start laughing so hard they have to hang onto each other. Zia is guffawing into the chair seat. Even I'm smiling.

'It's not fucking funny,' Skid moans. 'He once got me to scrub the pub toilet before he used it – with a toothbrush.'

This makes matters far, far worse. Saucy falls from the sofa, laughter rolling from his lips. George starts banging the armrest, crying for Skid to shut up. The twins collapse to the floor. Zia is now bent triple and I'm laughing my head off.

I almost miss the knock at the door but it's so loud and insistent that it manages to cut through the hilarity.

'Quiet,' I say.

It has little effect. There is just too much relief in the room, and the look on Skid's face would cheer up a depressed night-soil man. The knocking gets louder, and my brief dalliance with light-heartedness vanishes. There can only be one person who wants in so badly. I slip from the room, leaving them all to their hilarity, closing the door behind me.

I unlock the front door. The Capitán is standing there.

'Daniella, I'd like you to—'

'—accompany you to the station,' I finish.

'Yes.'

'Give me just one minute to let Zia know.'

The Capitán walks in behind me, not wanting to let me out of sight – which tells me a lot about how serious this is. That and the two officers he has brought with him.

The room falls quiet at speed when the Capitán appears. I tell Zia not to worry and that I'll be back as soon as I'm able. The Capitán doesn't venture how long that might be. Zia is crestfallen, and I take his head in my hand and kiss him. But, deep down, part of me knows things have changed for good. Zia may not be a killer. But he has lied to me. Lied a lot.

The Capitán escorts me away. I take a look at the living room as I leave and I wonder if I'll see it again for a while.

'Zia,' I say as I leave.

'Yes.'

'Make sure that bloody front door on the pub gets fixed double quick.'

'Sure.'

'And I'll need a house key.'

He digs it from his pocket and hands it to me.

And I'm gone.

22

A Need for Evidence

The air outside the police interview room is intensely fresh. Eye-wateringly fresh. Cool. Fragrant. My clothes are stuck to me, sweat bonding them to my skin. Eight hours in the police station and I'm amazed that I'm free. Amazed and worried. Very worried. I've promised things that I will probably regret. I've danced on the edge of a cliff that's crumbling at the edges, sailed close to a force-twelve storm – or one of many other analogies that place me as either very smart or dumber than a lobotomised chicken. I've been in the interview room all night and more than once was close to never leaving the station but I'm out now – but for how long?

I wander down to the seafront. It's dawn and the sun is cresting the horizon. I watch it rise, letting the early morning heat wash over me. The weariness in my bones is deep, and I can feel a weight like a truck full of bricks pushing down on my shoulders. I turn my back on the sun and head for home.

To prepare.

When I open the front door I can hear faint snoring. Otherwise, all is still. I enter the bathroom and fire up the shower, stripping my clothes and carefully unwrapping the bandages around my chest. I bundle the clothes into the wash basket and lay out the bandages in the sink. I spend twenty minutes under the water, scrubbing myself raw before sitting down in the cubicle. I put my head under the water and let the warmth envelop me. I study the bruises on my chest, massive wheals that will preclude the wearing of a bikini for a good few months. When I eventually get out I have a flashback to the intruder at Mum's place. Did I lock the door this time? I peek out of the bathroom and breathe a little easier when I see the security chain door is hooked.

But a clever thief would replace the chain. Wouldn't they?

Crossing to the bedroom, hair wrapped in a towel, I enter. Zia's snoring is much louder in here. The bed looks inviting but something is holding me back from crawling under the sheets the way I usually would. I spend a few minutes re wrapping the bandages as best I can and drop into my dressing table chair. I look out at the small wood beyond the window. If I lean back I can see the front of Pat Ratte's old house. And that brings back the promise that I made during the interview with the Capitán.

'Daniella?' A sleepy voice.

'Who were you expecting? Toyah?'

Zia has a thing for Toyah Wilcox.

'Nah, she left a few hours ago. Couldn't stand the pace.'

'In your dreams.'

'Do you know that might just be where I met her?'

'Was it good?'

'I've had better. What happened with Lozano?'

'A million questions asked a million different ways.'

'Did he tell you if Stoker left anything in your mum's flat?'

'They noticed the hole in the carpet. I think Stoker called it in. He probably thought that the blood would be in the flat. He wasn't to know I dumped it.'

Zia sits up, pulling the sheet up to his chest – a feminine action that I find odd.

'Lozano must have been suspicious about the carpet?'

'He was but he has nothing. I just kept telling him that Pat must have done it when he lived there.'

That wasn't quite how the conversation had gone.

'So, you've been let go?'

'For the moment.'

'And Stoker?

'Free and out there somewhere.'

'And did his name come up at all in the conversation?'

'No.'

A lie. An outright lie.

'Why are you asking, Zia?'

'Just curious. So Lozano doesn't know who killed Pat?'

'No.'

God, another lie.

'No word about me?' Zia asks.

'You? Why would he talk about you?'

That unsettles me. The need for reassurance is a norm for him, but to jump so quickly to talking about himself could be nerves, or my thoughts on how our dynamics have changed between us is right.

'A lot of talk, Zia, but if he suspects any of you, he said nothing about it to me.'

'And you are no longer a suspect?'

'Hard to say. I'm certainly not off the list.'

At least that's the truth.

'And where does this leave us?' he asks.

'Us? Do you mean you and me?'

'I mean all of us.'

'Still facing Stoker. He wants to own this town and he needs to control our pub to do so. He may not have the leverage he thinks he has, now you all know the blonde woman nonsense was a scam, but he won't stop.'

'He still thinks we all killed a woman?'

'No, he doesn't.'

'Sorry.'

'What did you lot talk about last night. The weather?'

Zia pushes the sheets down and rubs his stomach. Unconsciously, I reach down and rub at mine and feel a little less fat there than usual. Imagination, or is it the lack of food in the last few days? I'm ravenous. I can't remember the last time I ate.

'Zia, Mum must have wiped your noses and kissed your skinned knees for a living. I think you all stopped thinking for yourselves when she was around and haven't got the ability back. Of course, Stoker doesn't think you killed anyone. He knows what Pat knows, exactly what Pat knows, and that means he *knows* it was a scam. He just doesn't know that you know that now. How dumb are you all?'

'What?'

'How long ago did you go to that party where the blonde *died*? Two years, was it? And in all that time none of you talked to each other. All you needed was one, just one, conversation with any of the other Ex-Patriots, and you'd have all been suspicious as hell.'

'None of us wanted to talk about it. At least I didn't. I thought I'd killed someone.'

'As did all the rest, but, in all the talk about Pat in the last two years, none of you broached the subject of why everyone was kowtowing to him?'

'No.'

'Boy, did he land lucky with you lot. Ready-made idiot-fodder.'

That's a statement too far. Something I'd never have done before today.

'That's not fair,' he says in his best schoolboy voice.

'I'm tired, Zia. I just need sleep. Are you getting up?'

'I am. The joiner said he'd be here early this morning. He thinks he can get the door back up and running before we open if he gets going first thing.'

'Okay. Can you take care of that and let me grab a few hours' kip?'

He waits for me to reach over and give him a cuddle. I wait for him to get out of bed. I win, and, as he gathers his clothes, I slip between the sheets and close my eyes.

*

There are no dreams that I can recall but when I wake up I have a nagging sense of doubt over my conversation last night with the Capitán. I rise, slipping on my dressing gown, and wander to the living room. The sun is already out of sight, meaning we are well past midday. I fire up my phone. Two thirty. I've been out for seven hours. If I was ravenous this morning, I'm positively famished now. I raid the freezer for a family pizza, rack up the oven to lava hot and slide the monster meal in. I flip the kettle on and neck a good few inches of full-fat Coke straight from the bottle to slake my thirst.

I can hear the distant sound of the pub from below. I risk calling up the messages from my answer service on the phone. Apart from one, they are all people I'd have expected to have been looking for me yesterday. The one exception is a call from my friend 'Trine back in the UK, asking me to give her a call. A long-time-no-talk type of message. I check my texts but they aren't much more exciting. Nor is the email inbox. WhatsApp is dead, as is Messenger. I think that there are just too bloody many ways to get in touch nowadays.

I wipe all the stuff from the phone I don't need. An act that always makes me feel better. A cleaned-up phone adds to peace of mind. I was half expecting something from Stoker but he's not stupid enough to leave anything digitally incriminating. I plug my phone into its charger as the kettle flips off the boil. Strong coffee is the order of the day. Instant. Two heaped teaspoons to a mug and plenty of milk. I check the pizza. Another ten minutes and it should be good to go. I use the time to try and wrestle my bed hair into some shape. I forgo make-up when the ping of the oven tells me my pizza is ready.

Once the pizza is on a plate, I put it on the living room coffee table and switch on the telly to catch the BBC news channel. I nip back to the bedroom and pull on some black jeans, a black T-shirt and my favourite boots before slumping in front of the telly to practice osmosis on the pizza.

It's gone in fifteen minutes.

I polish off the last of the Coke as I burp my way through the sports bulletin. I've learned exactly zero from watching the news other than that the world is in the same shit state it always is. I give my food half an hour to settle, vegging out in front of an ancient episode of *Friends*. I don't laugh once.

When I hear the key in the door I jump. Zia walks in a few seconds later to find me on my feet staring at the door, intruder on my mind.

'It lives,' he says.

'That's a new meaning for the word "lives" that I've not yet come upon, Zia. But a pizza and a few hours of sleep means I'm probably just north of being a zombie. How's the pub door?'

'Swinging like a good one, and with a lock that will keep out Genghis Khan and his supporters.'

'Is the pub busy?'

'Not bad. Are you going down?'

'No. I have a few things I need to do. I'm on shift tonight.'

'We both are.'

'I'll be back in time.'

Another lie.

'Where are you going?' he asks.

'I've a few calls to make and I want the air. 'Trine also called and I'm due her a natter.'

'She's not been in touch in a while.'

'That's why I want to talk, and I'm better at gossip when I'm walking. Are you going back down?'

'Once I've eaten, I need to tidy up after the joiner. It took longer than he thought. He's only just finished.'

I give him a kiss on the cheek, aware my breath is none too fresh. He tries to wrap his arms around me, and disappointment washes across his face when I pull away.

'No time for a quick cuddle?' he says.

'Later, Zia.'

Cuddle is a euphemism.

I leave him frustrated and nip into the bathroom to brush my teeth and dab on some perfume. As I grab my purse and coat I know my exit is too swift and my mixed emotions around Zia aren't coalescing in a good way. As soon as I'm out of sight of the pub I call the Capitán and arrange to meet him as planned.

'Are you really ready for this, Daniella?' he asks.

'Absolutely not,' I say.

Ten minutes later I enter the offices of the Guardia Civil; half an hour after that I'm back on the street.

Sweating cobs.

I decide to walk to my destination rather than the more appropriate taxi. I make the journey even longer by choosing to walk along the seafront.

The promised warmth from this morning hasn't materialised and I'm glad I brought my coat. The walkers around me, apart from the very hardy, are also wrapped up. The sun is now behind the front-line buildings and the shade makes things even cooler. I walk slowly, adding even more time to my journey. As I reach the beach end of the bay I call Antonio. He's not pleased to hear my voice.

'Antonio, I'm sorry about any issues I cost you with Stoker.'

'He shut Héctor's hand in a door. Now he makes him clean the toilets and empty the bins. He was a good waiter and in line for his boss's job.'

Fuck.

'Jesus, Antonio. I really didn't mean for that to happen.'

'And what did you mean to happen, Daniella?'

'Look, I'm really sorry but I have another favour to ask you.'

'What?'

'I need to find Stoker again.'

The phone goes so quiet I think he has hung up.

'Antonio.'

'Are you serious?'

'Antonio, I'm only asking because I don't know anyone else who will know.'

'I cannot believe this.'

'I don't need you to do anything but tell me who I can contact who will know. I'll keep your name out of it. Otherwise I'm going to have to go up to the Muirend Club and take my chances.'

'I cannot help.'

'I need to see him, Antonio. And I need to see him soon. And . . .' I hesitate.

'And what?'

'You don't want to know. I just need to see him.'

'I cannot afford your friendship, Daniella.'

'I promise I will not let him know you helped.'

'You cannot make that promise. You cannot keep it, and you know it.'

'I can and I will. I just need to find him quickly.' Then I finish with, 'But I can't force you to help.'

This call is mad. I really don't know this man that well, and if his nephew is nursing crushed fingers then why in the hell would he help? But I need to find Stoker, and Antonio will know where he is.'

'He will be at the club.'

'He will?'

'There is a dinner on tonight. Black tie. Some charity event. The same charity that the El Descaro Classic raises cash for. Stoker has flown in a few of the long-term participants. And they are not all nice people. That's all I can tell you.'

'Thanks.'

'I'm not telling you anything that you couldn't have found out if you'd really wanted to know.'

'I owe you.'

'Goodbye, Daniella.'

The Muirend Club it is.

I'm about half an hour from the club by foot. Assuming the function kicks off around eight, I want to get there a few hours after. Around ten. Let the thing get rolling and see if I can get Stoker on his own. Not a plan that makes the slightest bit of sense. But it's the best I have. I make a quick call to the Capitán and update him on what I'm going to do.

I hang up and walk the backwaters of the area, seeking out a bar that is more locals than expats, and when I find one I order up a large glass of wine.

I know what needs to be done. I know what the risks are and I'm shit scared.

'Hi, Daniella.'

The voice makes me jump. I look up, and Saucy is standing next to me.

'Saucy? What in the hell are you doing here?'

'I fancied a change of scenery.'

He's fairly steady on his feet for this time of the day. I doubt he's sober but he's sober for Saucy.

'Do you mind if I sit down?' he says.

'Of course not.'

He signals for the waiter and orders up a large whisky. When it arrives he lets it sit. And sit. It's the longest I've seen a poured drink survive in front of him.

'Why are you here?' I ask after a few moments of nothing.

'Why are any of us here, Daniella?'

'Philosophy, Saucy?'

'Life.'

'I'm not in the mood.'

'So Zia thinks.'

'What does Zia think?'

'That you are not in the mood.'

'Is that why you are here? To give me relationship advice?'

'Daniella, can I tell you a short story?'

'Short, yes. Long, no.'

'Short it is. Let me start by saying a thanks from everyone. We never got the chance to say it because of Lozano's arrival.'

'It wasn't that hard to get to the bottom of.'

'A lot harder than you think. Pat played us well.'

'I get that, but what is this story?'

He still leaves the whisky alone.

'A few years ago I got a call from Pat,' he says. 'I'd done his books for some of his businesses off and on and he wanted some advice. I met him at his house. This was before the blonde woman who didn't die stuff. Pat gave me a slew of paper to sort out. All about some new business he had acquired up the coast. He let me use his office to sift through it all. It was a real mess and it took me an age to get some sort of order to things.'

The whisky is still untouched.

I can't help but comment. 'Saucy, I'm thinking of photographing that drink and sending it to the *Guinness Book of World Records*.'

He picks it up and necks it in a oner. 'Do you want me to finish the story as well?'

'Go on.'

'Anyway, I'm knee deep in numbers and I hear the doorbell go. And you'll be interested to know who walked in.'

'Who?'

'An eighties pop star accompanied by an owner of café not a quarter mile from here.'

'Zia and Antonio?'

'Exactly.'

'But Zia hasn't known Antonio long. At least that's what he told me. When was this?'

'Two years ago.'

'Okay, you've got my attention, Saucy. Where is this going?'

'There was a fourth person who turned up that day as well.'

'Who?'

'Stoker.'

'Stoker, Zia, Antonio and Pat were all together?'

'And it wasn't the first time from what I gathered.'

'What were they meeting about?'

'I never found out. Pat shut me in the office and they all talked in the living room. I wasn't let out until they left.'

'And that was two years ago.'

'Yes, and that wasn't the last time either.'

'They met often?'

'I think they were in your mum's place only last week.'

'When?'

'You were at the wholesalers.'

'Monday.'

'If you say.'

'Zia, Antonio, Stoker and Pat were in my mum's house last week?'

'The reason I'm here is to warn you that whatever you have planned with Lozano for Stoker might be best kept from Antonio'

My heart sinks.

'I've nothing planned with Lozano,' I say.

He raises his hand to order another whisky.

'Sure you have,' he says. 'I heard Zia talking to Lozano on the phone about you. He knows you went to see him earlier.'

'Jesus, what did Lozano want with Zia?'

'I don't know, but I heard your name and Stoker's and put two with two.'

'And you figured I'd come to this bar, tonight, at this time?'

'I fancied you were going to see Stoker and I fancied a walk and happened to fancy walking the same way you were walking. Then I fancied a chat with you and I fancied a drink and now I fancy another drink and then I fancy another drink and maybe another and then I fancy getting a taxi home.'

'Fancy all that. Why have you not told me about Pat, Zia, Stoker and Antonio before now?'

He clams up and orders up a second whisky.

With another drink in hand, Saucy is in for the haul. I worry about him. I've seen my fair share of alcoholics since I got here, but Saucy is a storm drain to booze. His liver has to be shot, as does his brain, yet somehow he shows no signs of deterioration on either front. He's by far the smartest of the Ex-Patriots. When he's sober he can run rings around them all. Even drunk he can hold his own. His wife recently sent him for a private health screening. For his age he got a clean bill. Some people are born to be the exception and Saucy is one.

'I didn't say anything about Zia and the others because it was none of my business,' he says at last. 'Until now.'

'So, Saucy, what are you telling me?'

'Stoker probably knows you are coming tonight.'

'Who says I'm going near him?'

'Why did Lozano let you go?'

'He knows I didn't kill Pat.'

'And he knows who did.'

'He didn't say.'

'So full of shit Daniella. So full of shit.'

'What do you think Zia, Antonio, Stoker and Pat were meeting about?'

'I've no idea. But it can't be good. Not with Stoker and Pat in the same room. They had little time for each other. Two Alphas in town are never good.'

'And you are saying Zia knows Antonio of old.'

'He knows Carmen better.'

'Say that again.'

'Carmen and Zia had a thing going a few years back.'

My jaw drops. Every bloody day in this place is a school day.

'You're kidding.'

'I'm not, and it was while Antonio and Carmen were an item.'

'Carmen had an affair with Zia?'

'Messy at the end, so I hear.'

'When exactly was this?'

'Four, maybe five years back. Had to be because Antonio's dad was still alive and working in the café. Antonio found out and called out Zia. As I said, it all got a bit messy.'

'But when we met Carmen and Antonio a few months back Zia said he hardly knew Antonio.'

'Do you and Zia talk?'

'Obviously not as much as we should.'

'I've noticed it more in the last few days. Up until now I thought you two were doing fine. I always thought the age difference would be hard to handle, but you both seemed to sail through any issues. Until Pat's death – but there's more to it than that. Isn't there?'

I'm not given to crying on shoulders. Mum taught stoicism in the face of emotion, but I've no one to talk to at the moment, and my nerves are shredded from the thought of a meet with Stoker. And so I talk. 'I thought Zia and I were fine. I mean really fine. But then the wheels came off with his lying over Pat's death, this stupid blonde woman thing and now you tell me he had an affair. It's the lies that hurt. A few small lies I can handle, but his are whoppers. Two days ago I thought we were a long-term thing – now I'm thinking the opposite.'

'But even without the lies you've still known something was out of sorts for a while?'

'Now I look back I can see that I've been putting a coat of gloss over life here. George accused me of swinging the lead, and he was, is, right. I've been living a holiday life, not a real one, since I got here.'

'Holiday romances never last.'

'I'm beginning to think you're right on that. I honestly thought it was more than a fling with Zia, but today has thrown everything into perspective.'

'Do you love him?'

'I thought things were heading that way. I loved, still maybe love, being with him. He makes me feel good, but all I can think of now is how much of all of it is a lie, a front. Were his words ones that I wanted to hear as opposed to words he wanted to say? And the more I find out about him of late, the less I like.'

Saucy rubs his eyes.

'I'm not one for doling out love advice, Daniella. But me and the wife have been together for over forty years, and she puts up with a lot. I love her to bits and she loves me and that's what gets us through. It's a maxim for relationships like yours and Zia's. No love, no future. It's a rule.'

'Whose rule?'

'The universe's rule. The Beatles were full of crap when they said, All You Need is Love. You need a damn sight more – but without it, relationships are for shit.'

'You've been married forty years?'

'Forty-five just past, and they said it wouldn't last.'

Time after time I learn stuff about people around here that surprises me. It's not realistic to expect to learn everything about everyone in such a short time. My problem is that I'm not even learning the really important stuff.

Living in a nice little bubble.

Isn't that what George said to me down at the port a lifetime ago? A bubble is a good way to describe it. A bubble that keeps everything out and me in. Safe. Secure. Hidden.

'Are you warning me off trying to fix this mess?' I ask.

'I'm telling you that Stoker is no mug and whatever you've cooked up with Lozano is probably not going to end well for you.'

I touch my chest and trace the wire beneath my top to the small box buried in the small of my back. Good for five hundred yards, the Capitán had said. We can listen in to everything that is happening, he'd told me. We can be there in minutes if things go badly, he'd promised. Just get Stoker talking and let us do the rest, he'd said. But, beware, you are on your own until we get there, he'd finished with. It sounded so simple early this morning when I'd agreed to be wired up. Anything sounded better than jail. It sounded less simple when I'd popped into the station earlier to have the transmitter fitted. Now, with Saucy telling me Stoker is expecting me, it all sounds too dangerous for words. Especially now I've blabbed to Antonio about wanting to find Stoker and, no doubt, the Capitán's call with Zia has not helped either.

'And your advice, Saucy?'

'I charge for advice, Daniella.'

'I'll pay for your whisky.'

'For the night?'

'As long as you stick to one bottle.'

'Deal. My advice is simple. Turn around, go back to Se Busca and pour yourself into a bottle of wine. It's not your job to fix us.'

I don't need to fund a bottle of malt to know he was going to say that. I just needed to reward him for caring.

'Saucy I'm not trying to fix you. I'm trying to fix me. And if that helps others, so be it.'

'That so sounds like your mother talking.'

We sit for a short while, watching each other, saying nothing, while Saucy creates a stock issue that some Scottish distiller will happily fill.

'Saucy, I'm off for a walk.'

'Which way?'

'I'm not sure yet.'

'People usually regret not taking my advice.'

'I know.'

Out on the street I look left, which is home and then right, which is the Muirend Club. With a glance at Saucy I turn left. And as soon as I'm out of sight I cut up an alley, reach the back of the building and head back the other way.

For good or bad I'm stepping into the lion's den. This needs finished.

I'm fairly sure Stoker will have been warned I'm out looking for him again. I know this is a risk but I'm out of other ideas. The Capitán had floated the idea of wiring me up after almost four solid hours of me insisting that I had nothing to do with Pat's death and that he should look at Stoker. He'd agreed that I was being made a patsy. The pub key and the note made no sense to him but the carpet did. A fit-up. The photo of me being shoved by Pat that was hidden in the pub in the wall was just icing on the cake. The Capitán is under huge pressure. The death of an expat UK gangster has stirred up the old 'Costa del crime' stories in the British and Spanish press, and the Spanish authorities are more than a little keen to get those headlines off the internet. Pat reminds people that Spain is still home – despite the best efforts of both countries – to the unwanted.

'Capitán, do you really think I killed Pat Ratte?'

'I have no way of knowing.'

'No, I mean deep down. What is your gut saying?'

'That we need to sort this.'

'And how do we do that?'

'Are you willing to cooperate fully with us?'

And the deal had been sealed. About three in the morning. When I was at my weakest. Me, to be wired up. Me, to visit Stoker. The Capitán, to listen in. By the time the idea was floated I was so tired I'd have agreed to milking the Duke of Sutherland's nipples in public. Now the idea seems close to insane. And that's exactly why it might work. *Has* to work. I don't need much from Stoker. I'm not looking for an all-out confession. That isn't going to happen. If the Ex-Patriots fess up to the Tyvek photo nonsense, that would put Stoker into police custody – but that alone isn't enough. If the Ex-Patriots do tell the Capitán about what happened, they also run the risk of them all being accused of being involved and orchestrating a cover up. As a minimum, Stoker will cry foul. And even with the crap about the blonde woman binned, none of the Ex-Patriots are going to go up against Stoker if he turns nasty. Stoker just won't take well to the Ex-Patriots talking. He'll find a way to hurt me and hurt the Ex-Patriots if he thinks he's being pinned for Pat's murder. So this is my best bet. All I have. All I can do. A real sixty-yard conversion into the wind and late in the game. I have no idea what Stoker might or might not say, might or might not *do* – I just need something that will get Stoker into police hands and something that will convince the Ex-Pats to sing about the photo – and send Stoker down.

I slip from the back alley onto the road and, with no pavement, I keep to the left and flip on my phone light to give oncoming motorists some sort of warning that I'm there. I try and envisage the conversation with Stoker and this makes me feel less confident with each step. So I stop that thought train.

When I reach the driveway that leads to the Muirend Club I've been passed by a number of high-powered, high-euro-value cars. I slip from the road and skirt the land that surrounds the club. Set well back in a clearing in the trees, I can see headlights and tail lights weaving their way towards the club but I can't yet see the building. I use the car lights to guide me, and when the building appears, lit up like an oil cracking plant, I cut in and find a spot to observe.

I wonder if the Capitán can hear my heart through the microphone. Certainly my breathing must be a giveaway to how nervous I'm feeling. I'd insisted on making my own way here when I'd called in. And he had said he would use that time to set up camp close by, but now I'm near the club I'm wondering where close by is. The driveway to the club is a quarter of a mile long, and I'd seen no parked vehicles near to the entrance. He could be in the woods, but that seems unlikely.

The club is a sprawling single-storey affair. From where I'm located I can only see the front. A hacienda-style building with an ornate columned entrance. The cars are pulling up at a large double door made of sheet glass. A man dressed in full evening gear is greeting guests as they arrive, and somewhere inside there's a small string band playing. Everyone who exits a car is dressed to the nines. I'll stand out like a mutt at Cruft's if I try and walk in. I spend a few more moments watching the arrivals. Will Zia and Antonio be on the guest list? Zia has an outrageous pink dinner suit from his pop star days that still fits him. He put it on for me when I'd discovered it hidden in the back of his wardrobe. With purple lapels, cream piping and frilly orange cuffs it was designed, in the excess of the eighties, to stand out.

Before starting to look for another way into the club I pat the small receiver and trace the wire once more. I feel so self-conscious of the wire that I'm sure Stoker will catch on.

At the rear of the building there's a swimming pool. A massive affair that must be close to Olympic proportions. The pool sits next to a glass wall, inside of which a room is laid out with over a dozen eight-seater round tables for Stoker's event. There must be a reception room for the guests beyond the room, as the only people I can see through the glass are staff prepping the place. Next to the pool is a breeze-block wall; from behind it I can hear the clinking and clacking of a kitchen in full flow. Keeping to the shadows, I pass the wall. A line of bins runs along the other side, and the door to the kitchen is wedged open. A couple of people are standing near it, grabbing a quick fag before the main event starts. I complete a near circuit of the building and can see no other way in. I return to the pool area as the guests begin to trickle into the dining area. A small podium has been set up near the glass for a speaker to stand at. Stoker walks in. Black on black on black his choice of colours for suit, shirt and bow tie. He glad-hands everyone he sees, wearing his warm and welcoming face. I reckon there will be over a hundred in the room when it's full. I've timed this badly. I thought the event would be well underway by now but Stoker is working on Spanish time. Late start, late finish. It's just gone ten o'clock, and they haven't even sat down to dinner yet.

It's cold out here. Even with my jacket on I'm starting to feel it bite. It could be another two or three hours before the dinner breaks up and I get a chance to get Stoker on his own – if I can find a way in. I can't spend that time out here. I'll be an ice block by then. A thought flits across my chilling brain. With Stoker otherwise occupied, maybe the wiretap isn't the way to go. Stoker must have an office in the club, if he now owns it. With everyone at the dinner I might be able to get in and have a look. Who knows what might be lying in there that could help me? He's not dumb enough to leave anything obvious. It would be nice to find the knife, blood caked on the blade, his prints clear and waiting to be found, but that won't happen. But even the smart can trip themselves up. Back when everyone was 'fessing up to the dirty deed with the blonde, Saucy called Stoker a cocky bastard. And cocky bastards can be over-confident. And that can make them lazy. Anyway, it's either that or walk back to civilisation and find a bar for a few hours.

I return to the kitchen door. It's still open but the smokers are gone. I approach and scan the walls for CCTV and spot one high up above the door, then another near the bins. I pull up the hood on my jacket and bend over as I walk. Not much of a disguise but better than zip. I reach the door and no one appears. Inside is the chaos that precedes serving a hundred guests. I slip in through the door, whipping off my jacket as I do so.

I'm dressed all in black, as are the staff. I bundle my coat up and walk straight through the kitchen, eyes front, as if I have all the right in the world to be here. The melee around me doesn't miss a beat as I pass through it and out into a corridor beyond. I turn a corner and can hear the buzz of conversation from the dining room. The band has just stopped playing. To my left are toilets, and I slide into the ladies. I pick a cubicle and sit down. I hear someone come in, and I wait as they go about their business. I stay until I hear the clatter of trolleys rolling along the corridor. That means that food is being served and everyone will be seated. Now's my chance to explore.

I open the toilet door and have to dodge a loaded drinks trolley being pushed by a young waiter. Pre-dinner drinks, not yet food. It's going to be a very late night. If the waiter is surprised at my jeans and T-shirt look he says nothing. I wait until he has gone and follow the corridor along. It opens out on what must be the waiting area for the dining room, now empty of guests. The decor is low key and classy. Subtle and expensive looking. Touches of gold, where gold doesn't look gaudy, and strips of silver to complement it. The space holds a couple of dozen chairs and sofas – all black leather. The carpet is dark grey, and LED lights buried in the coving cast the scene in a warm glow. There are a couple of massive quadruple batwing doors, both closed, guarding the dining room. One is pushed open, briefly, by an exiting waiter, revealing the seated crowd. The waiter ignores me and scurries off down the hall.

'I'm in the building,' I whisper.

They are the first words I've spoken since I arrived here, and they're aimed at the Capitán on the other end of my mike. *If he is listening.* The Capitán made it clear that being wired didn't give me permission to break the law. So far, I might be guilty of a bit of trespassing, and that might be worth Stoker completing a *Denuncia* and sending it to the Policía Local, but I doubt he will. He'll have other plans if he catches me.

I walk away from the dining room and find myself at the reception. It's laid out like a hotel lobby. The reception desk to one side is staffed by a single man. Chairs are scattered around for people to wait in. I can see the doorman through the glass doors, standing outside, waiting on stragglers or errant members. To my left is a set of double doors, heavy oak affairs with gold lining. Another corridor stretches away to my right. I take the corridor, half waiting for the receptionist to shout out and ask what I'm doing here – but there is nothing.

The corridor is lined with doors and there is no obvious way of knowing what lies behind each one. I push open the first door and look in on a bar. I say bar but in comparison to Se Busca we are talking a five-star leather-laden, chrome-polished, two-inch-thick carpet heaven. A few men look up and I close the door. The next door is a reading room and once again a few bodies eye me suspiciously. The next two rooms are meeting rooms, the fifth is a small cinema. I open the last door, marked private, and reveal another corridor. If my geography is correct this runs parallel with the corridor leading from the kitchen. I go in.

The decor in here is more two-star, cheaper, industrial carpet, scuffed panelled doors and more intrusive lighting. This is for the staff. If I'm discovered I'll claim I'm lost, that I was here to pick up a car and couldn't find anyone. I knock on the first door and get no response. I open it to reveal an office crammed with half a dozen desks, all unoccupied. The next door reveals a small cupboard hosting a coffee machine and a fridge. There are three more doors beyond this one. One is marked up as the toilet, one leads to a room lined with lockers, and the other door is locked. And I'll put cash on the locked one being Stoker's office.

The door leading to the corridor behind opens and I dart into the toilet. I hear the door to the office with the desks open and, a few seconds later, footsteps pass me and I hear the click of a lock. Whoever is out there has entered the locked office. I wait in a cubicle hoping they leave and don't lock the office door but a few seconds later the door slams shut and the lock is thrown. I risk dashing from the cubicle and looking onto the corridor. I catch the back of them. It's not Stoker but another man who I don't recognise. He goes into the office with the desks and leaves a few seconds later. I'm thinking that the key to Stoker's room might live in the desk-filled office, given the man's actions.

When the man has vanished, I return to the desk-filled office and look around. If the key is here it has to be within easy reach. The man was hardly in here ten seconds. I scan the wall for a key box but there is no joy. I look on top of three filing cabinets lining one wall and then check each of the desks' surfaces. Nothing. I'm now thinking top drawer of a desk. I begin with the one nearest the door, ears open for any noise. The drawer is an explosion of stationery, crammed to the top but no obvious key. The next two are all but empty, but the fourth houses a Yale key attached to a black BMW key fob. Just the sort of fob Stoker would use. I grab it and let myself back out of the office. I hear the door to the next corridor begin to open again. I dive into the toilet once more and jump into one of the cubicles. Again, I hear the office door open and close. Only this time the person is in the office for a while, and when the door reopens I hear swearing as the person leaves the corridor.

I give it another few seconds and emerge from the cubicle. I have to dive straight back in as I hear voices approaching.

'The bloody key was there not one minute ago,' says a voice as the door to the corridor is slammed open.

My little theft has just been discovered.

A SECOND VOICE: 'Why didn't you put it back in the safe?'

FIRST VOICE: 'Because he's had me in and out of his sodding office all day with this fucking dinner. I got sick of spinning the bloody safe dials so I stuck it in my drawer.'

SECOND VOICE: 'He'll be mad.'

FIRST VOICE: 'No shit?'

SECOND VOICE: 'You must have dropped it. Did you go anywhere else? The toilet?'

FIRST VOICE: 'No.'

SECOND VOICE: 'Go check the office again. Maybe it's under a desk.'

FIRST VOICE: 'I put it in the fucking drawer. I'm sure of that.'

SECOND VOICE: 'Go check.'

I hear the desk-filled office door swing open and shut. I sit in the cubicle, still as a deer having just heard a twig crack.

SECOND VOICE: 'And?'

FIRST VOICE: 'Nothing. I put it in the drawer and it's gone.'

SECOND VOICE: 'How? Who could have taken it? There's you, me, Martin at the reception and the kitchen staff.'

FIRST VOICE: 'A member?'

SECOND VOICE: 'Did you see anyone in here?'

FIRST VOICE: 'No.'

SECOND VOICE: 'Well, I didn't see anyone come along the corridor and I saw you come back. So if someone took the key they have to still be here.'

I open the cubicle door and look out to the wash area. The only other exit is a tiny window, high up on the outside wall. I might be able to pull myself up to it but I can't see me fitting through. But all that's moot, as it's locked tight with a padlock. With only the desk-filled office, the cupboard, the locker room and here to search they'll find me in seconds. I move to the toilet door and hear one of them re-enter the desk-filled office. The other one opens a door, and I'm guessing it's the locker room. I dive out and push through the door to the corridor beyond. A voice shouts out, 'Hey, you!'

I sprint down the corridor, slamming the door behind me – heading for the reception to find the doorman showing two people in. He spots me running. I swing left, back towards the dining room. As I do so the receptionist looks up, his face creases, and his mouth opens. I turn my back on him and run back to the waiting area outside the dining room. When I arrive there I try to exit via the hallway leading to the kitchen but three waiters, trolleys piled high with food, block my way.

'There she is,' shouts the first voice.

I spin. Two men are standing between me and the reception area.

'Coulstoun,' cries out a voice from the direction of the kitchen. I spin again, and Malky Robertson and Cauliflower Ears have just emerged around the corner and are standing behind the waiters, who, trolleys in front, have stopped to watch what is going on.

I'm trapped.

'I told you she came in through the kitchen,' says Cauliflower Ears. 'How did you miss her?'

'I needed a piss,' replies Robertson.

I'd seen neither of them out back or in the kitchen. But it's crystal clear that Stoker has had them on the lookout. Saucy was right on the money. Antonio talked.

Robertson and Cauliflower Ears push through the waiters, and the two from the office area also move in. A pincer. I've one choice and I take it, barging through the nearest batwing door and into the dining room.

23

Confession Can Be Bad for You

A few heads swivel as I enter but most stay focused on the speaker.

'Ladies and gentlemen,' Stoker says from behind the podium, 'I am not presenting myself as the new leader of our group but I would like to—'

He spots me as Robertson and Cauliflower Ears clatter into the room. He looks at me and then at Robertson and Cauliflower Ears. He lifts his hand waving Robertson and Cauliflower Ears away. They hesitate before backing off through the doors. Now everyone is looking in my direction.

'Good evening, Daniella. A little underdressed for this evening?' Stoker says.

I walk towards him. Weaving through the tables. One of the glass doors that looks out onto the pool is slightly open. The only escape I can see.

'And to what do we owe this pleasure, Daniella?' Stoker has his shit-eating grin on.

I reach the front of the assembly, a few yards from the open glass door.

'I'm a pleasure to see am I, Mr Stoker? I thank you for the compliment,' I say.

The guests, with a mix of confusion and mild amusement written across their faces, are centred on our exchange.

'But,' I say, 'I'm not really here for your pleasure.'

I pull my phone from my back pocket and draw up the camera app. I hit the video button and begin spinning the camera around the room, filming. Stoker immediately leaps down from the podium, and I back off, still letting the phone capture the people in the room. As he reaches me I ram the phone back into my pocket.

'Thank you,' I say.

There is a murmur from the crowd as talking breaks out. Stoker turns to them all and raises his hand. 'I am so sorry about this interruption. Dinner is about to be served. Please enjoy your meal while I have a quiet chat with Miss Coulstoun.'

He grabs me by the wrist and pulls. I yank away.

'Don't touch me,' I bark.

He leans towards me, whispering, 'Come with me. You have no idea who is in this room. If you try to run, there are far nastier people in here than me who will come hunting you.'

A bear of a man in a dining suit two sizes too small for his bulk rises and crosses to the open glass door. He pulls it shut with a click and then stands there.

'Thank you, Constantine,' says Stoker.

Stoker grabs my wrist again. I try to shake it free, but he has one hell of a grip.

'Out,' he says.

I flick my arm hard and he lets go. I walk back through the crowd with him at my heel.

'Where are we going, Mr Stoker?' I ask. 'For a chat in your office?'

'Shut up and walk,' he says under his breath, smiling at the odd guest as he passes them. As we reach the batwing doors they part and the waiters begin to swarm in. I'm ushered into the waiting area beyond. Robertson and Cauliflower Ears are there, but the other two men have gone. As soon as the doors to the dining room are closed, Stoker draws me in close.

'What the fuck are you doing here?' Stoker grunts, the grin gone.

'Mr Stoker, if you don't take your hands off me I'll do a lot more than video a few diners,' I say.

He doesn't release me.

'I'm warning you, Mr Stoker. Let me go. I just want to talk.'

This time he does let go.

'Now?' he says. 'You want to talk now? Right in the middle of my fucking dinner?'

'I had no idea there was a dinner on.'

'How in the hell did she get in?' Stoker asks Robertson.

'Through the kitchen,' he replies.

'You were supposed to be watching there.'

'I needed a piss.'

'I'll deal with you later,' says Stoker.

'So you were expecting me?' I ask. 'Now, how would you know I was going to be here?'

'The back-office, now,' he says, ignoring my question. 'I need to be with my guests sharp.'

'Why not talk here?' I say.

He points to the dining room doors. 'People will be in and out for the toilet and, after you pulled that trick with the phone, they will not be happy.'

'A wee video and I'm upsetting your guests?'

'Office and we chat. No office and you are out of here in a fucking body bag. Your choice.'

'Office, I think,' I say.

My words sound a bit clunky but they'll alert the Capitán to my whereabouts, I hope.

'Go with these two,' Stoker orders me, 'and I'll be there in five minutes. And give me your phone.'

'My phone?'

'I'll have these two take the fucking thing off you if you don't. I need to show that lot that you've not broadcast them to the world.'

Robertson grabs my collar and pulls me off my feet.

'Okay, okay,' I shout. 'Take it. But I'm not unlocking it. Just show them it and tell them you've had me delete it.'

I pull out the phone and Stoker whips it away. He re-enters the dining area to the sound of clinking knives, forks and the drone of conversation. When the door is closed Robertson surprises me by letting go. I look down at my T-shirt, worried that he might have exposed the recording device. I can't see anything.

'The back-office,' says Robertson.

I take a breath and walk towards the office area.

'Where's the key?' asks Robertson when we reach Stoker's locked door.

'What key?' I say.

'Funny girl. Joe says you have it. Just hand it over.'

I fish it out, and Robertson takes it from me. As he unlocks the door, Cauliflower Ears holds back. Robertson pushes the door wide and lets me in. The interior is disappointing. I'd expected something classy. What I get is stripped bare and functional. One small desk. One chair. And that is it. The walls are plaster grey – the roof painted concrete.

'Tell the décor consultant that they have nailed the *how little can you get away with* look to a tee,' I quip, trying to hide my fear.

My attempt at humour gets nothing in response. Robertson has followed me in but for some reason Cauliflower Ears is loitering outside.

'Would it harm the ambience if we added a few chairs here?' I enquire?

'We'll wait on Mr Stoker.'

'What has he got on you, Malky?'

Robertson raises an eyebrow, very Roger Moore. 'What are you talking about?'

'Stoker's almost certifiable. You know that. A real down in the dirt psycho. Maybe even Joker-level psychotic. Not right. He'll do you over as soon as look. It'll end badly for you. That I can guarantee. What has he got on you? Or are you stupid enough to think you're going to stay in his good books for the rest of your life?'

'I'm not going to grace that with an answer.'

Robertson is used to a lot of rough and tumble, the rougher the better. But he's a doer not a thinker. A cash in pocket, point and shoot, do and worry later type of a guy. Not that I know him at all. I just recognise the type. There are many around here of his make-up. Muscle, lacking brains, too much sun and booze and a hell-of-a-Friday-night people.

'Fair enough,' I say. 'You don't strike me as the smartest whippet on the race track, but even so I'm fairly sure you know that hanging around with Stoker isn't good for your long-term health. So I'm assuming whatever it is he has on you is enough to keep you on a nice tight leash.'

'The fuck you know about me to insult me?'

'I know enough that you got all light-fingered in Se Busca and my mum kicked your arse out. That you are helping Stoker roll Davie Brost and steal DB's from him. That you're dumb enough to tell me to leave town in front of an audience up at Lenny's. That you're dumb enough to steal Zia's car and enough of a muppet to clean up the road smash by tipping the debris off the cliff because Stoker told you to do it. Am I wrong?'

'Fuck off.'

'I know all that and more. You were the one who dumped the blood in Mum's flat. Weren't you? And what? Did you see me naked? Is that why you came to my own home later? To have another *peek*? Turn you on, did it? Or did we disturb you when you were trying to plant more evidence for Stoker? I know it was you in our house – I thought I recognised your skinny frame legging it when we caught you. Or am I wrong about all this?'

'You are talking through your arse.'

'Am I hell,' I say. 'And you know it. When I tell you things are not going to end well for you here, you might want to listen.

Because Stoker must have your dick in a vice for you to do so many dumb things in one week.'

Stoker pushes Cauliflower Ears to one side as he enters, just in time to stop Robertson trying to punch my lights out. There is no real reason to wind up Robertson other than to try and turn him against Stoker. It can't hurt. Can it?

'Let's get this done,' Stoker says.

'What? No foreplay? No kissing and cuddling?' I say.

'I'm not in the fucking mood,' he says. His voice cuts straight through my defences. Scary biscuits and all that. 'And I have ten minutes,' he adds. 'Let's sort one little issue out right now.'

He's lightning quick. He grabs my T-shirt, lifts it up, grabs the microphone wire and pulls it from me. With another swift move he rips the transmitter from my jeans. He wraps his hand around my mouth as he does so.

He hands the mike and transmitter to Robertson and says, 'Big office and stay there. Say nothing.'

Robertson smiles and takes off with the recorder. Stoker closes the door. 'Now we can talk. Your policeman friend might be a bit confused at that conversation and the silence but it'll take him a little while to come check.'

My heart drops through the floor at the change of dynamic this has delivered; I'm totally alone with a nutter.

There's a knock at the door and Cauliflower Ears peeks in. Clearly this room has his nerves on edge. Maybe bad memories. Maybe this isn't an office. More a place for a chat with menaces.

'He's here,' says Cauliflower Ears to Stoker.

'Send him in,' replies Stoker. 'And get your arse in here as well.'

Cauliflower Ears pushes open the door, and I groan as Zia walks in. Cauliflower Ears follows behind slowly.

'Zia, what in the hell?' I mumble.

He says nothing. Does nothing. He just stands. His eyes on the floor.

'Right,' says Stoker. 'Let's get this all done and dusted. I'm tired of dicking around. You've been a right pain in the arse, Daniella. Let's forget whatever chat you thought you could record and cut to the way it's going to be.'

'Zia, why are you here?' I ask.

Stoker replies for him. 'He's here to make sure you do as you are told. You might act the brave little bitch, but doing that now is going to have real consequences. I'm going to show you what defying me means by hurting your boyfriend here. Just to make sure you get the message.'

The first punch from Cauliflower Ears hits Zia low in the gut. He doubles up and Cauliflower Ears stands back. Zia coughs and wheezes.

'Again,' says Stoker.

Cauliflower Ears winds up.

'Don't,' I shout.

Cauliflower Ears rabbit-punches Zia in the back of the head and Zia collapses to the floor.

'One more,' orders Stoker.

I leap forward to protect Zia, but Stoker whips out an arm and clotheslines me across the throat. I bounce back, choking. Cauliflower Ears delivers a kick to Zia's leg. A bone breaker of a kick.

'Okay, Daniella. This is what I want,' says Stoker.

I can't respond. My throat is half closed from the blow.

'Your pub is now mine. The papers will be with you in the morning. Just sign them and we can forget the others in your little syndicate. You own more than fifty per cent of Se Busca and that will do me. Then you leave town. You get the fuck out. And you don't come back. Is that all clear?'

I rub at my throat. 'No way.'

Cauliflower Ears boots Zia again. This time in the thigh. Zia screams.

'Stop hurting Zia,' I shout.

'I'll hurt whoever the fuck I like,' says Stoker. 'And to show you that I really mean business here's a small token of my esteem for you.'

He slaps me across the face and I reel backwards.

'You know what I need you to do,' he says as I tumble into the wall. 'So just do it.'

I try and recover. Try to think.

'And if she doesn't do what you want, Stoker, are you going to kill her like you killed Pat?' whispers Zia from the floor.

Cauliflower Ears winds up for another attack but Stoker raise his hands. 'Wait.'

Cauliflower Ears backs off.

'Pat fucking deserved it,' Stoker says. 'And if your girlfriend doesn't do as I want, she'll get the same bloody thing. That fucking video stunt in the dining room cost me a lot, and I'm tired of playing games.'

Zia rolls over. 'All this to be king of the hill.'

Stoker begins to walk around the room. 'Ratte's gone and that lot in there are looking for a new leader. Come the Classic that will be me. It's my time to be number one.'

'And to get it you killed Pat in cold blood,' says Zia.

'He wouldn't fucking listen to reason. An old man hanging on to power by his bloody fingernails. I should have offed him years ago. He fucking pleaded with me not to kill him. Pathetic.'

'Big brave man, you are. Killing a man twice your age when he was unarmed,' says Zia.

'Are you looking to go the same way, MacFarlane?' Stoker spits. 'There are plenty knives in the kitchen.'

'Carl,' I say, finding my voice. 'There's no need for any more violence.'

'Sure, there is,' he shouts. 'You're hardly going to walk out of here and sign away your life, are you? As soon as you leave you'll call Lozano. So I need to impress upon you that getting him involved isn't an option and signing the pub over to me is the only way this ends. I reckon a few fingers ought to do the job. Go get me a knife.' He points at Cauliflower Ears.

Cauliflower Ears doesn't move.

'I said go get me a knife, or I'll fetch it myself and you also lose some digits.'

Cauliflower Ears leaves.

Zia tries to stand and Stoker slams his hand down on Zia's head. 'Stay down. I've had enough. More than enough. Why in the hell I didn't just sort this out before now is beyond me.'

He turns to me. 'And if you had just fucked off as you were told to, then this would all have been sorted by now, and I wouldn't be ignoring my guests. My *important* guests. And all to clean up this sorry mess.'

I have massively underestimated this man. I said he was certifiable. He's more than that. His eyes are blank holes. His soul the same. He is truly off the scale.

'Do you know how much this dinner is costing me?' he screams. 'Do you know how hard I've worked to get here today? Do you?'

He aims a kick at Zia, but Zia rolls away and it only half connects. But it's still enough for Zia to cry out.

'Forget the time and effort I've put in to make my money,' he continues, now pacing round the small space. 'Forget the hours dealing with arseholes and dickheads. Forget the shit I'm expected to deal with, every fucking day. Forget I've done all that, and I've still put in a shift that you couldn't imagine.'

I eye the door. I might be able to make a run for it. Get help.

'And look at what you made me do, Daniella. Why did I bother trying to set you up? That idiot Lozano couldn't find his own arse with both hands and a mountain guide. I handed you to him on a plate. The note. The key. Fuck, even that fucking photo of Ratte pushing you over in his own fucking house. It was left on the table for him. On the fucking table. What else did the dickhead need to arrest you? And don't talk to me about Pat's own blood. Fucking plastic sheets to catch the shit. For fuck's sake, do you have any idea how hard it is to put that crap in a bottle? They don't teach you that at school. Why the hell didn't—'

He's passing me and aims a slap at the back of my head. I duck. He adjusts his shot mid strike and clips me hard round the ear. My head stings and my ears ring.

'—I just take the easy route and double up on Pat. RIP Daniella Coulstoun.'

He is completely losing it. Spit is flying and his arms are flailing. The cool, collected Stoker is gone. The true Stoker is out and flying.

'I gave you a break, Daniella. More than one break. Breaks because I respected your mother. I gave you a warning to get out of town. Your mum worked with me well, and if you weren't Effie's daughter I'd have just taken what I wanted and been done with you. So I gave you some breaks. A few warnings. But you thought you could beat me.'

Zia is watching, and I'm wishing we were telepathic. While Stoker is ranting he's not paying attention to either of us. Together, if we could coordinate, we might be able to bring him down and then run.

'Where the hell is that knife?' Stoker shouts. 'Fuck it, Daniella, I'll just use this.'

He picks up the chair, an ancient wooden affair with a vinyl seat cover. He lifts it high and smashes it against the wall. Two more blows and he is standing on the remains, trying to wrench one of the legs free. With his attention on the chair I signal to Zia with a balled fist – pumping it back and forward in Stoker's direction – signalling to attack. Zia gets the gig and begins to rise. Stoker finally breaks the leg free and flips it over to grab it by the narrow end, a makeshift baseball bat now in hand. He swings it to and fro in front of him. Getting used to the weight. He smiles. Happy in his head that the leg will do the job he has in mind. I leap at him, no plan, just body weight, momentum and a need to do something. I crash into his shoulder and the table leg goes flying as he tumbles away from me. I try and grab his head with some vague notion of bouncing it off the wall. Stoker strikes the wall with his back and grunts. I slam my palm into his nose. The crack as the bone breaks is a gunshot in an echo chamber. Loud. Sudden. Memorable. Stoker screams as a blob of blood rushes from one nostril. The table leg is at my feet and I bend down to pick it up. Stoker lashes out and lands a kick on my forearm and I lose all feeling. I try and grab the table leg with my other hand. Stoker dives on me and we both collapse to the ground. He slams my face with his palm and grabs the table leg. I try and grasp it but he blows out his nose, blood rinsing my eyes, as he lifts the leg high.

Stoker rams the table leg down, and I throw up my arms in defence. The leg tears into the fingers of my right hand. I scream as fingers break. Then I hear the door slam open. Stoker flies away. Lifted clear of me. I look up and the Capitán and two officers are pinning Stoker to the floor. The Capitán stands up as the officers cuff Stoker.

Stoker is screaming the air blue. 'Get the fuck off me, you pricks. I've done fuck all. Get your pissing hands off me.'

The Capitán signals for the officers to lift Stoker off the floor.

'Take him away,' orders the Capitán.

Stoker swears his way out of the door and is still swearing when the door closes behind him.

'Robertson is in the next office,' I say to the Capitán.

'Señorita Coulstoun,' the Capitán says, 'we have him safely tucked away. His small friend with the bad ears as well.'

'Robertson and the small man are the ones that tried to ram us off the road up at Lenny's and I'll put money on them knowing where Zia's car is.' I pause, adrenaline still pumping, numbing my fingers, two of which, my forefinger and middle finger, are bent back at an impossible angle.

'We need to get both of you checked out at the hospital,' says the Capitán.

'You took your time, Capitán.' It's Zia's first words since Stoker kicked him.

'Señor MacFarlane, as soon as he confessed we moved in.'

'Confessed?' I say. 'How do you know he confessed? He took my recorder off me.'

Zia stands up and lifts his T-shirt up.

A wire runs from his chest to his back. A microphone at one end, a transmitter at the other.

24

The End?

'Are we finished?' asks Zia.

Zia and I are sitting near the El Descaro harbour, backs to the sea, squirrelled deep into the corner of a café. There are no other customers nearby and that's a deliberate choice. I'd rejected five possible venues before agreeing to this one. Zia had suggested talking at home, but I'd dismissed the idea. I wanted a neutral venue, and for that reason Se Busca was a no-go as well. If I'd had my way I'd have postponed this chat for a few days until the dust settled. Although I doubt it ever will. Stoker is far from bang to rights. The Capitán has his confession on tape, but Stoker has cash, and George reckons his expensive brief will go for entrapment or claim Stoker was boasting. But he also 'fessed up to the note, the key and draining the blood, although I'm sure Stoker will lay all the blame on Robertson. After all, Malky Robertson planted most of the evidence. He was seen up at Lenny's with Zia and me. He was even there the morning that Pat was killed. Holding a gun. The Ex-Patriots' statements will be key, but Stoker will almost certainly find ways to pressure them. And there's the photo that Stoker has of the six of them dressed in Tyvek over Pat's body. That'll be kept up Stoker's sleeve for the right moment. The Capitán has told all of them that a holiday out of town for a few weeks might not be a bad thing. None of them has gone. It will be months before the trial. A few weeks away now will do little to avoid Stoker's retribution when it comes. There's a witness protection programme, but that's far too hardball for them. At the moment, they have all agreed to wait and see. My view, for what it's worth, is that Stoker would be insane to try anything if there was the slightest risk of getting caught. It would be a cast-iron skillet of a way to demonstrate his guilt. George thinks I'm naive. He's probably right.

'Do *you* think we are finished, Zia?' I reply.

Everything about his demeanour says he doesn't want to answer in the affirmative.

'It's about what you want,' he replies.

'You lied to me, Zia, time and again. About the murder. About Carmen. About seeing Pat, Antonio and Stoker. About a lot of things.'

'And every time for good reason. I couldn't tell you about the murder while I thought Stoker had the photo and the gen on the blonde woman.'

'And the other stuff? What about your affair with Carmen?'

He winces at the word 'affair'. 'She made me promise to say nothing to you. Antonio thinks the world of her, and she told me that I was a mistake. Antonio was willing to forgive if we all forgot. I never meant for us all to become friends.'

'Are you sure? Still holding a flame for Carmen would seem a good reason to see her again. And I would be a good excuse. I can't think of any other reason why you'd want to see her, given you were fucking her behind her husband's back.'

Words to hurt. A real ice-cold stab there. I can't help myself.

'That's not fair,' he says.

'Fair, Zia? What's fair about what you did to Antonio?'

'It was before I met you.'

'And that makes it okay?'

'It was a while ago,' is the best comeback he has.

'And then there's you seeing Stoker and the rest of them behind my back. Your little meets with Pat, Stoker and Antonio.'

He bends his head, almost touching the table, and mumbles something.

'What?'

'I owed Stoker.'

'Owed him for what?'

'Owed him money.'

'For what? Betting?'

He nods, slowly.

'How much?'

Another mumble.

'Zia, this is not going well. I need clear answers.'

'Twenty-three thousand.'

'Euros?'

'Maybe a bit more.'

'And you never said a word to me.'

'I thought I could pay it off, but the interest rate was insane.'

'And Antonio?'

'He was into Stoker for more.'

That makes me wonder if Antonio's cousin Héctor really did have his fingers slammed in the door. Or did Antonio just phone Stoker from his café and grass me up?

'What the hell were you gathering them all about at our house last week?'

'The El Descaro Classic.'

'What in the hell is it with that stupid race? Everyone seems obsessed with it.'

'It's a big deal, Daniella. A real big deal for Pat, at least it was, and it's now a massive deal for Stoker. It's a meeting of some of Europe's biggest criminals. They use it as cover for an annual meeting.'

I remember what Stoker was saying when I burst in on his dinner.

I am not presenting myself as the new leader of our group . . .

Wasn't that what he said?

'And Pat was king,' I say. 'Stoker, the eternal prince. And with Pat gone he was the man of the hour. Is that it?'

'Stoker called the dinner to position it that way. At the meet after the Classic they all elect the king for the future.'

'And Ratte had to die for Stoker to step in.'

Another nod.

'And why the hell was Stoker at your meets at all? Pat hated him.'

'Pat was in for a slice of the betting action, and that was a fair slug of cash. Pat needed to keep an eye on that, or Stoker would have stiffed him.'

'And all of this, Zia, I mean all of this, stayed behind those sweet lips of yours.'

'None of it affected you. Not really. Apart from Pat's death, which was only a few days ago, the rest was old news that I was dealing with.'

'You owed a criminal over twenty grand, and Stoker was pulling your string. You thought you'd killed some blonde woman and Pat was pulling another string. You were arranging to see Carmen. Someone you clearly wanted to see again. And all this is old news that wouldn't *affect* me. Do you really expect me to sit here and believe any of that?'

I stand up.

'Where are you going?' he asks.

'I'm not sure, Zia. Right now I'm not sure, but listen to what you've just told me. Think on it. All of it. What would you do if you found out that lot about me? Eh?'

'Do you not think that I've been worried sick by it all? That's why I volunteered to get wired up by Lozano. I just knew you were going to do something stupid with Stoker so I called Lozano. 'Fessed up to him about Pat and Stoker. Told him that Stoker would haul me in if I contacted him. That if I could be some form of back-up, I would. He jumped at the chance. Come on, Daniella, you saw how crazy Stoker was. Lozano was wrong to do what he did with you. Stoker is not right in the head. Lozano should never have suggested wiring you up at all. If I'd not put myself on the line Stoker would still be free and you'd most likely be dead.'

'And what are you saying? Being a shining knight makes things right? That I should forget all the other stuff? That we should go back to our holiday romance? And things will be wonderful?'

'I'm saying that I need to make this right.'

'I know what you did with Stoker took guts, but making this right? Is that even vaguely possible, Zia?'

'It could be.'

He so wants that to be true. I can hear it in his voice. See it in his eyes. Smell it on his breath.

'Zia,' I sigh, 'I asked you an aeon ago about talking. About how couples talk. I've given you more than enough time to sit down and tell me all of this. When we moved in together would have been the time.'

'I couldn't. I'd have lost you, and we'd only just started.'

'And what did you think? That all this could be kept under wraps? Or did you plan to take me to some fancy restaurant one day and lay it all out on the table?'

'Everything was so messy. And too dangerous.'

'Sure, and letting it build up was the right call, was it? And do you know what? Even now you're playing games with me.'

'I'm not.'

'Yes you are.'

'I'm not,' he repeats.

'Okay, Zia, I'll give us a chance. One chance if you want to take it. Answer one single question truthfully, and maybe we can work on this. I'm not saying it will fix things but I'll sit down and talk.'

'Anything.'

I know before I ask the question that he's not going to be able to reply. I know that he's not going to answer the question truthfully. I know that I'm setting him up for a fall. I almost want him to *fail*.

'Okay, Zia, one question. Just one.'

'Shoot.'

'The truth?'

'The truth. I promise.'

I look down on him, expectation and trepidation dripping from his sweat glands.

'Zia, there was Pat, there was Stoker, there was Carmen, there was the gambling, and you said nothing to me about any of them. Zip. So I'll ask you once and once only. Is there anything else, even vaguely in the same ballpark as any of that lot that I should know? Something I don't know about? Another secret or secrets. Something that you want to tell me right now. In detail. The works. All of it. Leave nothing out. I am opening the confessional door again to you. That's the deal. I want to know everything else right now. I don't care how bad. How awkward. How hard to tell me it is. I want to know now, right now.'

I look down at him again and know, deep in my bloodstream, that he's not going to be able to answer. There has to be more. He's been here for two decades, living and breathing the air in Se Busca. Skulking in the bad corners of El Descaro. Hanging with people who will treat the last few days as a source of amusement. Stories to be told. Gossip to be exchanged. Death and violence the currency of choice when words are bandied about. That's where Zia comes from now. He was once a minor eighties pop star but now he's a fully paid-up member of a club that has warped his core. And because of that he's been part of other stuff that will have consequences. He can no more answer that question than stop breathing for an hour. And that begs another question, do I still want to be part of it all? Do I want to leave my holiday time behind and really take up residence in this swamp? For that is where this is all going. Zia, or no Zia, if I stay here I'll become one of them. An Ex-Patriot. And if that's true, there's only one role I'm going to fulfil. That of my mother.

Zia doesn't look up. He doesn't move a single muscle. And, worst of all, he says nothing.

I push the chair back and move away. 'That was your chance, Zia. That was your last chance. That was *our* last chance.'

He still says nothing and at that moment a seagull lets rip with a wail.

A sound that is long.

Hard.

Painful.

ACKNOWLEDGEMENTS

By the time I reached my ninth novel (not counting the half dozen unpublished ones that lie deep in my computer) I would have expected things to have become easier. They haven't. There are still days when I look at the screen and wonder what in the hell is going on in the story. Still days when I think I'll never get the thing finished. Still days when I have to force myself to sit down and write – despite the fact that an unmissable repeat episode of *Homes Under the Hammer* is about to start. What helps are the people out there who are willing to give over their precious time to read my work. Take my beta readers for this book – Sharon Bairden, Irene Sutherland, Lucy Sampson, Tracy Hall, Gwen Jones-Edwards and John Calderwood – whose feedback has been immense and who spotted everything I didn't, and for the thoughtful comments of my son and daughter, Scott and Nicole. My copy-editor, Alison Irvine, needs thanks for ensuring that Daniella's second outing is even better than her first. Helen White, in Javea, ensured my Spanish wasn't gibberish. My wife Lesley read the roughest of first drafts and encouraged me to polish and polish. And Alison Rae at Polygon provided the guidance I needed to get it all done. Paul, Scott and Raymond Davidson have my endless thanks for being so supportive over the years. There are a myriad of others who have provided succour and sustenance – and to all of them a big thanks.